Memories of Bronze

Books by Ryan Matthews

Sophia Tate Mysteries

Memories in Bronze

Release Day Saga

Release Day
Kano's Grasp
Arjun's Path
Zephyr's Hope

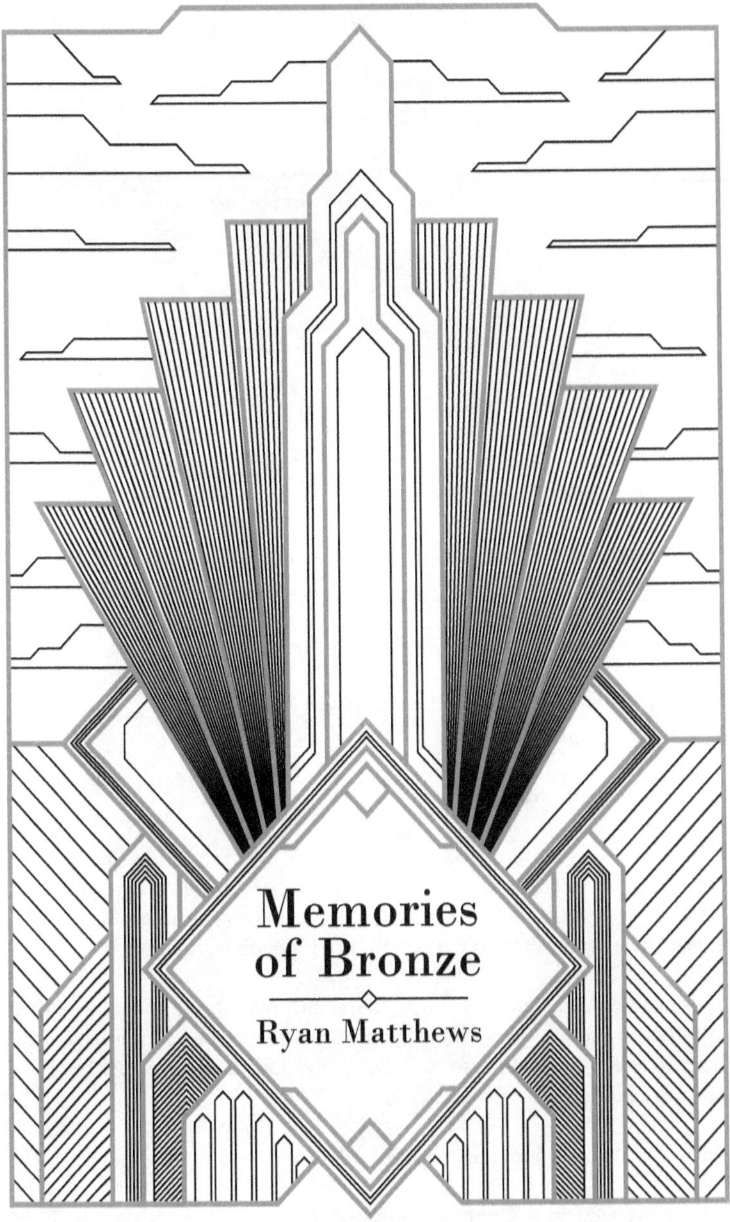

Memories
of Bronze

Ryan Matthews

All rights reserved. Published by Battlehill Press.
Friendship, Tennessee.

www.ryanmatthewsauthor.com

Layout and cover design by Ryan Matthews.

Library of Congress Control Number: 2025927741
ISBN 979-8-9901005-2-7 (paperback)
ISBN 979-8-9901005-3-4 (hardcover)
ISBN 979-8-9901005-4-1 (ebook)
First Edition: February 2026

for my mother, a lifelong lover of mysteries

Prologue

The winter wind stirred the dry leaves that had accumulated in the alley, the last vestige of the past season. Dorothy Tate stepped into the quaint little shop tucked away at the end of the brick alley in Central London, her six-year-old daughter Sophia tightly clasping her hand. A tiny brass bell hung from a curl of iron above the oak door tinkled, announcing the new visitor's arrival almost as loudly as the creaking floor beneath her feet. If she hadn't known of the shop's existence, she likely would have never found it.

"A single blink and you'll miss it," Oliver had said as he had laid next to her in bed, sweaty after their vigorous activity. Her illicit tryst had been a success in more ways than one, providing her with the information for which she had longed. "Wilfred has everything you can imagine, from intact Corinthian seals to chandeliers removed from the Palace of Versailles itself."

The world of antiquities was a gentleman's world, not to be trifled with by the likes of a widow whose only duty should be seeking a well-to-do husband to provide for herself and Sophia. Someone who would be as willing to overlook her fanciful interest in relics as the fine wrinkles beginning to accumulate at the corners of her azure eyes. She had reason to seek out such treasured objects, believing the most sought-after to hold the reason for her unexplained gift, and therefore, her existence. When she had serendipitously learned of Northrop's, an antique store rumoured to deal with the most difficult-to-obtain wares, she knew where destiny was leading her. Discovering its location had been a complex task all of its own.

Dorothy had given birth to Sophia later in her marriage than was typical, her deceased husband's virility to blame. Not his virility, *per se,* but rather the gender toward which he felt it. Stewart had needed a wife to mask his shunnable proclivities, and Dorothy had needed a husband to remove her overbearing mother from her life. Despite the rare times Dorothy had managed to bed the inebriated Stewart, he had been unable to complete his task. As a result, Sophia had ultimately been the product of one of numerous affairs.

Dorothy scanned the store's wares, taking in the room packed to the brim with objects spanning from ancient history to modern by prehistoric standards. It was difficult to turn without her bulky winter coat rubbing against a priceless object or the furniture on which it rested. The space was dim, lit primarily by the rays managing to worm their way through the few undersized windows, igniting the motes of dust swirling in the air like sparks and only adding to the place's mystique. The collection was impressive with inventory from every corner of the globe. She could not imagine what a number of the pieces were doing outside of a museum.

She leaned down to Sophia's level. "Don't touch anything," she whispered to her daughter as she smoothed her strawberry curls. *For more than one reason,* she thought. Dorothy's ex-husband, Stewart, had come from money. However, once Dorothy had paid his plentiful debts in the wake of his death, she was left with little more than what she needed to start a new life in the English countryside. Should Sophia damage any of the priceless artefacts in the shop, Dorothy could see that future evaporating like the morning fog over the Thames. Ironically, Dorothy had chosen to visit the shop for exactly the action she had warned her daughter against—to touch.

"May I help you?" The voice emanated from a withering gentleman that had to have been Wilfred. The elderly man stared over gold-rimmed, half-moon spectacles as he set a yellowing ledger onto a wooden desk that stretched across the rear of the showroom. The scents of pipe tobacco, moulding pages, and aged leather filled her nostrils, disguising the subtle metallic odour of bronze and brass, the metals she had crossed the city for on this dreary English morning.

"Just browsing. Thank you." Her eyes swept across the aged clerk as he leaned on the worn wood, waiting for a refusal that never came. Dorothy did not know exactly what she sought but knew beyond a doubt that it would reveal itself in due time.

His eyebrow arched as his lips cracked open, but not another word broke the silence thick in the stuffy air. He feigned interest in his accounting scrawls, but his eyes never drifted far from the stranger. Wilfred sat on his stool, its dry-rotting upholstery completely split. He kept the dreadful piece beyond the view of his prestigious clientele, but everyone had their creature comforts. Despite its dilapidated appearance, its buttery soft cushion was the only surface his backside could tolerate these days.

The woman who had wandered into his shop was unfamiliar to him, and he rarely forgot a face. He stared through the reversed black and gold lettering on the glass of the door. The narrow entrance to his antique shop was obscured by a brick wall from the street, preventing the average Cockney from stumbling into his place of business by accident. He had worked hard to build his reputation and cherished being difficult to find by the common consumer.

Child aside, his newest customer could easily blend in with his less distinguished patrons, the only reason he had allowed her to remain. Apparently a woman of means, her single-breasted long coat was tailored to her motherly figure, protecting the organdy dress peeking from beneath it. The rose gold curls that spilt from underneath her cocked pillbox hat would have had any sane man thinking about them draped out across his pillow, glistening in the morning sunlight.

Dorothy's eyes grew wide as she gravitated towards a turn-of-the-century candelabra, its base ornately carved with the head of a lion. With gloved hands, she lifted it into a ray of natural light as she gently blew the dust from its patinated limbs. Her pursed lips raised the hair on the shopkeeper's neck, causing him to turn away before she noticed the reddening of his cheeks. Wilfred's opinion of her rose as he watched her examine the piece in great detail. Only a connoisseur would wear cotton in such saturating weather to handle such a mundane piece when compared to the other artefacts in his possession.

The bronze fixture had been relegated to the rear of the early Victorian display cabinet over the last several years as more desirable wares took its place of prominence. Wilfred had kept the piece solely because of the immaculate craftsmanship, a disappearing art as the decades slipped through his withering fingers. It was only due to that superb craftsmanship that he had bothered with the restoration of the bent limbs it had on its arrival. Despite its imperfections, he still appreciated the piece's simplicity, even when compared to his more precious inventory.

Even though his priceless collection could rival that of the Tower, there was little need for security. Wilfred had always hoped that his son would join the trade, but to his chagrin, Simon had become somewhat of a fearsome racketeer. Fortunately for Wilfred, no one on this side of the river would think of pitting themselves against his ilk. The corner of Wilfred's lip curled up in a smile. In a manner of speaking, he *had* joined the family business. Wilfred hoped that if he could ever pry his younger son away from his mother's tit, he would be of some use in the trade.

"Mummy, can't we please go to the shops? Mr. Tuggles wants a lemon lolly." The little one withdrew her hand from tugging on her mother's coat. She squeezed the ragged bunny closely, burrowing her head into the plush toy that had no business being anywhere but a dustbin. One bogey-covered finger on anything in the shop and, connoisseur or not, the pair would find themselves mercilessly ejected out on the street.

"May I?" Dorothy had set down the candelabra and was removing her glove by the fingertips. Wilfred found himself strangely drawn to the sensual motion, the pale velvet skin of her hands as alluring as a low neckline on a lady of refinement.

Wilfred nodded his approval. The morning had been slow, many of his regulars financially recovering from the previous day's auction at Christie's, and the forgotten candelabra could use some attention. He himself was still reeling from the purchase of an Egyptian gold and lapis lazuli pectoral. At least this one had its proper documents. If she did not purchase the piece, once she departed, he would wipe it down, careful not to over-polish and mar the rich warm patina it had developed.

With a tentative motion, the stranger reached forward. Her fingertips barely had contacted the alloy before her hand rocketed back, stunning her as though she had touched a live wire. Her face grew deathly white as she hastily muttered an apology and fled from the shop as though her life had been threatened. Practically dragging her daughter by the arm, the woman slammed the door so hard that everything in the shop trembled, including himself. Her white glove remained among the objects cluttering one of the walnut drum tables centred in the room.

The damp air grew cool in her absence, once again spiking the fine hair on Wilfred's arms, this time for a more nefarious reason. Despite his favoured red and grey checked sweater vest, he rubbed his hands to discourage the chill cooling him from within. He made his way to the discarded bronze which no longer held the warm lustre it had. As a matter of fact, the entire shop had taken on a cooler hue, likely from the accumulating rain clouds threatening to make the afternoon as solemn as the morn.

Wilfred reached out cautiously, hesitated, then picked up the woman's glove to use as a barrier against whatever ill haunted the antique and stopped short. "Ludicrous." He flung the glove into the bin and wrapped his hand firmly around the candelabra's base, hesitating for the briefest moment before lifting the piece as if expecting something to happen. "Bloody gypsies." He shook his head as he replaced the candelabra in its forlorn, forgotten position where it sat until he died several years later.

Chapter I

I palmed my shoulder, the dull ache returning when I recalled how my mother had jerked me out of that antique shop on a dismal winter day not unlike this one. Whatever terrifying vision the vintage bronze had given her had driven her to madness. Peace had become a superfluous concept in our lives from that moment forward. Not that our lives had been the epitome of tranquillity before. After my father's death, my childhood had been one chaotic flight after another as we drifted from one location to the next. Every moment had been filled with Mother's incessant search for some sort of spiritual gratification that I did not understand, a search which eventually led to that one object—a nondescript flameless candelabra that had been burned into my psyche.

Given the economic depression and slow recovery from the Great War, antiquities were not at the forefront of anyone's mind save for the most affluent. Making matters worse, tensions were rising in Germany. Disturbing news travelled faster than ever before, and if there was any truth to the concerned headlines of every major periodical, the country's new chancellor was going to lead the entire continent into another war.

I pulled the tall collar of my coat tightly around my neck as I made my way up the steep gravel drive to the modest country convent, the warmth of the wool shielding me from the biting cold of early December. The gravel crunched underfoot as the wind rattled the barren trees lining the drive in an impromptu symphony, an ode to winter. I could have taken a taxi to the rural nunnery, but after so many years, I had learned that nothing calmed the mind like a lengthy stroll. The grounds were only a few kilometres from the humble town's edge. After a lifetime of searching, not unlike my Mother's, I had finally located the quaint little shop from which she had never truly escaped. We had fled not only the establishment but London entirely. Mother couldn't put enough distance between herself and the evil she had sensed in that antique fixture, but the time had arrived to follow her footsteps—wherever fate might lead. For that, I had to leave Luffield.

Stewart, who I considered my father, had left us with barely enough resources once we had paid his prolific debts to see us through our northern migration and had meagrely supported us as Mother's mental health declined. Dorothy Tate may have been a resourceful woman, but we owed much of our survival to our friends at Grafton Nunnery. They had taken us in when much of the town had shut their doors in our faces the night we had arrived with nothing more than two battered suitcases and no trace of a plan. I had spent my youth in Luffield, running between row after row of beautiful stone homes with thatched roofs embedded in an idyllic countryside that one would think could cure all ills. Not that we had lived in the lovely stone cottages or had a view of anything other than the backside of a factory. We, like so many others, lived on the opposite side of the Nene, our existence taking on a supporting role to those who lived across the river.

I stared up at the sanctuary, perched atop one of the many rolling hills for which the county was known. Under dreary skies that pulled all life from nature's hues, the isolated convent's exterior had fallen into disrepair and no longer appeared as welcoming as it had in days past. The warmth of its hearth and that of the nuns inside was unrivalled, especially in a town that was as cold to outsiders as the wind clawing at my skin. The church's original foundation dated back to the eleventh century though the majority of its construction had been done in the 1200s when Luffield's population had seen substantial growth. Each successive building had been linked to the next by cloisters in the shadow of a respectable three-storey bell tower. Even now, the relatively small convent was too much for its few remaining inhabitants to care for.

"Get inside, dearie." Mother Superior held the heavy oaken door open, letting me and the brisk wind stumble into the small sanctuary. "It's so good to see you again." I stepped onto the ochre tiled floor and shivered. The nun disguised the fact well that her black habit did little to impede the penetrating cold. As long as I could remember, the nun had sweated through the summer and shivered through the winter. Fighting the stout wind, the pudgy woman closed and barred the door, the closest thing the antiquated building had to a lock. "I don't know why on God's Earth you insist on walking here in weather such as this. You'll always be our stubborn little Sophia." She shook her head, chuckling to herself. "I suppose you'll be wanting to see your mother?"

"Please." I smiled politely as I moved to the large fireplace ensconced by a worn relief of Christ's passion. The abbess fetched me a cup of her obligatory black tea with fresh milk from the nunnery's cow, Annette. The entire convent had gathered around the massive hearth to knock off the chill as omnipresent at this time of year as the Lord himself. I greeted each of them in turn like the family they had come to be.

"I suppose I can't expect you to remain inside all winter. You're like your mother in that respect, you know?" She rubbed a cluster of my copper curls between her fingers before brushing it behind my ear. "The spitting image of her, God rest her soul." She crossed herself and passed me a worn ceramic cup, thick swirls of steam curled up from the vessel before being thrust away by a harsh draught. The malty aroma filled my very soul with the nostalgia for my youth.

"This will be my last visit for a while, I expect." I held the scalding beverage to my lips, still far too hot to consume.

Several of the women sighed in disappointment. Mother Superior cracked a knowing grin as she collapsed into an old rocker. The nuns may not have had belongings, but as a general rule, no one sat in "her" chair.

"I knew this day would come. You have your mother's spirit just as you do her strong will. Frankly, I'm surprised you lasted as long as you have in this stuffy little town. Such a wee lass when you were brought here." She gestured with her hand not much higher than her breast. "Where will you go?"

"London. Mother left a matter unresolved, and it's my responsibility to take care of it." I neglected to mention that the matter was the same that had driven her to madness. "It would be dishonest of me to say I wasn't looking forward to visiting the city."

Sister Therese, a lanky novitiate, spoke up. "My brother lives in London. Best guard your purse." Mother Superior gave her a look of reproach, and Therese lowered her head chagrined.

"The Lord didn't put us on this Earth to expect the worst from His children. Sophia," she began, leaning close so as to smooth down my collar. "London can be a hectic place with many… challenges for a young woman like yourself to navigate. Keep your wits about you and you'll be fine." She smiled, her grey eyes twinkling in the crackling firelight. "Now, best not be keeping you from your mother."

With a grunt, she rose from the rocker and took me by the hand. I ducked as she led me out of a shoulder-high side door as old as the sanctuary itself. I followed her into a garden-sized graveyard holding fewer than fifty souls, fenced by a low stone wall. In many places, the stones lay dishevelled on the dry grass, their abundance of moss revealing how long they had sat displaced. The fact that my mother had a place among the other graves was nothing short of a miracle. Only the Reverend Mother, Sister Agnes, and I knew her cause of death—one on which the Catholic Church was not particularly fond. The abbess, who had been old then, had neglected to mention that fact or her checkered past when she had petitioned the bishop to have her interred at Grafton, one of the only places Mother could ever find solace.

I owed everything to the sisters of Grafton Nunnery who had welcomed us in our hour of need. We had fled from London to Luffield as my mother desperately tried to outrun that which was inescapable—her mind. Under the arched eyebrow of then much younger Mother Superior, Sister Agnes had ushered us in, nursing my mother as she had slipped further into the all-consuming darkness. Her days alternated between lucid and dissociated. On the better days, I recalled trips to the market and strolls through the park, always with the support of Agnes. On her worse days, she was bedridden, screaming so fiercely that the nuns wore out their rosaries. Not even the holiness of the nunnery could dispel the haunting thoughts plaguing her mind.

I knelt at the foot of a weathered grey headstone, now almost black with mould, unconcerned about the overgrown grass that might find its way onto my dress. The inscription read: Dorothy Tate 1887-1922. "I found it, Mother," I began. "The antique shop." I could almost sense her distressed body clawing its way up, desperate to stop my pursuit of the artefact that had ultimately driven her to take her own life. At any moment her withered hand would reach out to grasp my coat, anything to keep me from going. "I can't imagine what you experienced that day, but I have to think it'll be different. I can't live my life without knowing." I wiped a tear with my woollen glove, darkening the fabric as the hilltop winds stabbed between the folds of my coat. "I never told you, but I have your gift. It *is* a gift. I'm convinced of it." I trembled, not solely due to the cold. At the factory, they had thought I was barmy when I told them I was quitting my position to move to London and chase my dreams. I believe my floor supervisor's last mumbled words were, 'Lost her bloomin' mind, she has.'"

I chuckled to myself. Maybe I had lost my mind. Perhaps what I considered a gift was the first sign of a fragile mind, already winding down the path of deterioration. Sometimes I wondered if Sister Agnes had understood more than she let on. She had spent countless nights cradling my mother's head as she tossed and turned in a restless sleep consumed by terrors, unable to ignore her unconscious speech. She had been the first to discover me sneaking into the holy tabernacle to embrace the nunnery's bronze chalice. My first communion had been the moment of awakening, not religious so much as spiritual. When Mother Superior had offered me the simply engraved gold-plated vessel, I took a deep draught, my tiny fingers grasping its polished edges. A wave of emotions jolted through me, a raging torrent of the thoughts of every parishioner who had interacted with the holy cup. Pure peace. Mother Superior herself had led me back to the room I shared with my mother, taking my daze to be the work of the Holy Spirit.

Long after that initial communion, whenever I craved relief from the woes of the world, I sought out the chalice, often sneaking into the darkened holy space of the sanctuary where it was stored to caress the bronze artefact. Sister Agnes often found and scolded me, yet not once did she report me to the abbess. Then came Mother's death. After years of battling her demons, she succumbed to the darkness. She was found at the base of the old bell tower. Sister Agnes had taken great care to erase all traces of her demise from the irregular cobbles paving the courtyard. Though I had not witnessed the event, I avoided the spot to this very day. Only two years after Mother's death, Agnes' fiery spirit had dwindled down to embers. It was no surprise when she came down with influenza that winter and joined my mother in the afterlife.

The nuns of the convent took me in, caring for me as the child none of them were allowed to have, until I reached adulthood and moved into the Women's Lodge in town. For years, the communion cup was the only object that affected me so. Other items constructed of bronze, brass, or copper would do little more than tingle in my fingertips. I had always operated on the assumption that only a fraction of my mother's ability had passed to me, diluted by my unknown father's contribution to my existence. With the chalice, I had concluded that copper alloys must have to be imbued with such intense emotion for my weakened sensitivity to detect it.

I ran my hand over the granite headstone's rough surface. I missed Mother terribly, but something about being near her, even in death, calmed me. I spoke to her as if she knelt beside me, aching for her to run her fingers through my hair as I laid my head in her lap. "For the longest time, I questioned this gift—our gift. Why would the universe provide us with such an ability with no practical purpose? I've dedicated what little spare time I have to researching all of antiquity in search of objects or people with similar attributes. I'd all but given up until a recent trip to the marketplace revealed what I believe to be its true purpose.

"On a trip into the town centre, I came across a small set of brass weights. Thinking that we could use them in the kitchen of the Lodge, I reached to examine the smallest of the set. Disgust surged through my veins. Instead of profound peace as with the chalice, a thick film of corruption seemed to drain down my body. Unlike before, the sickening sensation left behind information in the form of a hazy vision." I shook off the chill that came from the recollection. Between it and the winter wind, I was anxious to be back inside by the roaring fire. "My legs buckled and I collapsed to the ground, causing unwelcome judgement from the nearby perusers. The weights' previous owner had accumulated much of his profit from the opium trade. Furthermore, he had altered weights, pocketing the difference from a lifetime of dealings. As contempt bloomed in my chest, I could only hope that the afterlife would provide the dishonest trader with the same imbalance on the scales of judgement."

I laughed. "Now I understand why you always wore gloves." I forced a smile, looking up at the sky to hide the forthcoming tears. "I have to leave you. I have to understand what it was you saw that day when you picked up the candelabra. I will do everything in my power to find that piece, even if it means returning half-sane to the nunnery with nothing but a pence to my name. I couldn't bring peace to you, but maybe I can bring it to someone else. I love you, Mummy."

I rose and jumped when I saw Mother Superior lingering outside the short door. "I didn't mean to eavesdrop. I came to bring you this." Taking my hand, she placed a small leather sack into my palm and closed my fingers around it. Inside I could feel the clink of coins. "It should last you a few weeks, and it's yours by right. Eight pounds in crowns. Everything left after your mother's burial. We've kept it safe, and now it's yours to use as you will." She sighed. "You know, I've never understood the gift you and your mother have."

My mouth gave way in shock.

"You don't reach my age blind to your surroundings." She winked. "We aren't meant to understand all things, are we now? Your mother didn't always conduct herself...," the Reverend Mother paused, searching for the correct word, "in the most Catholic manner, but she was a good soul. A fact I hope the Lord takes into account despite her shortcomings. All I ask of you is that you use this ability for good. There are too many unfortunate souls in the darkness who could use some light in their lives."

I nodded, the weight of the nun's heavy commission on my shoulders.

She wiped a tear from my cheek and tightened my scarf. Blessing me with the sign of the cross, she guided me to the nunnery's door and saw me out. "You do the Lord's work, whether you realise it or not."

Chapter II

The abbess did not let the disagreeable weather keep her from watching me as I descended the meandering path from the convent. The surrounding hills stretched into the distance, their normally rich and verdant green fields now appearing devoid of life. Despite appearances, winter was a time of renewal, the first throes of a new year after a time of harvest.

Before I was out of sight of the convent, Sister Therese's voice echoed among the leafless trees. I turned to see her shuffling down the hill, habit hiked up above her knees, her hair beginning its escape from the tight headband. The younger nun hustled to catch me, struggling for breath, not used to anything more physical than the slow-pace of spring gardening. "Please, Miss Sophia, allow me to escort you to the station." Her freckled cheeks coloured from exertion.

I smiled, my own cheeks growing more tender by the minute as the cold breeze harassed my face. "You are too kind, Sister Therese. Only if it's not any trouble. I'd happily take you up on your offer."

"No trouble, Miss. Really. We've nearly exhausted our food stores and could use a good replenishing. I've been tasked with visiting the market to collect barley and potatoes, as bland and unappetising as they are! Oh, I shouldn't have said that," she scolded herself. "Mother Superior is constantly reminding me I need to guard my tongue."

The burst of laughter warmed me from inside out. "Your secret's safe with me, Sister Therese."

She smiled graciously. "Please call me Therese. At least as long as we're outside the convent." The nun had caught her breath and began leading us back up the slope. "Why don't you go back inside where it's warm while I get Mathilde bridled and hooked to the cart?"

"I'll be fine, Sis— Therese." I chuckled. "But I insist you call me Sophia. I'll accompany you. I don't see much sense in warming my hands only to have them subject to the cold again. I'm already used to it."

"If that's what you want." Therese shrugged and trudged on towards the stables.

The stables were inside a simple building constructed from reclaimed boards that had most likely been donated. The stables from my childhood had burned due to an unfortunate lightning strike years ago. All the livestock survived thanks to some quick-thinking nuns. The impoverished country nunnery had little in the way of means. If not for the meagre generosity of the community, it would have been forced to shut its heavy doors long ago. The lethargic drizzle that had begun on our return to the grounds rolled down the building's tin roof, playing a pleasant melody as it tinkled through the rusting gutters. The uncovered paddock was empty, its occupants seeking shelter inside from the dreary weather.

With some effort, Therese twisted the iron latch and opened one of the wide double doors leading inside to a space bathed in the warm glow of a lantern. Therese's steps were softened by the thick layer of hay strewn across the dirt floor as she made her way toward the cart nestled in the rear. The odour of dry straw and fresh dung clung to the air of the confined habitat, an unnecessary reminder to watch my step after spending my formative years within the nunnery's walls. I made my way to Annette, the teenage jersey, that still managed to keep the nuns in milk despite her age. I stroked her mottled head, the action sparking recognition. "You're still beautiful, old girl." She pushed her ear towards my hand, which I indulged with a thorough scratching.

"Mother Superior tells us vanity is a sin, but since she also teaches us that animals don't have souls, I suppose there's no harm in a few compliments." Sister Therese grinned, her smile fading when she noticed me eyeing the cow's overly visible ribs. "Like the rest of us, they aren't strangers to deprivation. Brother George is growing older. He's been having a more difficult time managing the grounds during the winter. We've been purchasing feed in town, but with less funds to do so…"

"No donations?" I pulled the heavy leather horse collar from a stake in the wall and gently slid it over Mathilde's taupe head, careful not to trip over the ladder to the loft. The horse whinnied, palpable excitement at the prospect of a morning journey.

Therese shook her head. "During the colder months, the local farmers do well to keep their own livestock in grain. The only merchant is that wicked man, Mr. Augustus Klemp, charging us exorbitant prices knowing we have little choice."

I arched an eyebrow at the nun's uncharacteristic anger.

"Oh, nuns are allowed to be upset by unfair commerce." Sister Therese's face darkened. "I see no difference between my anger with his behaviour and Our Savior's anger at the temple merchants."

"You have every right to be upset." I was. As I retracted my arm, the exposed skin of my wrist came into contact with the brass hames on the horse collar. My mind flooded with tender images. I recognised the warmth of the old stablehand painstakingly brushing the horse's light mane, the same stablehand now buried not far from my mother. "You miss him, don't you?"

"What was that?" Therese had replaced two old galvanised milk jugs in the cart with fresh ones and hadn't heard over the clang of the metal. The sale of milk was one of the few methods that the nunnery had left to generate its paltry income. Frankly, I was surprised that Annette still produced enough surplus to sell.

"Mindless musings." I traded a knowing look with the shire horse, and with a pat, joined Therese in pulling the heavy wooden cart out from its niche. "Whew." I brushed a curl from my face and adjusted my dress. "If I wasn't warm before, I am now."

Therese grinned, revealing her normally hidden dimples. "I have to be mindful about when I complain about the cold. The abbess will have me mucking out these stables, quick as a beat, going on about how hard work warms the body and the soul."

I chuckled, recalling George repeating a similar mantra about chopping wood. As the novitiate of the convent,

Therese was often relegated to the myriad less desirable chores. She took a healthy pride in the Lord's work of serving the poor, but she was still learning to accept the more mundane challenges of life as a nun.

Once prepared, Therese had Mathilde trot the cart out from the stable. I swung the heavy doors closed behind us as I bid farewell to Annette. I climbed into the box seat to join my companion, and we began the trundling journey down the hill to the town as the cart bounced along, every clatter questioning the wagon's integrity.

Upon our arrival into the town proper, many of the locals ceased their daily routines to wave as we passed. Politeness towards the nuns was a common occurrence, but I couldn't help but feel the cold gaze of the townspeople once their eyes drifted from Sister Therese to me. They had always beheld me differently, the shift of each face from one of welcome to one of scepticism was overt. It was an amicable scepticism, but a deep uncertainty nonetheless.

Ever since Mother's and my arrival, we had never felt like part of the Luffield community, even after years of residence. The locals had never been particularly fond of outsiders, but especially not ones who did not fit inside their moulds. We had lived what many would consider a nomadic existence after Father's death. We had stopped attending the Church of England, which Mother had done only to appease Stewart. I had always found his devotion a touch ironic, given the church's lack of acceptance of him. That did not keep Dorothy Tate from being spiritually active, though not in the manner of which the deeply Protestant Luffield would approve. Even the Catholic convent had always been relegated to the outskirts.

"Is something amiss?" Therese gazed at me with soft,

brown eyes laced with traces of concern as she pulled the cart to a stop.

"It's nothing. I suppose I'm nervous about my upcoming journey to London." My fingertips had gone numb as I realised that the locals had never trusted me.

"I would say you could always remain in Luffield, but one look at you and anyone could tell this isn't your place." Therese blushed. "I'm sorry. I spoke out of turn. I only meant that—"

"It's quite alright." I took the nun's hand in mine, smiling. "This isn't my place. Luffield has been an important part of my life, but my future lies elsewhere." I embraced Therese, parting with her reluctantly. We had grown closer in the months since she had devoted her life to the church.

"Take care of yourself, Sophia." Therese smiled, and with a flick of the reigns, she and Mathilde were off down the street, already disappearing amongst the bustle.

The second she had vanished around the corner, my pleasant attitude dispersed like the ominous clouds above refused to do. I marched directly to the storehouses lining the far side of the River Nene where the locals purchased the tools, goods, and materials for their trade. I had every intention of sharing my mind with the good-for-nothing supplier who had been taking advantage of the nuns' precarious financial predicament.

The sprawling facility was sheltered under a wall-less metal and glass roof the size of a football pitch, which offered no protection from the cold or damp. The further inward I travelled, the more chokingly humid and ominously dim the space became. Unease filled my breast. I shoved my way through the citizens perusing amongst the wares towards Klemp's sketchy booth, easily four times larger than all of the other vendors. When I arrived, the portly, greasy-haired gentleman was arguing with Paul Billings over the cost of goods. The interaction ended with the red-faced Billings slamming on his bowler and marching off in quite a huff.

"What can I help you with, Miss Tate?" All traces of his anger towards Billings disappeared, replaced by a vile infatuation as he stared from behind a wooden cabinet of his smaller wares, resting his hairy arm on the once lustrous brass rail lining the top, now patinated brown with age. "You appear rather chuffed."

"I absolutely am, Mr. Klemp! I find it unbelievable that a gentleman like you has the gall to charge the women of Grafton such—"

"Miss Tate, you're forgetting your place." Some of the colour rose back to his cheeks, almost perfectly matching the crimson shirt he wore under his dishevelled apron.

"And you forget yours! Those women are—" This time there was no interruption. In my anger, my hand had fallen onto the brass railing. Countless flashes of intense displeasure rushed into my mind—memories of extortion, bribery, and thievery, all with Augustus Klemp and a gooey brown substance at the crux. Each emotion corresponded exactly with the same sensations from the altered weights at the market. The anger transformed to a calm fury as I recalled Mother Superior's words, resolving to use my gift for those less fortunate. "Mr. Klemp," I began through clinched teeth. "You'll be donating hay to the convent as often as they need it, beginning with a delivery today."

This drove the dishonest vendor into a fury he struggled to mask as he undoubtedly questioned who was I to march into his place of business and order him around. He took a deep breath, audibly scratching his beard stubble as his gaze slowly followed my figure from top to bottom, eyes lingering longer at my waist and chest before eventually reaching my face. "Not unless you have something to make the donation worth my while." Bile rose in my throat as he subtly licked his lips.

"I'd rather be devoured by a rabid badger."

He smirked and shrugged. "Then the answer is no. A man's gotta provide for his family."

"And is your family aware that you provide for them by funnelling opium to the town's most vulnerable, often cheating them in the process?"

"Those are serious accusations, Miss Tate." His voice trembled. His face reddened with unrestrained fervour, his nose as violet as Saint Edward's crown. "I'm nothing but a humble businessman who's fallen victim to the jealousy of others. You will not shame me for my success! If you had a proper husband, he'd see to that mouth of yours."

"And if you had a proper notion of ethics, we wouldn't be having this conversation."

"You impertinent little wretch. I ought to—"

I gestured to a nearby bobby making his rounds as he spun a baton. "Perhaps I'll invite a friend to our exchange. I'm sure he'd be happy to learn of your hand-offs with his superior, your choice of goods, or that your new weights are just as inaccurate as your old ones."

"How could…? How dare…?" The man muttered a foul chain of obscenities, feminine company be damned. He pulled a dirty rag from his back pocket and mopped the profuse sweat beading on his forehead and shoved a fat finger into my face. "Everyone knows you're a witch, they're just too kind to say it to your face! I don't know how you know, but one day you'll get what's coming to you. And I hope I'm there to watch."

"You *will* cease your despicable side trade and you *will* keep the nunnery supplied with free hay. Do I make myself clear?"

Augustus seethed at his predicament. Judging by the rage in his eyes, the only fantasy he still held for me was to be found belly-up in a back alley.

I could not right all the wrongs Klemp had committed, but I could limit future ones and take care of my friends at the convent. I still had much to learn about my gift, but we had had our first victory. A small one, but a victory nonetheless. "Oh, and Mr. Klemp, they'll be needing a weekly supply of barley and potatoes as well."

Chapter III

I practically floated out from the market, elated to have used my inherited ability for good. Leaving such a dishonest vendor fuming in my wake, I considered an unexpected perk. The humid microclimate of the open-air building did not do the extensive green steel superstructure any favours. Rust coloured puddles gathered on the sweating concrete from Klemp's booth to the exit, but I glided over them as though they were the Sea of Galilee. Outside, I made my way along the flagstones worn smooth by centuries of traffic, my low heels clicking loud enough to be heard over the din of the workers hoisting the day's cargo onto waiting lorries and the sporadic horse-drawn cart. In the rural town, changeover to the noisy, dirty combustion engine had been reluctant and slow.

I paused next to an industrial brick building to watch a group of handsome young gentlemen use a hand-operated crane to maneuver their bulky, canvas-shrouded loads onto an awaiting cerulean flatbed. I returned their flirtatious smiles as they waved, basking in the attention until smoke plumed from a nearby Model Y as it puttered its way through the crowded street and concealed the men from view. I choked as the cloud of exhaust billowed straight into my lungs. Some of the town's more progressive residents claimed the piston engine to be far superior transport than its manure-dropping predecessor. I couldn't help but question their logic as I clung to a street lamp and caught my breath.

By the time the air had cleared and my eyes had stopped watering, the men had returned to their business and the lorry was nowhere to be seen. I pressed on, holding down my cloche hat against the icy gusts funnelled through the street by the tall buildings that bordered it. I passed a woman, her navy and beige ensemble bundled tightly as she watched her children play in her garden. I smiled politely, but her gaze held nothing but an apprehension as uncomfortable as winter wind. Gossip had not needed much help in a place where my mother and I would always be strangers, even after fifteen years.

I turned away from the woman, my eyes drawn to one of the taller manor homes on the far side of the river, the Hart-Watts residence. Mother and I would have had a much easier time assimilating into the quaint town's populace if not for the interference of particularly self-interested locals like the home's matron. Sadly, rumours were the currency that paid for friendship in Luffield, and Camille Hart-Watts had many friends. If the self-interested socialite had her way, Dorothy and Sophia Tate never would have stayed long enough to warm a park bench in what she considered to be her precious city. By her logic, outsiders—particularly mysterious ones like us—were nothing more than vagrants, marring the humble town's facade with their foreign presence, threatening to attract more of our ilk. As much as it pained me to please the wretched woman, the time had come to leave the pastoral village behind and make my way to London.

I set my sights on Citadel Station, questioning if I would ever return. The return walk to my flat at the Women's Lodge was not a short one, but I was not about to ask Therese, who would undoubtedly oblige, to go so far out of her way. Once I collected my few personal items, there would be little attaching me to the town. I made my way to the River Nene, treading carefully down the graded cobblestone slope that slickened more with each passing minute. The slow drizzle had transitioned into a light snowfall. Under the heavy sky, the matte grey stones now glistened like obsidian, not yet cold enough for the downy flakes to collect. I reached the base of the hill where I was met by the sight of the narrow river meandering its way through town, a sinuous border between the privileged and those living hand-to-mouth. The river was packed with the long crafts of traders. I moved along the elevated walkway that ran alongside the waterway, listening to the water lapping against its banks as boat captains barked orders to their crews. I dragged my hand on the slatted concrete barricade that prevented incautious citizens from falling into the frigid murky waters, feeling the smooth pebbles of aggregate pass under my fingertips.

In a neighbourhood such as this, it was all too easy to lose track of time. During the limited light of the winter months, the building-lined depression surrounding the river could nearly pass as night. For this reason, the town's gaslighters kept the wrought iron lamps lit around the clock to aid the area's illumination. Each burning mantle wrapped me in a tenuous warmth as I passed, a lingering homage to Luffield's reluctance to embrace the new. While the rest of the modern world had transitioned to electric lighting, our fair town still glowed with the brighter light of gas. I paused, leaning on the railing as I observed the workers moving about like ants a few meters below, poling their vessels through the crowded canal in effort to escape the jam, anxious to begin their return journey to Peterborough.

As excited as I was to reach London, there were aspects of the country village that I would miss. Once I reached the chaotic bustle for which every city was known, I imagined that I would miss the slower pace of rural life. I sighed, so busy soaking in every detail before my departure that I failed to notice the twin shadows approaching me from behind. When the sounds of a scuffle and loudly voiced complaints drew my attention, I turned to see two ruffians bearing down on me, eyes intent on their target. "Bloody hell." Panic jolted through my extremities as my body toggled between freeze and flight. With scarves piled high on their shoulders and cap brims drawn low, recognition was damn-near impossible. Augustus' goons, it had to be. *Did I honestly think I could manipulate such an immoral person without consequences?* I cursed my stupidity and began swirling through the slow-moving foot traffic and pull carts laden with produce in effort to lose the assailants. My erratic movements were anything but clandestine as each person dodged my advance or was shoved aside. Shouts of displeasure pinpointed my location amongst the crowd.

I snapped my head back to gauge the progress of my pursuers only to find them right on my heels. I burst into a sprint, violently shoving people out of my way, praying that each body would further slow the pair. The leaner of the two poured on speed to match mine. He chased me through the press of bodies crowding the thoroughfare, throwing them to the ground as they screamed obscenities from the puddles in which they had landed. *Why isn't anyone bloody helping?* Ahead I saw the entrance to Clifton's bookshop. The amicable owner would shelter me given how many hours I had passed amongst his dusty shelves overflowing with forgotten books. I dove for the alcove and was knocked onto the rough-hewn stone steps of the establishment and flipped harshly onto my back. *Why isn't anyone doing anything?!* Passersby were ignoring the scuffle happening before their very eyes, giving the altercation a wide berth. A boy, his denim overalls dirtied from a long morning's work, was riding in the rear of a passing cart when his eyes connected with mine. Without question, he darted away to seek help.

The hot stench of foul breath drew my attention to my captor, who covered my mouth with a gloved hand. His scarf had fallen low, allowing me to get a clear view of his jaundiced eyes, thinning cheeks, and thinning moustache. "Don't put up a fuss, love, and this will be over before you know it." He opened his coat and withdrew a razor-sharp stiletto, glinting in the lamplight.

When the assailant pulled back his arm to plunge the blade into my chest, my eyes caught a bundle of long-shafted keys at his waist. In an action of sheer self-preservation, I grabbed at the man's knife arm with my left hand, holding it at bay with every modicum of my strength as my right dove for his keys. At that moment, I couldn't have been more grateful for the strength I had gained from slinging hefty sheets of leather day in and day out at the factory. With surprising strength for his thin frame, the knife continued on its forward trajectory, advancing millimetre by millimetre towards my heaving bosom.

"What a waste," he murmured as the double-edged blade's tip made contact with my coat.

Not a moment too soon, my fingers closed around the brass ring. I ripped the iron circle from the leather tab on his belt, flipped the first key around between my knuckles and was almost overcome by the unexpected flash of an emotion-laden vision. A young couple pleaded in fear as their home was burgled, the thief brimming with thrill from his nefarious deeds. The victims' fear intertwined with my own—a nearly fatal distraction. With great effort, I returned my focus to the present. With as much force as I could muster, I jabbed the pointed key into my attacker's bloodshot eye. His remaining eye widened with shock as he fell to the ground, clutching his face.

In the brief moment of our entanglement, his portly companion had caught up and seen what ~~I had done to his companion.~~ "You rotten cunt!" He advanced towards me, his own knife flashing. The keys, still embedded in his friend's face, were useless to me. I rocketed back on my hands as fast as my sodden dress would allow, until my back was against the bookshop door. When I could go no further, the man's lips parted in a sinister grin. Before he could act, the blessed sound of a constable's whistle pierced the air. *The boy!* The portly mugger's eyes darted back and forth between his target and his companion. With a hateful glare and more obscenities, he collected his friend, and they hobbled down the stairway to the riverfront, vanishing among the palettes and bundles of cargo.

Chapter IV

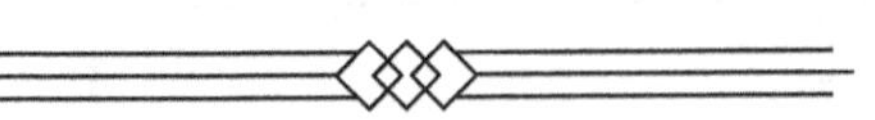

Everything after the attack on the street was a daze—nothing more than a blur. When the officers that the boy had brought arrived to question me, it was all I could do to remain focused. Clifton returned from his daily trip to the post office, and on seeing my shocked state, invited the three of us into his cramped shop for the remainder of the debriefing. True to form, he placed a scalding cup of tea in my trembling hands, offering the constables a cup as well. The familiar location helped to calm my nerves, but no matter how many times I washed my hands I would still feel the taint of blood on them. I was not sure what was worse, killing a man or not knowing if he survived. As vile as the attacker had been, I wanted him to live. I could not bear the idea of being a killer, even in self-defence. Making matters worse, I had no idea how many officers on the local force were recipients of Klemp's bribes. I nervously briefed the officer on the attack, attributing the incident to two would-be muggers. With his rigid hat under his arm, the greying Investigator Yarbrough listened intently, scribbling notes on a small pad all the while.

"Thank you for your cooperation, Miss Tate." The investigator impatiently smoothed his equally greying moustache. "We'll do everything in our power to track down these miscreants. I'll be in touch should we find anything."

His words felt more formality than honest commitment, making me all the more grateful I would soon be departing Luffield. Once satisfied, the constable introduced me to the freshly-minted Officer Jack Davies, whom he had thankfully assigned to escort me back to my home at the Lodge.

"I'm sorry you had to experience that, Miss. Quick thinking on your part though." The young constable did not elaborate further as he turned to face me. The gentleman's eyes were quite distracting, as blue as the sea on a sunny day. "If I'd been closer by…" He shook his head. Both men had been larger framed than he was and the officer a few centimetres shorter than myself. Only sheer chance had kept me alive given the odds stacked against me. All the more reason to escape this place. The town desperately clung to its idyllic reputation, but anyone who spent time here knew it had a wilfully ignored dark side. "I doubt they'll risk attacking you again, especially with it being a chance encounter as you said. Regardless, the captain has asked me to keep watch until morning." He smiled, pleased by the opportunity.

"That won't be necessary, Officer Davies." I struggled to get the words out as he led me to the front steps of the outdated building that was home to the Women's Lodge, forcing myself to retain my composure. "I'm departing the city by train this evening."

"Then I'll stand guard until you leave and escort you to the station."

We climbed the dated steps whose loose mortar testified to the brick building's age. Like every other aspect of the place, they were in need of repair. Taking more force than he expected, Davies tugged open the ill-fitting door and held it for me. The Women's Lodge was only the most recent of the edifice's numerous reincarnations over the last century. Hidden beneath the current sign over the entrance, the building still brandished the name of its illicit brothel past, Ishtar's, in a mosaic. The business had unsuccessfully masqueraded as a pub, even catering to many Luffield's council members who ignored its presence. The rumour was that the brothel had run afoul of a particularly licentious councillor who brought about its demise. The madam had ultimately fled town to avoid civil penalties.

True to the Women's Lodge name, any gentleman's access stopped at the door—not that the measure really stopped anyone. I bid the dedicated officer goodbye as I stepped inside. I turned to find the young man's eyes had not left me, but unlike Klemp's probing gaze, Davies' was one of care. I smiled politely. With a courteous nod, he descended the steps, assuming his post at the base of the steps next to the single remaining stone lion.

The moment I entered the all-female housing, Ms. Ruby dropped her crossword puzzle on the counter and rushed to greet me. "Oh, you poor dearie!" She cradled my face as I noticed the blood on my blouse for the first time. It had not occurred to me how frightful I must have looked. It should not have surprised me that she expected me in such a condition. Inspector Yarbrough had been a long-time suitor of the kindly matron.

After being widowed, Ruby Palmer had devoted her life to managing the facility, a home not only for single ladies, but for any woman down on her luck. For many of its residents, Ms. Ruby had become a second mother. The curly-haired matron often joked that because her son had turned out so poorly, she deserved a second chance like the rest of us. Removing her reading spectacles, she led me by the hand further into the sensuously red lobby, a holdover from its brothel days, towards a sitting room packed with plants.

"I'm fine. I…" My voice shook as the emotional walls I had erected crumbled along with my legs. I collapsed to the floor sobbing as my housemates rushed to tend to me.

Under the banner of solidarity, any uncertainty they may have held for me was swept aside as they consoled me—a woman who had fallen victim to the stronger sex. They guided me in towards the imitation gold velvet Victorian settee.

"I'll ruin the upholstery," I sobbed.

"Pish posh." The ever proper matron threw the decorative pillows onto the floor to clear my way and, with a glare, dared me not to sit. "Put your feet up as well. Edith, a cool towel."

Hazel played a serene piece by Satie on the upright piano that predated everyone but Ms. Ruby. Half of the notes were out of tune, but I appreciated her effort. In the privacy of the Lodge, Hazel had let her silky auburn hair hang loose, nearly reaching past the bench. Edith returned, placing the damp cloth on my forehead. She sat next to me on the settee, holding my hand until my sobs eventually subsided.

"Thank you."

"If we aren't here for each other, then what's the point?" She smiled down at me, sweeping her raven hair behind her ear.

In our years of living under the same roof, I had never thought of Edith as anything more than an acquaintance. Her personality, as cool as the rag on my head had been, had never led me to believe we were close. Perhaps there was more in Luffield than I gave credit. *The train!*

"I have to catch my train." I rose so quickly that my head spun.

"Enough with that nonsense, Sophia." Ms. Ruby returned with some of her homemade strong cider, another thing I would miss. "You're in no condition to travel. You'll be staying one more evening with us. Hazel, phone the station and have Sophia's passage transferred to the morning."

"But—"

"That's the end of it, and I won't hear another word."

Hazel darted from the room to the front desk where the building's single telephone was located and asked for the operator.

Ms. Ruby helped me lean forward as Edith drew the floor-to-ceiling curtains closed. In my last glimpse in the waning light, I could make out Officer Davies' silhouette diligently pacing in front of the building. Under the surprisingly good Gentileschi print above the mantle, I forced myself to relax as these women I had lived alongside, helped me out of my sullied clothes and into fresh ones from the suitcases that had awaited me upstairs.

After several hours of coddling and pleasant conversation over soothing piano music, I decided to retire. "I believe I'll be fine. Thank you for a most helpful evening." I rose to return to my room, nodding at each woman in turn, saving Ms. Ruby for last.

"You'll find your bed made with fresh linens, though with your things packed, your room won't be very inviting."

The matron eyed me with concern. "You're welcome to spend your last night in my flat if you'd care for company, though I can't promise I won't snore." She laughed and squeezed my forearms.

"If it's all the same, I'd prefer to be alone."

She nodded and smiled, watching me as I climbed the stairs. The women I had lived with for the last four years stared worryingly from the living room. Out of their sight, I wrapped my hand around the brass doorknob. Unlike before, the comforting flood of memories was all my own: the warmth of the sun and sand after returning from a day spent at Snettisham Beach, the comfort from visiting my mother's grave and my friends at Grafton Nunnery, the throes of passion from the occasional lover I snuck in after a few pints at *Trompe de Chasse* (recently renamed The Hunting Horn due to pressure from the patrons). I would be leaving all of that behind.

I inhaled deeply as I entered the cosy flat. The smell of lavender clung to the air from the fresh bedclothes. The space no longer felt like home without my personal effects adorning the walls. Everything of value had been sold to the others to help cover expenses. Anything unclaimed I would donate to the nunnery. Only a battered pair of leather suitcases held the meagre collection of belongings I would carry to London, the same two suitcases that had accompanied Mother and me so many moons ago.

I barely removed my attire before I crashed onto the mattress. Leaving the lamp on, I climbed deep under the covers, wishing to hide from everyone and everything. I cried silently into the pillow as I truly released the day's overwhelming emotions. Only then did I realise what had plagued me the most was not only the attack, but that image of the horrified couple I could not shake from my addled mind. I could still feel their terror gnawing me from inside out. Who were they? More importantly, had they lived?

I woke to a dismal grey horizon weighing on my already heavy mood. I made my way down the creaky wooden rug-lined stairs and joined the others in the former ballroom for what would be my second last breakfast with my companions at the Lodge. The mood was awkward, despite Edith's attempt to lighten it with her risque tales of endless spurned lovers as Ms. Ruby looked on disapprovingly. Nevertheless, her stories could always make us laugh. I refused to believe that Ms. Ruby's keen ears could not hear Edith's moans of late-night pleasure.

As a once young woman herself, I suspected that the wise matron had always known what was happening under her nose. She had taken over the Women's Lodge after her husband of forty years passed away in a construction accident. We never knew the full details of his demise. It had been gruesome enough that Ms. Ruby had vowed never to venture near a construction yard again. If she so much as spotted a crane in the distance, we would catch her crossing herself. As long as I had lived in the Lodge, I had seen the old inspector call on her from time to time, but the gentleman had always been turned away, crestfallen. I found it ironic that the woman who had lectured us so many times on the brevity of life was reluctant to take advantage of it herself.

With hugs to Ms. Ruby, Hazel, Edith, and my other housemates, I picked up my two laden suitcases, the dry-rotting leather handles threatening to snap under the stress. With a sigh, I took my first tentative steps towards London. During the eventful evening, I had forgotten about Officer

Davies, who still stood at the foot of the Lodge stairs, removing his uniform hat in respect and revealing his close-cropped blond curls.

"Miss Tate." He inclined his head slightly, weariness etched on his face by the dark circles under his eyes.

"Why Officer Davies, you look positively exhausted. What happened to your replacement?"

"I… I turned him away." Colour rose to his cheeks. "It didn't feel right leaving you. I felt like it was my duty to watch over you until your departure. It would be like abandoning my post."

I found the twinkle in his smitten eyes enduring. Devotion to duty had not been the sole reason Officer Davies had stood steadfast throughout the evening. He accompanied me quietly to the train station, all the while holding an umbrella over my head, a consummate gentleman.

Chapter V

Officer Davies escorted me through the winding streets of the waking town. Through open windows, sumptuous smells of sausage and eggs wafted into the street. The train station was located on the more prosperous far side of Luffield, a lengthy enough walk that would have me craving a second breakfast before long. As we strode among the affluent residents, my simple wool and cotton clothing stuck out among the furs and cashmere if my reputation did not. Closer to the river were the historic thatched-roof cottages for which the town was so well known with the construction growing more modern as one ascended.

While beautiful in their simplicity, the cottages required significant upkeep and boasted few amenities. We climbed the ascending streets, passing through the various neighbourhoods, each step carrying us among more and more wealth. Slightly higher were the ornate manors and their extensive, impeccably manicured grounds. From their higher vantage point, the less desirable side of town was cleverly obscured by conveniently crafted landscaping, providing an unsullied view of the rolling English countryside. Closest to the station were luxury flats for the carefully selected *nouveau riche* looking to escape London's hubbub on the weekends and a pristine park scattered with old-growth trees currently barren of their leaves.

Officer Davies and I cut through the park to reach the station, walking amongst those who chose to rise early and brave the frigid conditions for the serenity the expansive lawn offered. I paused in the centre to take in the spectacular view from the hilltop. Its picturesque skyline belonged on a postcard, both the reason Mother and I had sought solace here and why the gatekeepers did their best to maintain certain standards among the incoming populace. The bucolic view could almost give me the peace I sought. Before yesterday, it had been the perfect place to pretend all was right with the world. The town that for so long had been my home had taken on a more menacing air. The warm-hued stone of the manors and thatched-roof homes lining the river that imbued the location with such romance took on a haunting and unfriendly air under the ashen sky.

Neither of us had seen any sign of my assailants on our journey to the station, but that did not mean that they were not watching. A twitching curtain in a second story flat. A stranger staring on from a darkened alley. The constant feeling of eyes on my back. I found it hard to believe that the man I had stabbed would be anywhere other than convalescing, but the same could not be said about his partner or his need for vengeance.

I reigned in my fear, resisting the urge to rush to the station. I could imagine the villagers shaking their heads, the strange antics only adding to my perceived peculiarities. The last thing I wished was to give Luffield's more well-to-do further reasoning to detest those from the south side of the river. News of any unladylike behaviour on my part would spread like wildfire should Camille get a hold of it. I would not miss that wretched woman. Anytime I thought I was assimilating into the exclusive culture of the village, she had found a way to revive suspicion as though she had a personal vendetta against me. I had tolerated a great many names by unfriendly children in the school yard. Gypsy. Witch. Hussy. Adults were less likely to say those things to your face, but that did not mean they were not at the forefront of their thoughts. *Luffield's all yours, Camille.*

"This is it, Miss." The young constable stared at me in a doe-eyed manner that skirted unprofessional.

I stared at the brick chimneys of the station, puffing their plumes like old men and their pipes around a poker table. I turned back, facing the town. The action was not one of reluctance, but rather to absorb my last moments in the village that I had called home for so many years. Luffield was not without its redeeming qualities. Though I would miss them, they were not enough to hold me there any longer. "That it is, Officer Davies. I can't thank you enough for your assistance."

"Please, call me Jack."

"I don't think that's—"

He removed his hat, running it nervously through his hands. "If you don't mind me saying, when I am around you, my heart beats so hard against my ribs, I think they're going to break. When you return, I'd very much like—"

"*Officer* Davies. I'm quite impressed by your devotion to duty last evening. Your protection might have been the only thing that afforded me a decent night sleep, but—"

"But you wouldn't be interested. I understand." He tried unsuccessfully to hide his disappointment.

"Actually, I was going to say that I have no intention of returning to Luffield." I placed the tips of my fingers on his arm. "You're a dashing young gentleman, Officer Davies. I think you will make a fine suitor for one of Luffield's many eligible bachelorettes. Just not this one."

"I appreciate your candour, Miss Tate." He stiffened his lower lip. "Please don't mention—"

"You have nothing to fear, Officer Davies. Should we meet again, it will be as friends. Thank you for all you've done." I smiled, turning without giving him time to respond and walked under the patinated copper awning protecting those travelling as they entered the weathered brick building.

The station's interior had never been a bright one, but the oppressing weather outside only made the poorly lit space all the more foreboding. For a moment, the temptation to ask Officer Davies to wait with me until the train's arrival was almost too strong to ignore. The station was no busier than normal, but the waiting room held too many darkened corners, too many looming shadows, too many unfamiliar faces. After the previous day's attack, I suppressed the increasing panic and pulled my suitcases closer, hastening through the ticket claim and to the covered back landing where I could breathe once more.

As expected, Hazel had transferred my ticket to the next train departing for London, slated to leave within the hour. I passed the time anxiously, constantly glancing over my shoulder expecting to see one of Augustus' goons. Moments before the train's arrival, I noticed a familiar figure through the station's windows, pacing in front of the building. I grinned. Officer Davies had been guarding the station the entire time. A warmth grew in my bosom for the tender-hearted young man, allowing some of the nervousness to abate. *He's not that many years your younger, Sophia. In a few years, that will be nothing.*

I shook my head, muttering. "I'm not coming back to Luffield." Fortunately, no one heard. All I needed was for the last lingering rumour being that when I left town, I was positively batty and mumbling to myself. Although, what person does not talk to themselves on occasion?

I forced myself to stand still as I continued the interminable wait in the cold. I heard the clatter of the incoming train long before I could see it round the bend, felt its vibration through my soles. The countryside echoed with the heavy grind of steel on steel, the piercing whistle, the torrent of steam. Townspeople murmured about the fancy new LNER A4's design as it pulled to a halt in front of the awaiting passengers. More streamline than the boxy steam locomotives of the past, the black and blue behemoth more closely resembled Jules Verne's *Columbia* ready to carry its passengers to the Moon. Though I had no aspirations of setting foot on the Moon, at the very least, I expected to arrive at my destination in a fraction of the time.

With a look at his pocket watch, the white-mustachioed conductor shouted his call to board, jerking us from our awe. Judging from his grin and look of pride, our reaction must have been a frequent experience and one that he relished. A porter, uniformed in a black and blue matching the train, took my bags and offered his hand as I mounted the steep stairs into the passenger car. I gasped when I rounded the bulkhead and took my first tentative steps inside. The luxurious train's interior was as modern as what I had seen on the exterior.

"A brand new train, Miss," said the well-groomed gentleman, adjusting his cylindrical cap. "I thank my lucky stars I received placement here. It might be the first time I've been grateful to my father-in-law for something other than his daughter." I snickered at the porter's frankness as he examined my pass. He took off down the aisle, turning his head back to beckon me to follow. "Once we reach London, I'll retrieve your belongings from the baggage car."

"Thank you." I returned his smile as I slipped a sixpence into his hand. He grinned back before disappearing through the car's rear door.

I took my seat on the plush blue booth, scooting towards the large-framed window so as to give ample space to my would-be travelling companion. Every aspect of the decor was pristine, from the wood side panels to the velvety fabric lining the seats, not yet marred by decades of use. Moments later, a rotund woman wound her way down the aisle as she boisterously went on and on about the impressive quality of fresh haddock and Bordeaux in the dining car to anyone who would listen. I found her unrelenting enjoyment of the train's fare refreshing even as other passengers spoke condescendingly of her lack of decorum in hushed tones.

"Mildred G. Foster." The woman had stopped and stood over me, bathing me in her shadow, yet filling me with an inexplicable lightheartedness. "The G stands for Gertrude, so you'll understand why I don't use it." The woman was wrapped from head to toe in luxurious fur accentuated with elegant jewellery. Neither was overstated, but both alluded to wealth as ample as her personality and figure. She eyed me impatiently.

"Oh. Sophia Tate." I proffered my hand, having momentarily forgotten my manners at the intriguing encounter.

"A pleasure." Her voice was deep and loud even when speaking closely with someone else, her tone far from the reserved British formality expected among women of her social stature. "You headed to London, Sophia?"

"I am, Mrs. Foster."

"Milly, for God's sake. Only my mother called me Mildred. And it's Ms. Foster," she said, flashing her immaculate ivory teeth to the nearest porter. "That one has a backside I wouldn't mind waking up to." Her whispers were loud enough for half the car to have overheard and moan with displeasure at her impropriety. The porter's smile vanished as quickly as he did.

Milly was not unattractive, but I could see how her thicker figure, middling age, and forthright language among the stuffy individuals that comprised England's upper class had kept her unmarried all these years. Yet, I found the stranger's company endearing. Her unchecked honesty was a pleasant distraction from the unwelcome gossip around which I had spent so much of my life. Inexplicably, I felt like I had known the woman my entire life. "I think we'll get along swimmingly."

Chapter VI

A quarter of the way into the two-hour trip to London, I found a moment of solitude. As much as I enjoyed listening to my newfound friend, listening was all that I could do. Not to mention, keeping up with Milly's tales was exhausting. Once the lobster thermidor she had so thoroughly enjoyed began to digest, she had fallen sound asleep, snoring away as loudly as she had a tendency of speaking. At the moment, her head was resting on the seat back, her mouth open comically wide. I couldn't help but chortle every time a prudish couple across the aisle glared at her with disdain. Frankly, I had had my fill of people who considered themselves beyond reproach. A snore caught in Milly's throat, and for a moment, I could see the palpable excitement when the other passengers thought she would wake. To everyone's disappointment, she jostled and lolled her head to the far side. An audible groan could be heard above the muffled din of the train. I faced the window to hide the smile stretching across my face, holding back the fit of laughter.

The picturesque countryside rolling by drew me in as the train thundered along its iron rails. As muted as the sound was in the luxury liner, one could only mask the clatter of iron and steel to a certain extent. The once verdant fields that were so prolific in the rural counties were now filled with the pastel green growth of winter crops still crisp with the frost of morning. The forests, now draped in their uniform umber coat, were still teeming with life. Deer. Hares. Chipmunks. Foxes. A hunter's dream. I watched a small herd of deer search a barren field for breakfast before bounding off into the unknown, and my success dawned on me. Pride filled my bosom. I had taken the first step into a new world despite others' doubts. A shiver of excitement travelled pleasurably up my spine as I broke free from the mould that had tried so hard to snare me. Luffield might have been a haven for its prosperous inhabitants, but few of its less fortunate escaped, the cycle only repeating with their children. That cute visage that it prised so had a habit of occluding the backs on which it was built. The residents were blind to the poor conditions and struggles of the working class, the town council going as far as to keep them as physically separate as mentally. The factory where I had earned my meagre living was no exception.

My ears rang from the constant hiss of steam and clang of hydraulic presses. Even in the midst of the chilly season, the factory was akin to a sweltering Soviet banya. Sweat beaded off Geoffrey's brow as he pulled another unwieldy hide from the steaming press. Arching his back to compensate for its substantial weight, he lugged the hide towards me and tossed it on my station with a nod. When I had first begun work in the tannery, the noxious odour so pervasive in the building had been intolerable, but over the last few years I had grown used to it. The smell permeated my clothes, following me to the Lodge every evening. If not for her sense of propriety, Ms. Ruby would have had me strip on the stoop. As it was, my first stop was always the utility room, where I kept a fresh set of clothes to don after I threw the others straight into the wash. Once I had made the decision to move out of the convent on my own, naturally I had discovered the need for income. Despite my growing body of knowledge and skill, there was little choice for a woman with an informal education such as myself. I had taken the only position I could. I still remembered the look of scepticism on Raymond Wilkins' face through a haze of cigar smoke when I inquired after the job.

I stretched out the new hide across my work table, making certain to smooth every wrinkle from the damp leather. Carefully, I began the tedious art of dividing the leather into sections by quality, meticulously calculating so as to glean the most usable material from the defunct bull's skin. Without a doubt, should I fail to do so, the waste would be noted by Mr. Wilkins whose screams of displeasure could frequently be heard from one end of the thundering facility to the other. As a simple peon, much less a woman, I never had any option but to hold my head high whenever he berated me over the slightest inconsistencies in my work. The snivelling weasel was a top-tier bastard, but one who knew how few employment options Luffield held for me.

I spun the industrial compass with the deftness of experience, making one sweeping circle kiss the next without measuring each one. I may not have cared for the leather work or miserable conditions, but I took pride in what I did and did it well. As the tool grazed my finger, the warm brass amplified my boredom, anxiety, and displeasure, creating an emotional feedback loop that made it all the more difficult to focus. My only reprieve from the grind was the zen-like flow making the twelve-hour shift pass slightly faster. Day in and out I would accomplish my work, doing everything in my power to minimise detection by management. As much as it pained me, I needed the work. The Lodge rent was a paltry sum, but with no savings to speak of, the only chance of escape and opening the shop of my dreams revolved around this dismal factory. Antiques had long held such sentiment, often bringing great pleasure, memories, or history with them. For Mother and me, it was different. We could detect that provenance in ways no one could have imagined. My life's calling was to unite such relics with the ideal owners in a lasting relationship that would benefit both.

I completed tracing the various patterns on the warm hide and removed the hefty shears from the pouch at my waist, painstakingly cutting one piece from the next before the pieces would travel further down the line for the next steps in their production. During the Great War, the facility had temporarily been converted to create utility belts for the soldiers being dispatched to the continent. Rumour was already beginning to circulate about the escalating situation in Germany, and workers were curious if another such reconversion loomed on the horizon. The last thing the world needed was another war as terrible as the last. So many lives gone. I supposed that if there was a bright side to the tannery producing belts, it couldn't be simpler to trim straight strips from a hide. However, I would gladly accept the more complex patterns in lieu of another war.

History and art held endless fascination for me. Using what little energy remained at the end of a long work day, I would fall asleep reading old tomes I had borrowed from Clifton's bookshop. The older gentleman was aware of my limited funds. Provided that I purchased the occasional book, he allowed me to use his business as a library of sorts. As the open-minded person he was, if he believed the rumours about me that circulated like dead leaves carried by one gust after another, he never gave credence to them. Clifton had never greeted me with anything less than a warm smile stretching from one rosy cheek to the other. It was only natural that my literary interests culminated in a love for antiquity. Accompanied with my unique perception, owning an antique shop, not unlike the one Mother and I had run across in London, was the embodiment of my dream.

The women who I shared the Lodge with already believed my slaving away in a tannery was the epitome of unladylike behaviour. When I shared my plans of delving into the gentlemen's world of business, it was too much for their traditional values. According to them, a woman's place was in the home quietly supporting her husband. I had no immediate aspirations of marriage, though I was not opposed to the idea. I could live with being an old spinster like Betty had been before she passed, having spent her final years in the Lodge. At this point in my life, I found men nothing more than a pleasant distraction. No one was going to control my life, least of all the person I may or may not chose to share my life with. Ironically, the parlour was regularly filled with giggles as the women carried on about how much better the world would be if women were in charge. I will never forget

Ms. Ruby's advice: "Only let the men think they are in charge. After all, it is you who have the means of controlling them." The consummate lady rose and sauntered around, exaggerating each movement to howls of laughter.

I smiled at the recollection, stacking the freshly trimmed leather cuts on my station. With a grunt, I carefully lifted the heavy pile, making sure not to over bend the cooling leather. I trudged my way to Mr. Clayton's station where they would be formed. As I passed Mr. Wilkins, who had been marching between the rank-and-file scrutinising their efforts, I suddenly lost my balance. I cringed, watching the discs of leather fly across the greasy, mud-ridden floor, ruined by the runoff of the various processes. Mr. Clayton jumped to my aid, the gentle giant easily helping me to my feet. He began to ask if I was alright when he was interrupted.

"You fool woman!" Wilkins screamed, spittle shooting from his mouth as I brushed the excess filth from my work pants. The heavy-duty clothes, now saturated with the grime of the occupation, were beyond salvation and rendered worthless. Purchasing additional clothing would be yet another setback in a series of setbacks. As close as I was to my goal, I could never quite reach it. "That will come out of *your* pay! Not the wholesale price of the leather, but the cost of the finished products."

I fumed. "That's not fair! It was an accident." Before I could say more, the back of his gnarled, hairy hand impacted the side of my face, nearly shattering my composure.

"I tolerate your presence, but I don't have to tolerate your bloody mouth." Ire burned behind his eyes. "Clean all this up. Immediately!"

I nodded, my eyes burning. Anger replaced by humiliation and hurt. Exactly what he wanted.

He turned, walking away as he grumbled to his assistant. "As much of a waste of beauty as her whore mother." His harsh words drew heavy tears which rolled down my face uncontrollably. *If I had had the strength of a man...* That vile bastard made me cry several times a week, but I had resolved long ago he would never see me do so.

"Thank you, Mr. Clayton." I wiped my tears with the clean handkerchief he offered me. How he managed to keep anything clean in this environment was beyond me.

"That was no accident," said the broad-shouldered Jamaican, glaring over my shoulder in the direction our supervisor had departed.

Mr. Clayton was one of the few Jamaicans brought to England for the war effort who had been allowed to remain in the country. The quiet hulk of a man had worked in this very factory, producing the belts to supply British soldiers. When many of his fellow countrymen were deported, his immense size and strength bought him a position on the workforce, despite a great many protests from the locals. In a way, he had always felt like a kindred spirit, though his ostracization had been far more intense than my own.

I despised the factory, but I knew exactly how much money I had saved to the pence. My finances would be tighter than I had planned, but I believed that I had the minimum I needed to make my entrepreneurial dream a reality.

"Mr. Wilkins," I said, turning, all signs of weakness cast aside. The man spun on his feet, already bearing down on me, threateningly shoving his sleeves up past his elbows. I untied my apron and threw it into a puddle on the floor. "I don't think I will clean this up." The bustle of the factory died down as all attention turned towards me. "I've done all I ever will for you. I have a dream to fulfil, and you will play no part in it."

"A dream? You mean that asinine business idea of yours?" He and his assistant howled. "An uneducated bitch like you?" He moved close enough to my face I could feel the heat of his breath over that of the environment. "You leave here, and I'll make damn sure the only work you can find in this shite town is whoring on a street corner like your godforsaken mother."

Clayton's dark fist blurred across my vision as it impacted Wilkins face with the force of a freight train. "You don't speak to women like that, and you certainly don't hit them."

Wilkins slipped in the mire as he tried to rise, falling on his face once more. He struggled to his feet amid snickers, face beet-purple with rage, ready to deal out some savage blows. His normally slicked hair, dishevelled. Mr. Clayton took a step in front of me. With one look at the Jamaican's ample musculature, he shied away, backing down like the weasel he was. *What a coward.*

"You're both fired! By the time I finish with your reputations, you won't be able to find work in Ireland." He spat a rosy stream between our feet before skulking away to doctor his wounds and his pride.

Mr. Clayton and I collected our last compensation from the barred window on our way out, mine far less than I was owed. We meandered out through the quiet lot, heading back towards the town proper in the distance.

"You didn't have to stand up to him. Not for me."

"Too many like him." Mr. Clayton was soft spoken, a gentleman of few words with the poor grammar of someone who had never had even the informal educational opportunities I had. "I'm strong. I find work."

"Thank you." I stood on the tips of my toes to give him a quick peck on the cheek.

He blushed and waved as I departed. Sadly, Wilkins was correct in one respect. Finding another job in this tiny town after what I had done would prove damn near impossible, but I had no intention of staying. I may not have had traditional schooling, but between my educated father, wise mother, and knowledgeable Sister Agnes, I had an extensive education though I would never have the papers to show for it. More importantly, I had been taught how to learn by my numerous tutors and had quite the motivation to do so. Reading was my favourite pastime, and I had learned more than enough to run an antique business, even without a supernatural gift.

I grinned as I walked down the street, contentedly unemployed. Mrs. Ruby would have a conniption fit when she heard. I was sure the town gossip would see to that soon enough.

There was little point in dwelling on the past, but I could not help thinking how different my life would be had a few things been different. When my father's well-bred family discovered his sexual proclivities, they had disowned not only him but his offspring as well. The act had driven him to drinking heavily, ultimately flinging himself in front of a train. Mother's gift had her chasing relics throughout Europe, pursuing them like a drug and burning through her inherited wealth at an unsustainable rate. However, I would not change a thing. Their quirks and passions were what had led me to become who I was. After everything they had done, I owed it to them to use my gift to help others. It was my driving force. That was what I envisioned every time a Raymond Wilkins-type glared at me from under their furry eyebrows and receding hairline. Men like him still abounded in the world, but I could not wait to reach the city where open-minds were more commonplace.

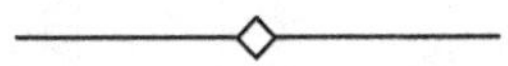

I didn't think it was possible to feel freer than I had in that moment when I had stood up to Wilkes, but as the speeding train passed through station after station taking me closer to my London, I absolutely did.

Chapter VII

"There it is, Merry Old London!" Milly leaned over me, pressing her ample bosom into my lap as she gazed out the window. The city's skyline sprouted from the earth, running from one side of the horizon to the other. The last time I had been in the city I had been only six. Even with my limited memories of the place, I was positive that it had grown since then. In the distance, I could already see the prominent lead-clad dome of St. Paul's Cathedral reaching above everything else in the city. My heart thumped with a sense of nervous excitement. "I'll never grow tired of seeing the place. Progress and all. Nothing makes me miss this crowded mess more than visiting these backwater townships. If not for my ailing sister, I'd never set foot out of London."

My garrulous companion had told me (loudly enough for the entire car to hear) all about her perpetually pregnant sister, her good-for-nothing brother-in-law, and their eight poorly-behaved children. *My God, I couldn't imagine living in such a household.* With as much as she disliked visiting their hamlet, she did it quite often. Her sister, Tabitha, had had a particularly rough bout with tuberculosis. She had barely survived the encounter, suffering a miscarriage and leaving her bed-stricken. As the illness took its toll the house and her family collapsed around her thanks to her "worthless drunk of a husband." If Milly was to be believed, her visits were the only thing keeping their lives from turning into a quagmire of chaos. Despite my new friend's complete lack of propriety and disregard for social mores, anyone could see that the woman possessed a heart of gold.

I nodded, finding it difficult to concentrate on Milly's never-ending monologue, distracted by the unending city blurring past my window, my body buzzing with excitement. It was not until the conductor announced our arrival at Euston Station that my focus returned to her.

"You never did tell me, what brings you here, Sophia?" She stood and bellowed for the steward to bring her luggage.

How could I? You hardly let me get a word in edgewise. I let out a little chuckle, receiving an arched eyebrow from Milly. "I'm here to inquire after an antique."

"Oh, I absolutely adore all things vintage. I could stare at them for hours, marvelling at what spectacles they've experienced, who's touched them, what role they played in history… I've been meaning to acquire some for my home, but I'm afraid an ignorant woman like me will get swindled. Promise me you'll accompany me to the Natural History Museum at some point—"

"Your bags, Madame." The porter handed Milly her gargantuan trunk and proffered mine, which looked like a handbag by comparison. "I took the liberty of retrieving yours as well, Miss." He passed my suitcase to me, his fingers brushing my hand with the slightest intent, and flashed a wide grin.

I returned the gesture with a polite smile as he went to tend to others. Another arched eyebrow from Milly.

"What?"

"Don't you 'what' me. You know good and well that that fine young man would love nothing more than to take you to Picadilly Circus as fast as his skinny legs would carry him. If I was half my age, I'd take him up on it."

I stifled a hysterical laugh, following her plump frame down the aisle. "He's certainly not hard on the eyes, but my business must come first."

"Antiques? You must be joking, right? Those things have been around this long, they can stand to wait a while longer while you enjoy a little romp in your fleeting youth. And believe me, it's fleeting."

I shook my head as she rambled on, oblivious to the fact I was no longer listening. I stepped off the train's steps and onto the crowded platform, breathing in the thick city air brimming with smoke and promise. Admittedly, promise did not smell quite as good as I had hoped. "It's important," I said when there was finally an opening. "I need to track down something that holds great sentimental value to my family."

"I suppose I can respect that."

I had never been surrounded by as many people as were present on the narrow concrete platform stretching between the parked trains. What I had considered crowded back in Luffield during the morning bustle paled in comparison to what London had to offer. For a brief moment, overwhelm washed over me. I stared at the sky through the expansive glass ceiling in search of reprieve from the chaos. At that exact moment that the sun peeked through the clouds, revitalising life itself before it returned to its place of hiding.

Milly dropped her trunk down on an empty luggage cart with a grunt before adding mine. "You'd think I'd eventually learn to pack lighter," she scoffed. She reached for my hands, taking them in hers. "I sense something different in you, Sophia. I can't help but think we were meant to cross paths. Call it fate." She eyed the suitcase. "Now tell me, where do you plan on staying?"

"Likely whatever hostel near the Thames is the safest and most affordable."

Milly's mouth fell open as she continued to roll the cart into the station's high-ceilinged great hall. For the first time since I had met her, she had been rendered speechless, and not from the impressive Greek-inspired architecture intertwined with Art Deco accents. "What type of friend would I be to let you stay in such squalor? You'll stay at my flat in Islington, you hear? A pretty lass like you can't wander the streets of London looking for a room to let. You'll have every bloody bedswerver from here to Croydon offering you a place to lay those ginger curls of yours."

I shrieked with laughter. Mildred G. Foster was anything but boring. "Thank you, Mildred."

"If you want to stay with me, you best stow that Mildred nonsense."

We exited the station out into the uninspired courtyard leading towards the gargantuan columned arch that made the station so recognisable. My newfound friend hailed a cab with a most masculine whistle and one screeched to a halt in front of us. She saw the surprise etched across my face and grinned. "I gave up on being all proper and ladylike long ago. You want to get things done in this day and age, you have to do it your damn self. The last thing I want is some man to do it for me, dragging me along by the hand like a bloody child."

"You and I think more alike than you realise."

Milly winked as the cabbie rushed out from the driver's seat. The short gentleman nodded in greeting, grabbing our luggage and placing it in the alcove next to his seat before holding the door for us as we took our seats.

"Thornhill Square, young man."

The car lurched off with a whine as he pulled into traffic without hesitation and began navigating his way towards Barnsbury at a good clip. Milly pulled out a compact to refresh her light makeup, and I took advantage of her rare silence.

"I understand that London cab drivers have bigger hippocampi to memorise all of the city streets."

"Hippo-what?"

"The hippocampus. The portion of the brain that's responsible for memory."

"You're saying they have larger brains?"

I nodded, noticing the cabbie following the exchange in the rear view mirror.

"Hah! They'd like to think so. You know, I dated a cabbie long ago, before I met Edward. God rest his soul. Possibly one of the most arrogant bastards I've ever known. No offence." She patted the driver on the shoulder.

"None taken." He smiled into the mirror without turning his head. "You have to either be an arse or plain barmy to drive in London for a living, pardon my language. If I'm honest, I'm probably a little of both."

We chuckled, amused by the driver's frankness. "It'll be so pleasant to be home again. And with markedly improved company. It'll be nice not to talk to myself day in and day out."

"Didn't you say you had hired help?"

"Mei? Yes. She says nary a word. The damn house would be on fire and the woman would tap my shoulder and point. Stoic as that statue of Robert Stephenson we passed in the Great Hall. Must be all that Oriental philosophy."

The further we drove from the sprawling city centre, the more the buildings decreased in size, no longer stretching themselves as far skyward. The cool tones of the concrete landscape transitioned to the warm hues of natural stone. Small swathes of greenery became commonplace as they intertwined with the roadways and crowded residences. People milled about on the sidewalks, volume unchanging, but businessmen and labourers had given way to caretakers, children, and the elderly. Each kilometre took on on a journey through time as we passed from one major architectural period to the next—Regency, Victorian, Modern—all strove for something new, but in many ways were homages to what had come before. I toyed with my gloved fingers, questioning if retracing my mother's footsteps would be something new or merely another revival.

The car eventually came to a stop at the side of an expansive park packed with evergreens, and the driver collected our bags. Milly slipped a handful of coins to the content cabbie, and he was off with a tip of his cap. The afternoon sun beamed down, warming my face. As anxious as I was to settle in after the day of travel, the park could not have looked more inviting. Uniformly styled brick buildings with whitewashed ground floors surrounded the park's perimeter. Each home's front windows overlooked the natural scene, a welcome respite in a city that lacked the rolling hillocks of Luffield. The neighbourhood buzzed with the voices of children as they played their games, the winter season doing little to dampen their merriment.

"That's us." Milly gestured with a finger, hoisting her massive trunk aloft without complaint.

"Wow." I would have been grateful for any place to stay, but Milly's townhome would be far from uncomfortable. The lot alone must have cost more than I would have made during a lifetime of factory work.

"Well, don't stand there gawking. Let's get inside where it's warmer." She led me up the wide stairs and into the checkered marble foyer. Her welcoming home had a fire roaring in anticipation of our arrival. Once I took a whiff of the marvellous odours wafting through the home, it occurred to me how long it had been since I had eaten. My mouth salivated to the homey aroma of chicken accompanied by the earthy aroma of porcini mushrooms.

"How did—"

"—someone who grew up in Tockwith afford this?" Milly harrumphed. "Didn't take me for a woman of means, did you? Strictly speaking, I'm not."

"I'm sorry. I didn't—"

"Don't apologise. I'm messing about. My skin's thicker than a rhinoceros. People have never loved the idea of sharing their walls with some uncouth Yorkshirewoman. Well they can bloody well get over it." Milly kicked off her shoes and motioned for me to do the same.

A short Asian woman emerged from what I took to be the kitchen, bringing more of the fragrant odours wafting behind her. Her apparel was sewed from patterned fabrics common to the Isles, but had been cut in a traditional Chinese manner. Her pale face spoke of youth, but the wisdom in her eyes indicated more years than Milly.

"Sophia, I'd like to introduce Mei."

"It's a pleasure to make your acquaintance."

Mei responded with only a slight bow, revealing a few grey strands among her jet-black hair, confirming my suspicions. The woman collected our coats and returned from whence she came.

"Everything I have I owe to my late husband, but I doubt that's a story that holds much interest to you."

"On the contrary. I'd love to hear about it."

"You aren't tired of me going on and on yet?"

I shook my head. I truly was not. Everything was so new, so different, that I felt overwhelmed. I was grateful to not be responsible for maintaining pleasant conversation.

"Where did I leave off? Oh, Edward had been contracted to do some structural restoration in Tockwith. A talented and much sought-after engineer, that one. Made good money. Real good money. I never did figure out what he saw in me, whether it was my ample curvature or my loquacious nature. Well, whatever it was, he liked it. We were wed within a year. Everyone from one side of Barnsbury to the other thought I was chasing him for his money. Truth be told, I hadn't known he had any until we returned from our honeymoon. I was about as shocked as you are now. When he fell ill, people assumed I'd poisoned him. God's honest truth, Edward was the only man who'd ever seen me as something more than a possession. Above all else, he was my friend." She dropped into a sitting room chair, her eyes growing distant.

"God. I can't imagine what it's like to lose someone like that, Milly." I crouched on my knees and held her hand. "I was so young when I lost my mother."

Milly waved off her loss, returning her focus to the present. "No point in moping now. I've learned to be my own woman and could care less if I ever have another man. I'll never have another Edward. There's only one thing I want a man for nowadays, and even that's only when I get tired of taking care of it myself."

"Mildred!" I failed to stifle a laugh. My face turned beet red as I cried with mirth.

"If I can embarrass you that easily, having you for a house guest is going to be a hoot!"

Chapter VIII

"That's unbelievably generous of you, but this is something I need to do alone." The restaurant echoed with the clink of silverware and porcelain over the hushed tones of morning conversation. I folded my napkin, placing it next to my plate. Seeing the motion, the server disappeared with my half-eaten entree of eggs Benedict. Chez Ranhofer, without a doubt, was the fanciest restaurant I had ever patronised. From the brocade curtains framing the windows to the gold-rimmed tea service, not a single extravagant detail was overlooked. I had been more than willing to pay my way at a more affordable venue, but Milly wouldn't hear of it. After the dismal fare from her romp through the British countryside to visit her sister, she had been craving "more refined" food.

Her face distorted into a look of scepticism. "I can tell when someone isn't being forthright, but I trust you have your reasons. Promise me you'll be careful, Sophia." Milly reached over and took my hand. "If you find yourself in a tight spot, don't hesitate to give me a ring."

I smiled as I nodded. "Of course." I had been unable to finish my food despite how incredible the gourmet breakfast proved to be. I hated to dwell on the cost of the food that had gone to waste on my behalf. My stomach was a bundle of nerves as I steeled myself to face the traumatic memories that had lingered in the back of my mind for a decade and a half.

Milly finished her Ossetra caviar-topped eggs and brioche and took care of the bill. Afterwards, we stood out front of the restaurant clustered tightly together, waiting for the frigid rain pitter-pattering onto the awning to lighten. Working-class Londoners passed by the fancy establishment's windows, casting glares from the sidewalk towards those who were oblivious to their daily struggle through the economic recession. Though Milly had done everything possible to welcome me into her life, I felt out of place in the rarefied air. She noticed me staring at a bedraggled labourer ambling past. "A minute ago, I was thinking a shopping day was in order. Now that I think of it, perhaps a day of serving in the soup kitchen would be more beneficial." She playfully slapped me on the back, and I realised that it was no longer raining. "Well, don't just stand there, Sophia. You have a date with destiny, right? Off with you!" She cracked her trademark grin.

"Alright," I chuckled. "I'm going. I'll tell you all about it on my return."

"You bet your caboose you will."

I shook my head as I parted the woman's larger-than-life company. In many ways, her boisterous manner reminded me of the Americans portrayed in the radio dramas Ms.

Ruby played so often. Mildred Foster was unlike anyone I had ever met, making her all the more interesting. She was self-assured, brutally honest, and as kind of a woman as could be. Our paths crossing as they did could not have been more fortuitous.

I pulled my collar tight as I made my way through the busy streets, questioning my decision to walk over taking a cab. The rain may have ceased, but the wind had not. Unlike Milly's fur coat and muff, my wool was struggling to keep the stabbing breeze at bay as it whipped down the thoroughfare and fluttered my lapels. Lingering in the Baltic air may not have been the wisest idea, but I wanted to experience London firsthand, not removed as one was inside a vehicle. After spending years familiarising myself with the city's layout from the comfort of my flat in Luffield, the city felt strangely familiar, yet foreign. I let my feet carry me down towards the riverfront, all the while taking in the sights and sounds of the bustling city, so different from the tranquil countryside.

If the information from Ms. Ruby's son was accurate, the brisk walk from the restaurant to the antique shop would be only a couple of kilometres. Relying on him had not been my first choice, but my search had been filled with dead ends. Perry was a sleazy ingrate who often stole into the Women's Lodge late in the evening. Reeking of smoke and booze, Perry would prowl around the atrium in hopes to glimpse something he could never set his eyes on otherwise. When caught, Ms. Ruby would invariably drag him from the premises by his ear and throw him on the street, all as the grown man whined like a child.

The mysterious antique shop my mother and I had visited did not seem to exist, at least not among the legitimate businesses. With little alternative, I turned to Ms. Palmer's witless son, who had a tendency for bumbling his way through criminal activities as demonstrated by his lengthy hiatuses in the local penitentiary.

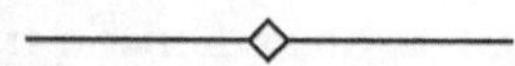

My stomach growled for the umpteenth time. After pulling a double shift in the tannery, I was desperately tired, but the leftover mulligatawny soup Hazel had made for dinner was proving insufficient to satisfy my hunger. My body was craving more calories after the hard day. I had already wasted too much time deliberating on whether to slip downstairs for a mug of milk from the kitchen or trying to go to sleep hungry.

I sat up with a groan, the narrow bed echoing my complaint as I dropped my feet to the rough oak flooring original to the building.

Aside from the clock, the dim atrium was silent as I padded my way down to the kitchen. I ran my hand along the crimson wall for balance. I regretted not having donned my robe, but at this hour no one should be awake. I had been too warm to consider it and appreciated the cool air wisping into my nightgown.

I reached the galley kitchen, large enough to prepare sufficient food for the building's current population of nineteen, and collected a mug from the cabinet. After filling it with milk from the industrial refrigerator, I turned to go back to my room. Halfway up the steps to the second floor walkway, I heard someone skulking about, breathing heavily. I would have been more alarmed, but the culprit's wooden-soled shoes always gave him away.

Amongst the potted palms that his mother was so fond of was Perry Palmer, his good eye illuminated in a vertical beam emanating from Edith's slightly parted curtains. The greasy-haired miscreant had returned in another desperate attempt to catch one of us disrobed. Judging from his rapid hand movements, he had been successful.

I cleared my throat, and the intruder nearly jumped from his skin. In great haste, he adjusted his clothing and turned to face me, his face flush.

"Ah, uh, Miss Tate. So good to… see you. Do you happen to know the whereabouts of my mother?" He took a second to catch his breath. "I've been looking all over for her and can't seem to find her."

The pig hid his intentions no better than a toddler.

"Have you tried knocking on her door?" I asked in an elevated voice, making him visibly uncomfortable.

As a dedicated residence for single women, The Women's Lodge was supposed to be a place where we did not have to be as concerned with our modesty and safety. Perry Palmer was the epitome of what the Lodge sought to protect us from. It was no surprise when Perry's eyes began to wander up and down my thinly veiled figure. When I realised how little I wore beneath my attire, I crossed my arms to better conceal my breasts, which were already responding to the draughty air of the open central space. "As a matter of fact, I'll do it for you." I began marching downstairs in the direction of the matron's flat.

"No, no." Perry struggled not to yell, scurrying to get between me and the stairs, waving his hands as his eyes focused on mine. Even from a metre away, it was apparent that his body was long overdue for a shower. "That won't be necessary, Miss Tate. I was on my way out, you see."

"Well, since you're here…" His yellowing eyes grew wide with excitement, opening a maelstrom in my stomach. I masked the disdain, but could not avoid rolling my eyes. "I need some information. I'm having trouble locating something."

"Hmm." He scratched at his scruff, feigning consideration. "What's in it for me? You could always pay me in pounds sterling, but you know I also have a fancy for gingers."

I burped up into my mouth. The grimy worm couldn't have appealed to me less if he tried. "I wonder who would be more interested in your voyeuristic escapades, Mr. Palmer, your mother or the police? Maybe your reimbursement should be that I won't divulge how often you hide amongst the fronds and peep into our rooms while—"

"Enough! Lord knows you couldn't have seen a damn thing in this darkness, but since I don't want you sullying my otherwise immaculate reputation…" He finished tucking in his shirt as if to appear more reputable. "What would you like to know?"

Dear God. I drew a slow breath, reluctant to share any more than I had to with the low-life git. "I'm searching for a business in London. A small antique shop. I'm having difficulty finding any record of its existence, but I'm positive it's there. I believe that it might deal in… illicit sundries." For some reason, I uttered the last bit in a whisper.

"Illicit sun… Flipping hell. You women and your posh drivel." Perry's annoyance grew. In his mind, it was clear that women had only one use. "If you mean nicked goods, why can't you come right out and say it?"

"*Are* you aware of it?" I marched closer, forcing his back

against the wall, my impatience waning. The reek of his unwashed body made my stomach grow queasy.

"Uh… Maybe." He shook with fear. I was a far cry from intimidating in my revealing evening wear, making the snivelling weasel nothing more than a lily-livered coward. "There are several."

I described the one from my memory as best as I could.

"That has to be Northrop's," he stammered. "Don't tell no one I told you, they'll have my arse."

"Where is it?"

"I can't. If Simon finds out, he'll send that goon of his. The nick will be the least of my—"

Still clutching the mug of milk in one hand, I grabbed his filthy ear with the other as his mother would and dragged him towards her door.

"Alright, alright! It's on a side street off Drury Lane, about halfway between the Thames and the British Museum. If they ask how you found the place, we've never met in our lives."

"If only that were true." I released his ear and let him fall to his knees. I turned on my heels towards the stairs as he placed his loathsome hand on my backside. Without thinking, I spun, shattering the half-filled mug of milk across his temple. He tumbled back on the floor, vacant eyes staring up at the ceiling as a trickle of pinkish blood made its way down his temple.

For a moment, I thought I might have killed him. When he blinked, I let out the breath I had not realised I had been holding. He recovered from his shock and darted out the back door before anyone could piece together what had transpired. The crash must have awoken those nearby as moments later, Ms. Ruby, Edith, and Hazel had joined me in the lobby, attracted by the hubbub.

I explained the incident as being so drowsy that I had clumsily dropped my mug. The other women believed me, but the twinkle of doubt never left Ms. Ruby's eye. If her sly grin was any indication, she had known exactly what occurred that evening. The longer I lived at the Lodge, the more I came to understand the matron's preternatural senses when it came to the goings-on within her building. I thought about a number of the less-than-proper things I had done over the years and was mortified by what all the woman probably knew.

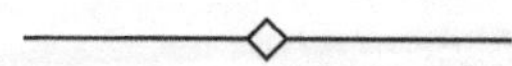

I meandered down Drury Lane amongst intriguing shops, eateries, and residences that hearkened back to London's past age. Businesses that had endured more than a century gathered here like old friends playing chess in the park, though not even they could distract me from my goal. As best as I could figure, once I was halfway between the river and the museum, I turned down a narrow side street that held a number of vaguely familiar storefronts. I was about to return to the lane and try the next street down when I saw it: a nondescript white-bricked alleyway, virtually unchanged after fifteen years. And somewhere at the end of it was a memory so haunting, it had driven my mother to insanity.

Chapter IX

I forced one tentative foot in front of the other, taking the first few steps down the narrow alleyway. The vivid flashbacks of being ushered away by my terrified mother crashed into my mind, so real that I could almost feel the little stuffy gripped tightly in my arms. During our flight so long ago, the alley had been left unguarded; whereas today, a motley pair of street toughs blocked the path. No sooner than I had made my intentions clear the shorter of the rough gents began his nonchalant approach. I was not a particularly tall woman, if anything, only slightly above average, making him no taller than about a metre and a half. The stocky gentleman barred my path. Judging by his coarse appearance and scarred face, his diminutive stature did not keep him out of regular tussles.

"Take a wrong turn, did you mum?" He smiled through poorly kept teeth, pulling his watch cap tighter against the drizzle.

"I dunno, Jas." A skinnier gentleman with greasy hair curling out from under a similar cap leaned up off the wall, gesturing towards me with a toothpick frayed from far too much attention. "Maybe she came down here to keep us warm."

"Stow it, Henri. How many times have I told you to conduct yourself as a gentleman?"

Jas muttered something under his breath before returning the toothpick to his maw.

"Forgive 'em, mum. He's not as refined as the likes of us." Even in the draughty alleyway, I could detect the stench on his breath. "Now, it's best if you find your way back out to the street, and forget this little alleyway ever existed."

"I'm here as a client." I held my head high, staring down the goon with all the bravery I could muster. I had come too far to be bullied away now by the two imposing miscreants.

"Wish more of the old man's client's looked like 'er," said Henri, mumbling about old men and hiked trousers.

"Well, well. Far be it from me to bar a paying customer." The man called Jas slipped an arm around my waist and steered me towards the door. "Forgive my colleague's manners, he doesn't fully understand how one treats a lady as lovely as yourself."

"And you do?" I shirked off his arm with repulsion. "I'd thank you to keep your hands to yourself."

Behind me I could hear Henri's wheezy chuckle.

"Suit yourself." Jas shrugged. "Door's down there on the right."

I spun on my heels and marched down the cobbled path that must have predated the surrounding buildings by more than a century, grateful not to hear pursuing footsteps. Dry leaves rustled as they swirled restlessly in the breeze, trapped against the alley's white-washed dead end. A sudden flash of a nearly identical image from the past nearly caused me to stumble. I reached the recessed oak door of the shop without further issue, shuddering from all the built-up tension. *Perhaps I shouldn't have turned down Milly's offer to accompany me.* The innocuous business front appeared anything but that of a criminal enterprise. The warm, ornately carved door frame and painstakingly inscribed lettering reading "Northrop's Antiques" on the windowpane showed a degree of refinement normally unheard of amongst illegitimate affairs.

Based on the hazy memories from my childhood, I had always assumed the shop to be a reputable establishment with a certain degree of refinement. After years of struggle to locate any record of the shop, the only conclusion left was that it must have been a less-than-legitimate business, its existence as secretive as the whispers and inventory that passed between its clientele. I questioned how such a bumbling fool like Perry had become involved with a business that catered to such prestigious customers.

I stared at the brass latch, sceptical and yet curious at what sensations I might feel upon that initial contact. Taking a deep breath, I depressed the heavy latch of the handle. As expected, my mind was awash in inseparable images and feelings of so many souls that had passed through that door. The majority of the mundane memories were that of routine business, but intertwined with them were darker, more sinister undertones. Like releasing an electric current, I released the latch with some difficulty. I stared at the brass with revulsion as I grasped the door by its wood frame and shut it behind me with a second tinkle of the brass bell that had announced my arrival.

Many aspects of the preternatural gift the universe had bestowed on me still held great mystique, leaving me with much to learn about it and myself. Clearly, stronger emotions left stronger impressions. As in the mind, they tended to linger in one's memory, not fading with time like others. The undesirable emotions from the latch had been distant, undefined, like tricks of the eyes that disappear when given attention. For that I was thankful. I doubted my ability to keep a straight face should I be confronted by a shocking vision with great clarity. Not only was I opposed to anyone discovering my ability, but in my vanity, I did not wish to appear a fool.

"Bloody thieves." A tall gentleman in a suit rushed by as he donned his hat, nearly toppling me over in his hurry to reach the exit. He made eye contact with me for the briefest moment before vanishing into the alleyway without so much as an apology. I had not needed unnatural abilities to see that the gentleman's teak eyes burned with fear-masked anger.

Trying not to dwell on the interaction, I wound my way through cluttered tables and shelves packed with lifetimes of knickknacks and tchotchkes. I gave a wide berth to the fragile Ming-dynasty porcelain, balanced carelessly on edges, separated from an untimely end by mere millimetres of tabletop. Every object in the crowded space deserved its place. Surrounded by the unrivalled beauty of relics spanning the world in their origins, I found it difficult to avoid distraction. *Magnificent.* A carved ebony Oba from Benin. A matching pair of Persian gold rhytons. A 17th-century Raeren salt-glazed jug. The shop's collection could rival that of the British Museum several blocks over; its wares, I suspected, equally desired as the museum's exhibits by the countries of origin from which they were removed.

Focus, Sophia. You're here for one item and one item only—the candelabra.

Unlike before, the pleasant lingering odour of spearmint pipe tobacco that I recalled had given way to the acrid odour of stale cigarettes. As I continued my search, the slick-haired man behind the desk that I had yet to notice lowered a newspaper boasting headlines about the escalating situation in Spain and cleared his throat.

"Looking for something in particular, Miss?" Taking one last drag, he mashed a cigarette into a handsome Baccarat crystal ashtray amongst a pile of other butts.

Smoke clung to the air, as thick as the tension I felt under his critical gaze, twirling in eddies between the simple bulbs poorly illuminating the dim space. The sparse sunlight that managed to escape the overcast sky's grasp was further inhibited by the tiny windows nestled amongst the shelves. From the dark recesses of a corner between shelves, a wide-shouldered hulk of a man began to emerge. With the slightest motion of a finger from the suit behind the desk, the foreboding figure faded back into non-existence.

"Yes." My voice squeaked. "Yes, I am." My second attempt proved far calmer. "I'm looking for a particular vintage candelabra, a fairly mundane object by your exceptional standards. The piece is solid bronze with ornately carved lions on its base. I understand the piece has been part of your inventory in years past. Does this candelabra sound familiar?"

The man leaned back, stretching after being slumped over the low mahogany counter for God knows how long. His shirt stretched tight with the hidden muscles beneath, and if not mistaken, the bulge of an automatic pistol in his waistband. The gentleman looked more than capable of handling any conflict that arose, making me question for what situation could he possibly need the hulk in the corner. "I'm afraid not. The real expert is the sad sop in the back." He gestured with a thick thumb towards the building's back room. "Peter, get in here!'"

Amongst the sweeping melodies of Bruckner, I could discern the sounds of someone rising from a squeaky desk chair, followed by a clatter of metallic objects and a few light curses. I stifled a snicker and received an arched eyebrow from the suit. A lanky gentleman with neatly-parted hair stumbled from the back room, nearly tripping over his own feet as he did so. Just as he regained his balance, the dark shadow gave him an extra thrust from behind, and Peter fell flat on his face.

"Are you alright?" I jumped to his side, all traces of humour lost. I helped him up as I glared at the menace's twinkling eyes between the shelves.

"I… I believe so." He stood, dusting off his chocolate and beige checked sweater vest and smoothing out the wrinkles of his shirt. I picked a fleck of debris from his dusty cheek. "Thanks," he muttered, blushing. "Did you need something, Simon?"

As I glanced between the odd pair, I noticed the slew of fraternal traits. Despite the wealth of differences in nearly every respect, the underlying similarities were undeniable. Brothers. I could only imagine that Simon had spent his youth bullying his brother to no end. The rail-thin Peter would have been helpless to fight back against the notably more powerful sibling. In the brief moment that I had been inside their store, I could not understand why Peter put up with such maltreatment.

"Dame's looking for some candlestick. Thought you might be able to help her out." With that, Simon returned to his newspaper without so much as a second glance but not before igniting another cigarette. Judging by the tray, either it was not emptied often or the man smoked nonstop throughout the day.

I returned my gaze to Peter and realised that I still had my hand on his arm and quickly withdrew it. Our eyes crossed paths and the gentleman immediately dropped his gaze to the ornate Farahan rug covering a wooden floor in desperate need of refinishing.

"A candlestick, Miss?" His voice quavered as he straightened his tie, struggling to appear professional after the inflicted mishap.

"Not a candlestick, but rather a candelabra."

"Ah." He smiled, amused. "My brother wouldn't know the difference."

"At least he knows a dame's tits from her arse," muttered the gruff voice from the shadow.

"That's no way to talk around a lady, Tim." Simon calmly scolded the man without raising his eyes from the paper.

"My apologies, Miss. I'm not used to polite company, is all." In the faint light, I could barely make out his stubble lining a recently shorn head which merged directly into his broad shoulders.

Peter led me through a pair of darkly varnished saloon doors into a storage room crammed with sundries, many of which in various states of disassembly. In the middle of the space he had constructed a small but functional workspace. He gestured to a stool in front of the battered wooden bench as he took the needle off the nearby gramophone, ending the composer's eighth symphony abruptly. Lit by a solitary bulb, the bench was scattered with bits, bobs, and a pair of magnifying lenses, but there was a meticulous order to what at first glance seemed chaos. Ignoring the mechanical grime, I took a seat, thankful I had chosen to wear more casual attire.

Looking more carefully at the room, I found the place strangely alluring and began to understand part of the reason Peter endured his brother's harassment to remain. He made his way to a bookshelf lined with thick leather tomes. After perusing for a minute, pulled one out, scattering enough of the fine dust into the air to make himself cough and causing me to chuckle once more.

At first, the gentleman looked chagrined, but then realised the humour of the situation and chuckled himself. "I suppose it's obvious I look at some of my books more than others." Peter smiled as he placed the book on the workbench in front of me, opening to the middle of a span of musty pages with still after still of candelabras in every conceivable style and age.

I gasped.

"It's quite daunting when you're faced with so many." He ran his finger over the black and white photographs as if he could sense the history through the pages just as I could with real brazen objects. "Every one unique and beautiful in their own right." He looked at me, then quickly diverted his eyes again before clearing his throat. "Now, let's find your candelabra."

Chapter X

"Lion heads, you say?" Peter rubbed a hand along his clean-shaven face, deep in thought as he tried to remember anything that fit my simplistic description. "I don't recall anything like what you've described, but I didn't begin working in the shop until I was sixteen, several years after your visit. Before Father's death, he'd run this place for nigh on forty-five years. There's no telling the number of pieces that passed through our doors during such a span. And you can confirm that this candelabra was in the showroom fifteen years ago, for a fact?"

"I'm certain of it." I fiddled with the strap of my purse across my lap. "I suppose it was silly of me to waltz in and immediately expect to be granted my desire." I harrumphed. I had spent years hunting down the antique, giving it more than enough times to change hands, possibly more than once. What was a store worth if it was incapable of moving its inventory? "Is it possible that you have record of its sale."

"Perhaps, but those records would be confidential. We have a number of clients who take their privacy quite seriously and prize Northrop's for our discretion. I'm sorry, Miss Tate."

"Please, Mr. Northrop. It's a family heirloom." While not strictly true, in a way, it had been part of our family's history for the majority of my lifetime. "I would be more than willing to reimburse its purchaser to have it returned."

Peter rubbed the back of his neck, uncertain. Oblivious to the thin film of grime on his fingers from the repair that I had interrupted, his touch darkened his neck. He was momentarily torn between satisfying the current customer or honouring his client's privacy. I could tell that my presence in his space made him uncomfortable. It seemed that the small-statured gentleman was far more accustomed to the company of inanimate relics than other humans.

Peter sighed, entertaining the idea of caving to my request. "I'd know if we'd sold an object matching your description during my tenure, meaning it has been gone for over a decade. Any sales records that old wouldn't be here, but rather at our warehouse."

"I'd be more than happy to help you search." I perked up at the notion.

He responded with a daffy chortle though I had no idea what he found humorous. "It's not that simple." He said once he had composed himself. "Simon uses the warehouse to keep his… personal effects. He doesn't even like me visiting the warehouse alone."

"What an unusual arrangement the two of you have. You're his brother and I presume half of this business, are you not?

His face flushed, anxious to please but struggling with the notion of denying my request. He squirmed in the awkward position. I had been too direct, a habit of mine that was not oft well received. I resolved to be more delicate in my approach so as to not risk losing the potential lead. I found Peter's quirks and innocence to be strangely endearing, a refreshing trait when compared with the brash and cocksure patrons found at The Hunting Horn.

"I am, but Father left Simon in charge. I may not always agree with my brother, but I respect his authority. He hasn't led me wrong yet."

It took substantial restraint not to take advantage of his treatment in the showroom. *Delicate, Sophia,* I reminded myself. I desperately wanted to encourage Peter to stand up for himself. I had little doubt that what I had observed was a common occurrence between the siblings. "If only he respected you as much as you do him. Your work is equally as important as his. Surely he wouldn't mind a quick trip."

Peter's eyes fell to the floor. Aside from the gusts rattling the shop's tin roof, all was silent. Afraid that I was losing my chance, I placed my hand gently on his knee. He almost jumped at the unexpected contact, trembling ever so slightly.

"If I happen to see any proprietary secrets, you have my word they shan't be divulged."

"I suppose you're right. The warehouse *does* belong to me as well." He raised his chin and smiled, his confidence growing. "I suppose no harm could come of it. The files are kept in the building's front office, so we wouldn't even need to enter the storage area itself."

"Unless there's any chance the candelabra is in the warehouse. Could that be possible?"

Peter shook his head, all the while not removing his eyes from the hand that had not left his leg. Unless I was imagining it, his forehead was beginning to bead with sweat. "The warehouse is reserved for merchandise waiting for showroom space or pieces that were sold as soon as we'd taken possession. People don't realise that much of our business is conducted off-site with little more than a handshake to seal the deal."

That realisation had very much occurred to me. What I had seen in the showroom alone illustrated that Northrop's Antiques sold all manner of items, many of which from dubious origins. A business that specialised in foreign and domestic ill-gotten relics would naturally conduct business in the shadows. Operating in such clandestine circumstances, it came as no surprise that Simon and Tim were both brawny and armed. I examined the younger Northrop. The gentleman obviously was quite astute and adept at his craft, but was the polar opposite of his sibling. Either Peter was oblivious to the true nature of the inherited family business, or he was wilfully ignorant. Regardless, any visit to the family's warehouse would not be without risk. Those who relish the darkness do not often enjoy the revelations brought by light.

"I understand. Nevertheless, could we still examine your archives?"

Peter sighed, glancing at the Fears timepiece on his wrist. "Perhaps while Simon's at lunch. On Fridays he tends to linger at the gentlemen's club afterwards cloaked in cigar smoke and bathed in brandy. I sincerely doubt he would note my absence."

I squealed with excitement, a sound that caught my host off guard.

Peter chuckled, shaking his head at the informal behaviour. "The warehouse is near the wharf. Perhaps it'd be better if we left separately so as to not draw unnecessary attention. Would you be willing to meet me at St. Anne's Limehouse at the top of the hour?"

"Nothing would please me more, Mr. Northrop."

His cheeks grew rosy as he smiled, revealing a pair of dimples. "Just Peter is fine."

My cheeks were beginning to respond themselves when Simon interrupted.

"Peter, haven't you taken enough of this lovely woman's time?" Simon stood in the narrow doorway, nearly filling the frame from one side to the other.

I retracted my hand as surreptitiously as possible, concerned about how long he had been eavesdropping on our conversation. "Really, Mr. Northrop, it's quite alright."

"Call me Simon. Would you care to join me for lunch? There's a little French bistro around the corner that serves a fine *confit de canard.*"

"Thank you for the kind offer, Mr. Northrop, but I really should be going," I said, ignoring the request to call him Simon. "Thank you for your time, Peter." I rose and made a beeline out of the shop, moving briskly past Simon's goons. I managed to make my way several streets over before the wave of anxiety began to abate and hailed a cab. On one hand, my nerves were frayed from the interaction and on the other, excitement bloomed in my chest at the prospect of being one step closer to my goal.

"Where to, Miss?"

The cabby had to repeat his question before he broke through the haze that surrounded my giddy mind. "St. Anne's Limehouse, please."

The driver shook his head, muttering as he put the black cab into gear and pulled away from the curb.

I had never intentionally spent time in the presence of such shady characters. This upper echelon of criminals lulled people like me into a dangerous sense of complacency. Luffield was no stranger to miscreants like Augustus, but they were far removed from the organised operation of Simon's and his underlings. I would do well to stay on my guard. Crossing someone who could instil such fear in grown men would be positively idiotic, and yet I was about to sneak under the veil shrouding his enterprise. I took solace in the fact that Milly somewhat knew my whereabouts, even if she was not present to watch my back. Should any ill befall me, I imagined that she would have the Yard hot on my trail even if she had to drag them by their ears. I giggled at the prospect, causing the driver to further question my mental integrity.

After a lengthy ride through the busy streets of the United Kingdom's largest city, I paid the gentleman and found myself staring up at the white stone edifice of a glorious eighteenth-century church. The towering Gothic structure was far more ornate than the simple convent in Luffield or the utilitarian cathedrals constructed in the present century. When compared to the extravagant architecture of St. Anne's, Grafton would appear as little more than a humble hodgepodge of stone, an edifice cobbled together over the centuries with little regard to aesthetics over function.

So intent was my focus on the church that I had not noticed Peter's arrival and advance. He caught me unaware when he tapped my shoulder from behind, causing me to lurch from my skin. Any anxiety that I had shed during the journey roared back as I started from his touch.

"Dear God, Peter." I clutched my thundering heart as I caught my breath. "You gave me such a fright."

"My apologies, Miss Tate. I had no intention of—"

"It's perfectly alright." I took a deep breath, laughing off my reaction. "If I wasn't alert a moment ago, I certainly am now. I think I'm on edge at the prospect of being reunited with a long-lost family treasure is all."

"It's pleasant to be around someone who is equally enlivened by the ancient as I." When he grinned, his amber eyes sparkled, a pleasant replacement for the ever-absent English sun. "Especially someone with beauty that Botticelli would struggle to capture."

My face instantly warmed thanks to the unexpected compliment. What I had initially thought to be a shy, bumbling individual was quickly proving to be quite charming. Intelligent, interesting, and above all, kind. I feigned a sudden interest in the cobblestones lining the street to obscure my blushing cheeks.

"Oh, God. I apologise. I've made you uncomfortable again." Peter timidly stared at the street. "Simon's always telling me to speak my mind. I must be a fool for entertaining his notions of conduct."

"You have no reason to apologise." I raised my eyes to meet his. "Truly, I'm flattered."

Peter forced a nervous chuckle. "You can tell I don't get out of that back room much."

"Well, I've spent too much time in the presence of men arrogant enough to believe that they can say anything they wish to a woman. I find your sincerity and self-awareness refreshing."

"Thank you, Miss Tate."

"Now, if we are going to be accomplices in this little escapade, I must insist that you call me Sophia."

A more authentic laugh escaped my companion. "Then right this way, Sophia."

I proffered my hand. After a brief hesitation, Peter timidly took it, handling it like he would a priceless vase from a long-forgotten kingdom. He led me down the street and over a few blocks as the residential area we had arrived in gradually transitioned to that of industry. As we neared the wharf, pedestrian traffic gave way to workers with hand trolleys, and passenger cars to cargo lorries.

After a lengthy walk, we arrived in front of a sprawling metal-clad edifice. Little attention had been given to the building's appearance. Here and there were the signs of structural repairs, but no effort had been made to blend the varying materials. I had not considered it, but I supposed that if the warehouse held an invaluable collection of artefacts of questionable origin, attention would be the last thing its owners would desire. Surrounding the entire facility was a menacing black iron fence supported by copious amounts of rough-textured concrete. Placed every few centimetres atop the barricade were needle-sharp spikes, as functional as they were decorative.

"Worried about thievery?" I spoke without thinking and silently cursed myself. From what he had said, Peter struggled with saying too little, whereas I had a habit of saying too much.

Peter was unfazed. "Simon's concern for our inventory has always bordered on paranoia, some of it well deserved. The contents of the warehouse would fetch a tidy sum if stolen, but thankfully few wish to cross my brother." Peter unlocked the bolt and, with a grunt, rolled one side of the heavy gate open far enough for the two of us to slip through. "Fortunately for us, he is also too cheap to hire a guard." Peter smiled as he closed the gate behind us.

I took a last glance towards the street in the nick of time to see a shorn head disappear among the bustle.

Chapter XI

It was my imagination, it had to be. I ignored the tingle raising hairs on my neck as Peter and I made our way to the building's primary entrance. Even if it had been Simon's goon trailing us, the warehouse belonged to Peter as much as it did his brother. *He has every right to be on his property with whomever he wishes,* I reminded myself.

I was pretty sure that Milly would scold me to no end if she had any idea how careless I was being at present. The rational part of me believed Peter to be a kind soul, but if my intuition proved incorrect, I would be in dire straits.

"It's this way." Peter stared at me patiently, and I realised that I had frozen in the middle of the treeless courtyard as I evaluated my predicament.

I nodded, smiling politely as I placed one hesitant foot in front of the next. I examined my host—his mannerisms, stance, attitude. Nothing about him came across as ominous or threatening, in fact, quite the opposite. I allowed myself to relax a bit without lowering my awareness. Ahead, Peter had inserted the key, grumbling as he struggled to get the door's formidable lock to acquiesce.

"Bloody…" With a satisfying click, the lock gave way. "There." Peter sighed, a look of embarrassment further softening his features. "It's normally not that troublesome."

The non-descript grey steel door swung open with the groan of under-oiled hinges and the crackle of breaking cobwebs. The building's interior was black as pitch and far from welcoming. Peter saw my immediate apprehension and led the way into the darkened entry, tripping over his own feet as he stumbled to find the light switch. With a snap, the caged bulbs suspended from the heightened corrugated ceiling began to glow one after the next, humming contentedly as they brightened.

"That's more like it." He gently shut the door and turned to me, all grins. "Ignore the state of things. Simon mostly stays in the warehouse portion and rarely steps foot in the office. I'd keep it tidier, but as I stated before, my brother doesn't prefer to leave me here unattended, so my time for organisation is limited."

"No judgement here." I raised my hands in mock surrender.

Peter chuckled, his eyes resting on my face for a split-second longer than natural, before clearing his throat and turning away. "I suppose I should start digging for those records."

Peter's disclaimers proved unfounded. Aside from a few scattered papers, the room appeared to be painstakingly organised. The only strikes against its cleanliness were that of its time uninhabited—cobwebs, mildew, and dust.

The illumination had revealed two large drafting desks in the centre of an expansive room. The brick walls were painted in a putrid lichen hue, a colour chosen more likely as a bargain than for a preference. Calling the space an office was generous at best. The room was clearly not that of those who wore ties to work, but rather those who had callused hands and grime under their fingernails. My tenure in the tannery had left me with a profound respect for hard-working people like Mr. Clayton who toiled away so that others could enjoy their more lavish lifestyles. When I imagined my future as a business owner, it was not one spent trapped behind desks such as these. I would be out in the world, collecting meaningful artefacts, researching their provenance, and connecting them with the ideal owner.

Peter made a beeline between the work surfaces towards a door in a partial wall that divided the office in two. As I perused, my eyes were drawn to a bay of windows that looked out upon the unlit warehouse. Unlike the permanently masked windows facing the courtyard, these allowed the office lights to reach the carefully stored wares. The glow cast by the bulbs struggled to penetrate the all-encompassing darkness, but I could make out the large panel of a Renaissance painting peeking out from beneath a shroud. The work featured a number of men on horseback with a cathedral in the distance.

"What a gorgeous piece." I stood, enthralled by the authentic masterwork. "Is that…"

"Best not linger." Peter lowered the blinds, obscuring the painting. "If I'm not back to the office before long, I'm afraid Simon might send someone searching for me." He ever so lightly placed a hand on my upper arm and prompted me towards the door that had opened, his gentle touch radiating an unexpected warmth.

"Searching for you? An adult?" I neglected to mention that I already suspected a follower.

"My brother can be very protective. Not only of his collections, but those under his charge. Honestly, I'd prefer not to have to endure a round of his questions. He makes even me nervous when he puts on his inquisitorial act."

"Does he not trust those he cares about?" We stepped into a room lined with shelves and cabinets overflowing with all manner of records and references.

"He doesn't trust anyone," Peter said with nonchalance.

Unlike the previous room with the desks of scuffed pine, the smaller room was packed with wooden shelving nearly as ancient as the antiques of which we were both so fond. Each sagging shelf struggled with the copious weight of countless boxes and ledgers recording the Northrop's long history of business. Peter paced up one aisle and down the next, periodically making the hum of one deep in thought as the sound of his shoes on the gritty floor echoed through the cramped room.

"Ah, I believe this is what we are looking for." Peter gestured to a large rack of old, leather-covered, spiral bound ledgers to which the moisture had not been kind. "These were Father's records." He ran his hand along their spines, his mind deep in the throes of nostalgia. He coughed, choking on the sporish dust that his contact had sent fluttering through the air. "As you can see, there are a multitude of them, some dating back ages. If only we knew more specifically when the item was sold…"

"I believe I can help with that. I have a habit of being lucky."

Peter shrugged, happy to allow any method that would see him back to work before Simon. Of course, luck had little to do with it. Each book was bound with a brass spiral, one which the book's author would constantly brush as they scribbled each hasty annotation. Beginning with what I assumed to be the oldest, I slowly ran my hand along the set. Records flashed in my mind one after another as though flipping through the pages of a book in search of a specific image. More than simply visual information, it was as though I had awoken an additional sense. As of late, each use of the gift served to enhance it, refine it. Suddenly, my hand stopped on one three-quarters of the way through the shelf.

"This one," I said matter-of-factly.

"Right." Peter dragged out the word as he pulled down the large-format book, arching an eyebrow but saying nothing more. He blew the dust off the ledger, carefully directing it away from my face.

Peter carried the wide notebook to one of the nearby drafting desks, its surface already angled, and placed the ledger on its rubber-coated surface. Though surely unintentionally, I found it humorous that the desk's green coating perfectly matched the unappetising wall. He slowly opened the cover to the music of the creaking leather and turned to the first few entries.

"This is Father's handwriting." He ran his fingers over the pencil marks lightly enough so as not to smudge them. "All we have left are the memories and his legacy."

I softly placed my hand on Peter's. When he stared into my eyes, his shy, clumsy manner drifted away, but when I massaged the back of his hand with my thumb, the awkwardness came rushing back. He gently withdrew his hand and focused all of his attention on the notebook.

"If you look here, this is where the sales entries begin. This will only take a few moments, assuming your lucky guess proves accurate. Feel free to wander about, but I would ask that you remain in these rooms."

I nodded, but he had already immersed himself in the ledger. Such a quirky, yet endearing gentleman. He was attractive in a subtle way, well dressed with a tidy appearance. Aside from a notable intellect, there was little that set him apart from average. Still, there was something about him that drew me in, be it kindness, dedication, or the fact that he was a kindred spirit in the love for the ancient. Apart from his mother, I had the impression that he had not spent any significant time in the company of women. Hunched over the desk, the normally timid gentleman could not have been more in his element. I found myself delighted that Peter and I had crossed paths. Without him, I did not know that I would have ever located the candelabra that I sought.

I meandered through the shelves of records, taking care not to brush my coat against any of the filthy edges. I suppressed the desire to explore further than my limitation, knowing full well that the objects hiding within the warehouse would fascinate me to no end. The brief glimpse that I had of the painting reminded me of the cheap replica of the Vera Icon hanging back in the convent. Art was a world of its own, existing within that of antiquity. It would take a lifetime to become an expert on paintings alone, but that signified neither art illiteracy nor lack of appreciation on my part. I respected Peter's restriction, but admittedly, my curiosity to explore the mysterious room was palpable.

"I may have found it." Peter looked up at me, surprised that my intuition had paid off. "Have a look at this."

I darted over, my flats clicking against the concrete floor obnoxiously loudly after the period of silence. I leaned over his shoulder, sweeping the coppery strands behind my ear which put our faces perilously close. With a hand on his upper back, I could feel his tension as I stared at the record on which his finger rested, reading it aloud. "May 1924: Victorian style gilt and patinated bronze candelabra. 19th century. Three lions' busts around base holding aloft five candle arms. Exquisite craftsmanship. Sold 15£."

"That's it! Peter, you've found it." I grabbed his head and kissed his forehead, leaving a faint trace of lipstick behind. "Does it say who purchased the piece?"

Peter was punchdrunk, but regained his composure after a few moments. With a daffy smile stretching from ear to ear, he forced his focus back to the record, and read it aloud. "Sold to A. Wilbanks of Harefield." He rocked back on his heels and dropped into a vacant chair, not bothering to dust off the seat. All of his previous gusto vanished like morning fog. He rested his hand over his mouth for an eternal moment before speaking. "I'm afraid the piece is no longer obtainable."

"Wait. I don't understand. How could that be?"

"The A. Wilbanks it refers to is Alexander Wilbanks, former shipping mogul. He passed away a number of years ago with more gambling debt than the Black Forest has trees. The dregs of his estate not already rotting away were ruthlessly parcelled out by creditors hoping to limit their losses. *If* any records were kept, it would be damn-near impossible to track down your candelabra. I'm sorry, Sophia. I'm afraid that your search ends here."

Chapter XII

"I can't stop here, Peter." I let my head fall into my hands with exasperation, gripping fistfuls of locks already dishevelled from the stout wind outside.

Peter stood and awkwardly patted my shoulder in apology. Given his proximity, I could faintly detect the melange of pipe spearmint, mechanical grease, and old books. A grandfather. Peter smelled like a grandfather.

I stared at the scuffed concrete of the warehouse floor littered with flecks of paint that the moisture had mercilessly driven from the walls. "I refuse to give up. Someone knows where the candelabra is."

"I think that it's highly unlikely that we'll figure out who that was. There is another possibility. I suppose it's probable that such a nondescript item escaped attention during the estate sale."

The glimmer of hope was all I needed. "You really think so?"

Peter sighed, the corner of his mouth turning upwards in a soft smile. God, he even smiled like a grandfather.

Standing there in his brown tweed sweater vest and pleated cotton slacks, he was the epitome of an English country gentleman. An old soul in a young man's body.

"I *think* I need to return to the shop before Simon begins asking after me."

"I understand." The guttering fire in my chest had reignited. I rose and planted another peck on my helpful companion's cheek. "Thank you for your help, Peter. I'll take the next Albion to Harefield," I said with newfound alacrity.

Peter swayed for a moment while colour rose in his face. I thought for certain that he would collapse once again into the wood-slatted rolling chair from which he had just risen. Instead, he stared at me dumbfounded before eventually speaking in a cracking voice.

"Right. Um…" His cheeks burned as he massaged the back of his neck. "I see there's no end to your ambition." He said, pausing with a grin. "I must be mad for even suggesting this." He muttered and chuckled as his amber eyes rose to mine. "If you are willing to postpone your bus trip until this evening, I will accompany you to the Wilbanks Manor. If we are going to pilfer his estate, I would imagine that it's best to do it after nightfall." He eyed my light-coloured attire sceptically. "Might I suggest you don something darker."

"I'll sort something out," I said, winking. Considering the way Milly shopped, she likely had every chifforobe in her Thornhill home packed with outfits for every size and occasion.

"Shall we say Tottenham Court Road Station tonight? Seven sharp?"

I nodded.

Peter mindlessly rubbed his palms together. For the partial owner of a well-established illegal enterprise, the slight gentleman standing in front of me appeared unsettled by the prospect of breaking and entering, a notion that I found quite ironic. Peter struck me as someone who had always kept his head down, doing what Simon asked without question. I could not imagine the man so much as placing a stamp upside down. I supposed that his work with the shop's inventory came with a certain detachment. Completing managerial paperwork and painstakingly restoring artefacts was a far cry from intentionally trespassing and stealing an item that clearly did not belong to us. Not to mention potential danger. I found the thrill of adventure nothing short of exciting, justifying our actions by thinking, *It isn't larceny if no one owns it.* I resisted the urge to squeal.

Peter led me out of the formidable iron gate where the cold air dragged each of us back to our senses. While Peter was fiddling with the lock, I searched carefully for any sign of Simon's minion among the labourers conducting their business outside of the courtyard gates but to no avail. I chalked up my sighting to an overactive imagination, though deep within, I did not fully believe it. *If it was Tim, why hadn't he stopped us?* I shook the thought from my head as Peter turned towards me.

"That's it then," he said.

"Until this evening."

We parted ways, smiling, and I began the lengthy walk towards Shadwell Station. I never turned back, but something told me that his eyes never left me. I rounded the first corner so deep in my own thoughts that I nearly knocked over a trench coat-clad businessman emerging from a telephone box. After a sincere apology, I used the remainder of the trip to calm my swirling emotions. The morning had been one revelation after another and yet had left me little further along than before. Making matters more difficult, every time I tried to clear my mind for a moment of reprieve, Peter's face would reappear.

"What a load of poppycock," I said aloud. "You just met the man, Sophia."

Due to my distracted state, the walk to the station passed by far more quickly than anticipated. Shadwell Station was easy enough to locate, though it was little more than a simple brick building where I could purchase a ticket and descend the stairs to the platform. The metropolitan line would conveniently deliver me nearly to Milly's doorstep. I waited for the train amidst a crowd of others, all lingering under the expansive arched brick ceiling. The downy hairs on my neck raised on end as the sensation of being watched washed over me like a cold draught. I swirled, examining each face in the crowd expecting to see Tim grinning back at any moment, but found nothing out of place. Still, someone was watching. Peter's welcome gaze was akin to laying under the warm summer sun, whereas the present sensation was icy daggers piercing me all over begging me to flee.

By the time I arrived at Thornhill Square, the unnerving feeling had abated. I suppressed any remaining paranoia and climbed the marble steps to Milly's front door. In less than a day, the woman had become like family and her house, my home. I listened to the children's laughter as they played down the avenue, and I grasped the door's wrought iron handle.

I snorted, the simple metal a welcome reprieve from my additional sense. The ability may have been responsible for extra insight into numerous affairs, but the flood of information could be exhausting. A railing here, a knob there… each saturated with nothing more than the mundanity of daily existence, but each took yet another toll on my psyche. I longed to experience the sensory deprivation practices I had seen illustrated on papyrus scrolls from ancient Egypt and Greece. Mother had spent so much of her life with gloved hands for this very reason.

My footsteps echoed on Milly's black and white checkered floor as I entered the foyer. Mei gently closed the door behind me with a soft click. Before the woman was able to collect my coat my clamorous friend barrelled into the room, arms spread wide for an embrace.

"Sophia, dear! You must regale me with your morning adventure over a cup of tea in the conservatory. I won't take no for an answer." She kissed my cheeks in greeting and jerked me towards the rear of the home. "Mei, another setting for Sophia. Mei is the absolute best, you know. A commoner hired straight from the Orient. Best damn money I ever spent. And a great listener to boot."

I glanced back at Mei who gave a nearly imperceptible polite nod. With as much as Milly dominated the conversation, everyone was forced into the role of listener. If not for the bottomless well of generosity and kindness, it would be all too easy to consider the woman obnoxious. In reality, Mildred G. Foster was quickly becoming my dearest friend.

Milly led me to a small whitewashed iron table in the middle of the bright room lined with red flagstones and absolutely brimming with greenery. Despite the cool afternoon, the sun's warmth kept the glass-enshrouded space at a comfortable temperature. Among the veritable jungle of exotic plants, it was no wonder Milly sought refuge here with such frequency. With the addition of a macaw or two, I could have imagined that I had been transported deep within the Amazonian rainforest. I could just make out the trickle of water during the rare lulls of Milly's explanation as to the origins of her more foreign plants. Her conservatory had a fountain! I almost vibrated with delight to be a guest in such a special place. Here it was the dead of winter, and I was in the tropics of South America.

Reminding me that I was still in Central London, the small-statured Asian entered carrying an engraved silver platter laden with tea sandwiches, mouth-watering scones, and a jaw-dropping Song-dynasty tea service. Judging from the crackled duck-egg blue glaze, it must have been authentic Ru ware kaolin porcelain. A woman of such humble means as Mei would never have had access to such a priceless, museum-quality set in her homeland. I questioned how she must have felt using the appropriated imperial tea service for a Westerner like her employer on what I presumed to be a daily basis. Milly undoubtedly preferred the set because it was exquisite, but to Mei it was an integral part of China's rich history.

"*Shee, shee,*" mispronounced Milly as Mei gently placed the cup and saucer in front of her, adding a healthy splash of milk. "That's 'thank you' in Chinese."

Mei nodded without voicing a reply, a slight smirk on her face at my host's poor attempt at Mei's native language. In years past, the Woman's Lodge had briefly employed an elderly Pekingese woman to help maintain the premises. She had assumed a grandmotherly role among the residents, even teaching me a few scattered words in the foreign language before eventually returning to China to care for an ailing sibling. A pleasant mirth filled my bosom as I recalled the evening she attempted to teach us to paint the complex writing system. Oh, what terrible students we must have been! It was from that meagre smattering of Mandarin that I knew Milly's pronunciation needed substantial improvement. Mei dismissed herself, vanishing into the kitchen.

Milly noticed the questioning smile that I mistakenly thought I was hiding as she lifted a slice of rye decadently layered with smoked salmon, soft cheese, and capers. "You might think she waits on me hand and foot, but you'd be wrong." Milly chuckled and took a large bite, relishing in the savoury flavour, before continuing. "You know that I consider myself an independent woman and tend to most of my own needs. My father was a miserable bastard. As far as he was concerned, his wife was good for one thing and children—nothing else. Never lifted so much as a finger to help us, so we learned early on how to take care of ourselves and one another. Now that I have means, I find her presence invaluable, but I'll never be helpless. And I compensate her generously. So long as you're under my roof, don't hesitate to ask either of us for anything. Or hell, do it yourself. My home is yours."

My life had been filled with all manner of people, but none as authentic as the woman in front of me. I grasped her hand, graciously thanking her for her unexpected hospitality towards me.

Milly waved it off. "Age has filled me with many revelations. One of which being it doesn't matter how much wealth you have, you can't buy good company. Money might make life easier to an extent, but in the long run, it's meaningless. Your only true value is what you bring to the world," Milly jokingly jabbed me with a finger. "I aim to leave the world better than I found it, by golly. I get that same sensation from you. Now, if you really want to thank me, tell me your story."

Between bites of the delicious petite sandwiches, I enthusiastically divulged the details from the morning and our plans for the evening, leaving out only the supernatural bits. My God, the food was exquisite.

"Oh, to be young again!" Milly clapped. "I have half a mind to go with you. These old bones could use some excitement, not that they could move quickly should the need arise. Not to mention, I would very much like to meet this bumbling fool who's clearly captured your interest."

"It's nothing like that at all. He's helping me locate the sentimental item I told you about."

Milly eyed me down, unconvinced, gesturing with a scone that had made it halfway to her mouth. "You keep telling yourself that, Soph. The man may be a clumsy recluse, but he sounds positively smitten and your feelings towards him are anything but neutral. Suppressed desire has a nasty habit of sneaking up on you at the most inopportune time. Plus, this Peter doesn't exactly sound like the type to resort to questionable activities on a whim. Look at you. You're Venus de Milo. Anyone not blind would be awkward around you."

I blushed at the praise, but considering how poorly I had been treated through my childhood in Luffield, I felt nothing near that level of confidence. "At least I have my arms." I laughed, reaching for one of the mouth-watering scones and demonstrating my superiority over the renowned statue. "Even if it's true, I assure you that he didn't need my help to be awkward. I do suppose that's what makes him so adorable."

"See. If I was a man a few decades younger, I'd be doing everything I could to garner your attention as well!"

"Milly, your candour is as unbridled as your charity."

She cackled so hard she shook long after the laughter had ceased. "Those are the compliments I strive for, Sophia. Now, let's get you upstairs and make you a little less conspicuous for your criminal debut."

Chapter XIII

When I arrived at Shadwell Station without a touch of colour on my person, I could not have felt more ridiculous. No one batted an eye, but that did not mean I was not self-conscious. *I should've worn a dress and veil,* I thought with a titter. *At least I could have passed as a mourning widow.* The dark reflection in an advert for Barbasol caught my eye. Milly had garbed me from head to toe in solid black (except the grey socks) to the point where my face was the only bright spot on my body. Even my fiery curls were tucked beneath the beanie I sported. *Forget the veil—a Crimean balaclava!* I chortled, garnering extra attention from the bald gentleman and his wife who were also awaiting the train. *Could you imagine?* People would be shuffling out of Shadwell as quick as could be, even under the fear of mugging, reluctant to break the renowned English calm. I could not take my gaze off of my reflection. I had never been a timid person, but I barely recognised the woman staring back at me—inside or out. Would this evening be an expression of profound bravery or exceptional stupidity? Focusing on the end goal, I put on a straight face as the train pulled in, suppressing the apprehension that gnawed at the back of my skull. I boarded, chalking my roiling stomach to the jerky acceleration as the cars gathered speed along their route into the heart of London. I allowed the adrenaline to course through my veins, arousing my senses.

A short walk was all that remained from the Underground to the agreed Tottenham Station where I would catch the bus with my would-be accomplice. The brisk night air cooled my flush face and overly insulated body. Aside from my downright frigid hands, I was sweltering, making for a strange juxtaposition. Like an overly concerned mother, Milly had made damn sure that I would not die from exposure on my foray into thievery. After being crammed inside the stuffy train, the cold evening air was a welcome reprieve. The thrill pulsing through my core was both unnerving and vivacious. When I arrived at the bus depot, I was wholly unprepared for the dashing gentleman that awaited me. Gone was the cashmere sweater vest and cotton trousers, replaced by a sleek pitch-black pea coat, turtleneck, watch cap, and wool serge pants. Peter raised his hand in greeting before promptly tripping over the sidewalk, nearly dropping his holdall. *There is the Peter I met.* Fortunately, he caught himself on a lamppost before stumbling to the ground. I grinned, noticing his boots were a size too large.

"Good evening." His voice shook with the same nervousness I felt. He followed my gaze down to his footwear. "They're Simon's."

"I could barely tell." I lied, my grin giving away my true opinion.

Peter smiled back at me, offering a hand as I climbed the curb to join him. Without thinking, he drew me close, our gaze bound to each other. My breath faltered. Not wanting to come off as too forward, Peter relaxed his grip. We broke our contact, each of us feigning the normalcy of the moment.

I had enjoyed the occasional lover, but gentlemen—true gentlemen—*that* was something my life had been lacking. Everything I had experienced had been little more than trysts, not a relationship by anyone's standards. The men of Luffield who had been willing to overlook my questionable reputation only did so for one reason. I often found myself caving, seeking the same fleeting satisfaction they desired. I had no illusions about how my conduct was perceived but doubted my character could be further tarnished. Apart from kindhearted residents like Michael Clayton, Ruby Palmer, and the Grafton nuns, few in the close-minded town ever considered me anything other than an unwelcome presence in their midst. Peter, however, had a certain *je ne sais quoi* that made him so endearing, an innocence without naivety. The gentleman possessed a fierce intelligence balanced by the universe with a significant lack of grace. I suppose that no one could have it all.

With a soft squeal from its brakes, the green, tan-striped Albion pulled to a halt at the curb. Peter motioned for the cluster of weary second-shift workers to board first. I watched as they ascended the stairs with slumped shoulders and empty lunch pails, aching for the comfort of home. What a relief to no longer be working in such conditions— honourable, but harsh. Upon seeing our suspicious attire, the driver gave us a severe look from under his bushy eyebrows, but with a glance at our faces and nonthreatening builds, decided that we did not warrant expulsion. I thought my near-funereal attire odd enough on its own, but with the two of us together, we appeared more like miscreants than either of us had intended.

"Back there." Peter gestured hurriedly towards a seat near the rear of the bus.

We began to walk down the narrow rubber-lined path as a final passenger boarded. With a harrumph, the driver gave the lever a jerk, closing the bi-fold doors.

As I sat, I couldn't help but notice the driver's lingering gaze in the rear-facing mirror as the last person aboard came to rest behind him. I averted my eyes to the woman across from me. The elderly lady pulled her clutch tightly into her chest.

"Oh my God. We look like petty street thugs." I whispered to Peter, cringing and giggling at the same time. I desperately wanted to hide my face, but worried about further arousing suspicion.

"Forgive me. I'm not accustomed to clandestine rendezvous and late-night burglary. Not exactly my forte, eh?" Peter chuckled. "The goal was to be inconspicuous, but I fear we are anything but. I don't believe there is cause for alarm. Once we are off the bus, the passengers will be more occupied with being rid of us than informing the Yard."

"But how do you think we will look if we board the bus dressed like this with an ornate candelabra in our possession?"

"A valid point. Fortunately for us I had the forethought to bring a change of attire. There's enough for the both of us, assuming you don't mind men's breeches."

"Why Peter, you are becoming quite the ne'er-do-well."

I giggled as I watched his cheeks redden. I had never been

one to take crime lightly, always striving to be a better citizen regardless of what others believed. The last thing I wanted to do was provide chinwaggers like Camille with the satisfaction of my having a criminal record. Before tonight, my most notable indiscretions had been sneaking men into an all-women Lodge. Yet, nothing about our scenario felt wrong. Had I been alone I would have no need for the bronze antique once I had absorbed all the information the candelabra had to offer. Given Peter's presence, I had no alternative but to bring the item with me or divulge everything and hope he would not have me committed. Legality aside, the fear of going mad like my mother chewed away at my insides. I sincerely hoped that I was stronger in mind than she. Though if I was to go mad, would I care anyway?

We stopped at the next hub and changed to the rural bus that would make the journey out of town to Harefield, experiencing many of the same reactions from other passengers as we had on the previous trip. We ignored them just the same.

"Did Simon say anything about your long lunch?" I asked, watching out the window as the bright lights of the city faded to the dark hillsides of the country. Road signs were all that broke through the obscurity in the nighttime winter landscape. Judging from what they read, we were moments away from our stop.

Peter shook his head. "I arrived at the shop moments after him." He rubbed his hands on his lap nervously, a habit he had done more the further from the city we travelled. "He did little more than glance up from his paper, make a rude comment, and return to his football statistics."

I turned away from the window, staring him in the eyes. "Why do you let him speak to you like that?"

Peter shrugged. "He's been doing it since we were boys. Father was of the mind that his criticisms would 'build my fortitude,'" he mocked his father's stuffy voice, "but all it did was undermine my self-confidence."

"I'm sorry, Peter." I took his cool hand in mine. "For what it's worth, I think you grew up to be a far finer gent than your uncouth brother."

"Thank you, Sophia." Peter smiled as the bus lurched to a stop. "I love my brother, but as you've noticed, he can be a bit of a cad. He's always taken care of me, so I ignore it."

We rose as the few passengers eyed us suspiciously. For the most part, they were too tired or preoccupied to care about two strangers dressed in black. We were the last to depart the bus. I could have sworn the driver sighed once we had our feet on the ground. Without nary a word, the doors slammed behind us and we were left in a cloud of dust as the bus' lights disappeared into the distance. When I turned, the other passengers had already made themselves scarce, anxious to leave our presence and return home.

"So, we're in Harefield. Where is this Wilbanks Estate?"

"On the outskirts of the town, believe it or not."

He continued his thought before I could voice complaint.

"On this side. Only a kilometre or so down that path." Peter pointed towards an under-maintained gravel road. "I hope you don't mind a walk under the stars."

"I do not."

For a moment I wondered if I had been too trusting. Even with Milly aware of our destination, I was allowing a complete stranger to escort me into the middle of nowhere under the guise of nighttime. God knows what my companion could do to me should he have ill intentions. As much as I had despised my work in the tannery, it had not left me weak. Barring a weapon, I suspected I could overpower Peter if it came down to it. I stole a glance at him. His hands were buried in his pockets as he whistled a merry children's tune. My fears abated.

Beyond the reach of London's numerous lights, I could barely tear my eyes away from the star-filled expanse. I could spend the rest of my days staring up and never tire of the awe-inspiring, humbling sight. In these moments I could feel humanity's connection to the vast universe. I rubbed my upper arms as the chilly air tried in vain to stab through my thick clothes. The full moon occupied half of the clear evening sky, bathing the vast open terrain in its soft glow. In the distance, sounds of pleasant evening revelry from the local pub echoed across the countryside. The night could not have been more tranquil.

Mutually appreciating the experience, we quietly made our way down the country path, the only sound gravel crunching beneath our feet. Peter's eyes would flit in my direction from time to time, always with a sheepish grin. Naturally, I could not help but return the gesture. Out here, away from his brother and the perception of others, Peter took on a more confident persona. For the first time, I saw the true Peter.

"I know we haven't known each other for long, but you seem more at ease."

"I am." Peter pulled his hands out from his pockets and rubbed them together. "I grew up in the city but would spend summers at my uncle's cottage helping with his sheep." Peter chuckled. "As you could guess, my talents didn't lie with farming. My mother and her brother shared a voracious appetite for reading. He had a veritable library, which I devoured. His place became my second home. I tolerated the animals for the opportunity to pass more time among his collection. Things were simpler in the country, surrounded by people equally disenchanted with urban conditions."

"What made you stay in London once you'd grown?"

"The shop. One thing led to another. Before I knew it, Father was gone, and Simon was my *de facto* caretaker. I didn't wish to cross him by leaving."

"Simon certainly doesn't act like he needs you. Is he not capable of running a business on his own?"

Peter laughed loudly. "Simon knows little of history and less of antiques. All he understands is money and force, which is enough to manage his dealings. Without my knowledge, the family business would fail. Perhaps that's the real reason I've never left. Northrop's Antiques means everything to me. I can't watch Father's legacy collapse under my brother's ineptitude. With my advice, he manages the business dealings. In return, I don't have to interact with anyone directly and am compensated well. Father at least had the foresight to make Simon pledge to watch over me."

"Have you ever reconsidered moving to the countryside?"

"My uncle willed his cottage to me when he passed. I pay his neighbour's son to upkeep the property. Though I have little interest in agriculture, perhaps one day I can spend more time there." Peter squeezed my hand and then froze in his tracks, staring towards a menacing silhouette on the horizon. "We're here."

Chapter XIV

I followed the direction of Peter's gaze. Through the leafless trees lining the property's perimeter, I could discern the looming manor in the distance from where it occluded the stars. The building's towers gave the edifice a menacing shape, its vast form existing in the absence of light making the vacant structure all the more foreboding.

"The Wilbanks Estate, or what's left of it. Such a depressing sight." Peter said, downtrodden. The same sight that had instilled me with fear filled him with regret. "One of the few Jacobethan revivalist homes left in England. Under different circumstances, I could think of no better place to house a museum. Truly heartbreaking, you'll see why inside. Disputes by debt collectors have left the property unoccupied and unmaintained for nigh on two decades. I'm certain the damage we'll find will be extensive. I should warn you, some of it may be structural in nature. Are you certain you wish to proceed?"

"I've never been more certain of anything." The candelabra—my future—was inside that house. I knew it. Though my ability could not transcend its tactile nature, there was something to be said about intuition. Dorothy Tate had instilled a deep respect in me for my instincts.

Peter led me to a pair of vine-wrapped iron gates, each with an ornate cast "W" in the centre. The letters were already rusting away where the paint had flaked, a visual representation of humanity's tentative coexistence with nature. With a few cuts from Peter's barely adequate pocket knife, the large intricately sculpted gates parted with a squeal that echoed across the hills. I winced at the profound break in what had been almost reverent silence. Considering the growth, we must have been the property's first visitors in ages. At least the first to use the main gate. I had little doubt that a ne'er-do-well or two had hopped the fence for some late-night jollity. Peter wiped the rust on his trousers before continuing onward. The sprawling grounds appeared uninhabited aside from a small herd of roe deer that fled once they noticed our presence. Nevertheless, we approached silently across the low hills towards the three-story manor.

We carefully adhered to the gravel path that, despite the prolific weeds that had managed to pressure their way to the surface, was somewhat intact. I couldn't say the same for the rest of the undulating hills. The dry grass reached my waist. Hundreds of birch and alder saplings stretched reedy branches towards the open skies, saplings that if kept unchecked would eventually reclaim the land for forest.

"How will we get inside?" My human voice felt like an intrusion into the natural soundscape of insects, disturbing a peace not meant to be broken. We idled for a moment,

Peter remained silent until the hoot of an owl returned us to awareness. I caught myself trembling and for the first time in the evening, I questioned our presence on the grounds. Something far deeper than the questionable legality of our impending infraction left me unsettled.

"It's been abandoned long enough that surely the local rabble has shattered a window or two. Finding a way in shouldn't be difficult."

My head swam with unease as we continued up the grade. I was chasing my undeniable destiny, but doing so felt like a violation of the deceased Alexander Wilbanks. *Am I being driven by anything other than selfish intent? There must be something more, something that haunted Mother to her grave.* I had been so caught up in my own thoughts I didn't see the broad-shouldered figure looming in the grass ahead. I loosed an embarrassing shriek and clung to Peter. *Simon's henchman!*

I waited to hear Tim's gravely voice utter a threat of violence, but instead felt Peter's chest bouncing in a fit of laughter. I jerked away and stared at the figure, identifying the source of Peter's mirth. Resting on a pedestal was a life-size statue of the Bodhidharma. In hindsight, the sculpture's meditative stance was anything but ominous. Peter must have instantly recognised the figure knowing Wilbanks' proclivity for the eclectic. I suppressed the flash of anger for his humour at my expense and began to laugh myself.

"I apologise for my amusement, but I couldn't help it." Peter's laughter faded as he grew more bashful.

"It's alright." I clutched my chest, trying to catch my breath after the fright. "I've been on edge since I left Milly's home. I suppose I should welcome the relief."

We continued our journey, falling back into silence, but in lighter spirits.

"Tell me about her. About Milly. How long have the two of you known each other?"

"Would you believe I met her yesterday on the train to London?"

Peter chuckled. "She must be quite… outgoing."

"That she is. When she found that I had nowhere planned to stay, she was kind enough to open her home to me."

"The world could use more people like that. People looking out for each other."

I smiled in agreement, but before I had to respond, we crossed through a giant pair of columns supporting a wide archway. Without realising it, we had arrived at the front veranda of the manor. "I guess we won't need to break a window."

The door was ajar, a large weathered chain and padlock hanging down limply. Peter held the end of the chain aloft, examining it in the low light. "Cut."

I glanced at the door, a new fear blooming in my chest.

Peter noted my expression. "I doubt we have anything to fear. Look, it's oxidised at the point it was severed. Whoever cut this chain did it months, possibly even years, ago."

"That's a relief." I pushed the door open with some effort, fighting the hinges as they refused to grant easy entry. The foyer of the home was expansive, opening up to a pair of twin staircases rimming the circumference of the room. Moonlight filtered in where the curtains had rotted and fallen from their windows. I slowly entered with Peter on my heels. What little furniture had been left by the debt collectors and looters was worthless—overturned and clawed to pieces by animals in search of nesting materials.

"Are you sure you want to do this?" Peter had a noticeable quaver in his voice, asking for his benefit more than my own.

"I would never forgive myself if I turned back now."

Peter's gulp echoed throughout the uninviting chamber, a space which resembled something from a penny dreadful. His fear evaporated once he became absorbed in the building's period architecture. I was examining the scrawling across the wall left by the rabble when he asked, "Where should we start?"

The thought occurred to me that we could cover more ground if we split up, but I didn't believe either of us was in a hurry to do so. "Why don't we take it room by room. There can't be much left, so I don't imagine it will take too long to search the premises."

Peter gave a wide-eyed nod. With his intense focus, his fear completely subsided. Though damaged, there was enough remaining detail to hold his attention as we searched. The tendrils of nervousness still writhed inside my core but could be ignored with so many fascinating sights to behold.

In its heyday, the manor must have been nothing short of astounding. Most of the rooms allotted for entertaining were trimmed out with polished mahogany walls. Though shrouded in a thick layer of dust, many remained, too difficult to remove by cretins seeking easy money. Each ceiling was more impressive than the next with intricate relief patterns that now drooped where moisture had taken its toll. The hand-carved marble fireplaces were some of the few objects that had withstood the test of time, only marred by the occasional chip. Judging from the prolific dustless bottles in each room, the local hooligans still used the home for occasional debauchery.

In one room, Peter paused to lift a picture frame from the floor, dumping the shattered glass from it onto the moulding rug. "Unbelievable. This was an original Egyptian papyrus. Priceless." He grunted. "Ironic given those seeking items of value left behind one of the most profitable."

The shredded piece was unexciting by modern standards. To the untrained eye, the piece was nothing more than old cloth with fading illustrations of birds and scribbles. I reached to touch a portion of the material and it disintegrated in my hand. "Oh, I'm sorry! I should've known better."

Peter put a caring hand on my shoulder. "It was unsalvageable before I laid eyes on it. You can't leave 4,000-year-old paper subject to the elements."

Even in light of that fact, he reverently leaned it against a wall. The consummate professional. Upon closer inspection, I noticed that the frame was abnormally thick. *Vacuum sealed.* Wilbanks may have had his shortcomings, but he was clearly no fool.

After more searching, we wound our way up the rightmost flight of stairs we had encountered in the foyer, having found nothing of note on the ground floor. We were equally disappointed by the second storey, but the third felt promising. The first several rooms were more of the same—scattered furniture, destroyed artefacts, piles of rubbish—but when Peter entered the fourth room ahead of me, his gasp made me panic. I darted into the room after him in such a hurry I ploughed into him, nearly causing him to tumble over and sending me careening to the filthy floor.

"Are you okay?" He offered a hand to help me up, but when I beheld the room's contents, I was equally in shock.

The library! The awe-inspiring room was one of the largest we had come across, still packed to the brim with books spanning the centuries. Burdened shelves lined the space from the warping parquet floor to the cracked glass dome embedded into the ceiling. Ivy had grown out of control, watered by rain cascading in from the broken dome. The greenery twisted and turned through the rolling ladders and around the room, worming its way into every conceivable niche. In the centre, a dilapidated desk was beginning to sink into the floor.

"Can you imagine this place in its prime?" I ran my hands along the spines lining a shelf, each fighting a losing battle against rodents and rot.

"It would have been a historian's dream. Now it's nothing more than a historian's nightmare. Few know where the real value lay in this house."

I pulled one of the more intact books from the shelf when a loud crack caused my heart to skip. Our intrusion into the room had been just enough to overwhelm the decaying floor. With a series of thunderous cracks, the wood gave way and the desk tumbled to the second storey and shattered, tilting the middle of the room—and Peter with it.

"Peter!" I screamed.

I struggled to balance on the shifting floor, listing like a ship mid-squall. I rushed to the furthest edge of solid floor.

Peter fell, clutching the floor's sharp edges as the ground beneath him angled steeply. "Stay back!"

To hell with that. I fell to my knees, reaching for Peter as concern overpowered any sense of self-preservation. "Take my hands."

Peter stared at the dark open maw behind him, then turned and nodded. He grasped my outstretched hands. As his feet struggled to find purchase on the smooth wood, I pulled with adrenaline-fuelled might. Between our combined efforts, Peter escaped the parquet crater, collapsing on top of me and gasping for breath. Our faces were so close that they were nearly touching. An eternal moment passed in silence as we stared into each other's eyes, each grateful to be alive. I leaned up and placed my lips on his, all thoughts of the brittle floor forgotten. Peter stared at me wide-eyed before rolling off and laying on the cool floor in a state of ecstasy.

"Well, I, uh, don't care to do that again."

"Was my kiss that bad?"

"Oh, God. No. I only meant that—"

"I know what you meant." I laughed in a state of bliss of my own. "Consider it payback for your reaction in the gardens."

"Touché." Peter grinned as his face blushed under the moonlight. "If you don't mind, can we leave this room now?" He climbed to his feet, offering me a hand up. Something about him had changed. Or perhaps something about me. We held hands as we carefully searched the remaining rooms, making easy work of the nearly empty spaces all the while giving each other furtive glances. Upon entering the last room, a forlorn master bedroom with a double-arched window and a collapsed Victorian canopy bed, he looked at me apologetically. "I'm sorry, Sophia."

That can't be right. "It's here, Peter. I can feel it." I would tear the house apart until I found it.

Peter examined me thoughtfully, noting my certainty. He nodded in agreement. "Then let's give the entire house another pass." Peter began to guide me from the room, then paused mid-stride. "A thought just occurred to me. We haven't found the servant's quarters. It's the perfect hiding place for an object not wished to be discovered."

Chapter XV

Peter escorted me down the creaking stairs in search of one of the myriad access points through which the household's servants would execute their duties unnoticed. Curling wallpaper reached out like claws from the wall, grasping at intruders disturbing the home's rest. Neither of us spoke as we padded down the dusty corridor like hunters pursuing prey, fearful that any stray sound might alert our quarry to our presence. Every few meters, Peter would turn to verify that I was on his heels as though his hand clasping mine was insufficient. Each smiling glance radiated a warmth through me that was unhindered by the icy current permeating the vacant manor. As thrilling as the unexpected kiss had been, the candelabra continued to dominate my thoughts.

We returned to the dining room, the sprawling space's deep green ceiling sagged to the point of partially masking the damaged hunting scenes that adorned the walls. Peter began examining the room as he had every centimetre of the hallway. Though I did not recognise the room's artist, the detail of the hand-painted mural had once been exquisite. Peter shattered the silence when he kicked aside a broken dining chair in frustration. "There should be an entrance around here somewhere." He began running his fingers along the panelled walls, feeling for the gap that would signal a hidden door as I watched patiently.

A bygone era. It was all too easy to envision the home as it once was: filled with life warmed by roaring hearths and swimming in the aromas of freshly prepared delicacies. All against a backdrop of fine art spanning the globe and classical music enriching the air. No corner of the manor had escaped the craftsman's attention. No, this must have been quite the place in its heyday. The idea of having to search for a door in any modern home would seem preposterous. This house, however, was from an age where servants were nothing more than hands serving the master's will, striving to be invisible. There was an inherent romantic quality to the way of life, provided that you were the master. Like every display of opulence throughout history, the home's appearance masked the dark secrets belonging to its owner.

A draught teased my now chaotic curls from behind, tickling the back of my neck and causing a shiver. The manor's interior had swirled with frigid gusts slicing through the broken panes, but the source of this current emanated from seemingly solid walls. I turned, waving my hands around in the shadows to find the draught's origin, drawing Peter's attention.

"I don't think he can see you." Peter chuckled as I noticed that from his perspective I was waving at a hunter standing in the wood.

I loosed a laugh myself. "I felt something. A soft blowing."

"Allow me." He drew a metal lighter from his coat pocket and used the flame as a guide.

Peter quickly isolated the source coming from the adjacent wall. "Here." Air trickled from behind a ripped painting taller than either of us which once depicted a traditional Japanese samurai. I lifted the torn segment back into place to view the piece as a whole. "Magnificent."

"Well, we've clearly established that the debt collectors and looters weren't connoisseurs. They were simply looking for easy quid." Peter felt along the edge of the simply carved frame cleverly paired with the painting. "This particular piece would've fetched a decent sum at auction." He shrugged, then stood back and began to laugh.

"What?"

"This painting may have been damaged before his death."

I arched an eyebrow.

"There existed a rumour that Alexander's wife, Lilith, invited no shortage of men into her bedroom in effort to garner attention from her husband. He was known for his obsession with gambling above all else, including romancing her, whose beauty was renowned." Peter began running his fingers around the frame's edge. "If there is any truth to the matter, she would become irate at his lack of interest, and would often go on rampages destroying his most recent acquisitions—the only other thing he cared about."

I harrumphed as a satisfying click rang out. Peter swung the painting open like a door.

"Unfortunate, but humorous, nonetheless." Peter said with one last glance at the painting. "After his death, I believe she ran off with an American."

"Do you know why he didn't—" My words were cut short by the inescapable icy tendrils that reached out from the dark passage ensnaring my very soul. The tiny hairs covering my skin stood painfully erect. Never in all my years had I felt a sensation from an object I had not yet touched. Every modicum of my being said, "Run."

Peter eyed me worryingly. It did not take preternatural abilities to activate human's innate sense of fear. He was equally reticent to enter the pitch black corridor, but his subtle nod said that he would follow me wherever I led. Mother's voice echoed in my head. "Everyone has gut instincts, whether they choose to embrace them or not." Not only was I about to not embrace them, I was going to flat out ignore them. I *had* to know what memories lurked inside that relic.

"It just dawned on me how silly I am to have forgotten a torch." Peter's voice quavered. "Let me see if I can find a candle."

In the middle of the lengthy dining table, he easily obtained a pair of cracked burgundy candles where they had been cast aside, unwanted. After a light dusting, he determined that they would hold together long enough to serve our purpose. Again, Peter pulled a lighter from his pocket, and after igniting them, held his aloft, and we entered the narrow passage. The irony of using candles to find a candelabra was not lost on me.

"You never struck me as the smoking type."

"An unhealthy habit I picked up from Father and a rare indulgence at that. Simon chides me that someone with as little grace as I have shouldn't be allowed to toy with fire." His open flame passed under a cobweb and it disappeared in a flash causing Peter to jump back towards me. He chuckled, "It's one point at times I'm inclined to agree."

"If that's your worst vice, I doubt you have anything to worry about."

Peter was silent for a moment as he reminisced. "It might sound daft, but when I use father's pipe, it's as though he's there in the room with me. Sometimes I light it and never so much as take the first puff."

"There's nothing daft about that at all." I squeezed his hand, bringing rosiness back to his cheeks.

Another Baltic wave smattered me with goose pimples, and any inkling of romance disappeared. The unaccoutred passageway was purely utilitarian in nature, a remarkable departure from everything that had preceded it. With each cautious step forward, the foreboding invisible haze thickened. The object I sought was near. I forced myself to place one foot in front of the other.

"As soon as we find your candelabra, I'd very much like to leave this place."

I needed little convincing. I faced him and nodded. We could not have travelled far, but time slogged like treacle, nearly as thick as the stale air encompassing us. Barely past the entryway into the servant's kitchen, I froze in front of an unassuming door. A presence, whether good or evil, rooted me to that spot. Reluctant to utter words, I simply stared.

In merely a day, Peter had learned to trust my intuition. With a shaky hand, he attempted to open the door's iron latch. "Locked. Perhaps there's a key nearby."

The idea of spending any more time cloaked by this cumbersome veil that had descended upon us was unbearable. I kicked the door with all the force I could muster. The aged wood splintered into countless shards as the crack and shudder echoed down the solitary corridor. Peter gulped as the hairs on his neck arched out mirroring mine. In the dim light of the candles, he looked pale as a bed sheet. The oppressive nature of the space was nothing short of terrifying. The faint orange glow cast by our twin flames struggled to permeate the thick darkness, illuminating little more than our next step. Being unable to see the room's furthest recesses was nothing short of unnerving.

The bedchamber was untouched. Perhaps the servants' passageways were so well concealed that they had never been found by the local rabble. Paint flaked from the lath and plaster walls as dated as the home's construction, making the room feel no less eerie. The railed bed was dishevelled, its mattress a haven for rodent kind, its sheets gnarled and ripped. At its foot was a simple trunk, clothes spilling out from under the lid as though the room had been abandoned in haste. Dresser drawers hung open, distorted by their own weight and the passage of time. Next to a pair of moth-eaten uniforms, a few empty hangers cast their long shadows on the closet's rear panel. *Only one place it could be.*

Peter nodded towards the trunk.

I dropped to my knees in front of it, knowing what lay inside. Pushing my sense of self-preservation aside, I took a deep breath. Proceeding slowly, I set my candle aside and placed my hands on the trunk's lid, leaning it against the foot of the bed. A sharp current of energy swirled the room. Nestled among various feminine undergarments was the distinct shape of a candelabra, protruding from beneath a shift.

Peter placed a gentle hand on my shoulder, the first time he had initiated touch since I had met the man. The candelabra exuded malevolence, freed by my mother that fateful day fifteen years ago. A malevolence so strong that it even filled laymen like Peter with dread. Remarkably, he remained by my side. I cautiously drew the discoloured cotton aside, exposing what I knew lurked underneath. Peter sucked in his breath as I demonstrated that my intuition was more powerful than he could have imagined.

A pit opened in my stomach as I stared at the candelabra. The piece was exactly as I remembered it. I was suddenly plagued with doubt that I would have the strength to remain grounded after touching such a foreboding relic. Whatever memories it contained had haunted Mother's mind through her last breath. Inner turmoil raged as I fought the instinct to slam down the trunk lid and set the manor ablaze, candelabra be damned. But I wanted answers. Before I had consciously made the decision, my arm had advanced of its own accord, drawn to the aged bronze like a moth to a flame. Before I could think twice, my fingertips made contact. Lightning jolted through my body, and my world went topsy-turvy.

Chapter XVI

Anoxious grey fog washed over me, twisting and churning, stealing my senses, suffocating me. Agony gripped my being, flooding me with immense terror. I tried to scream, but no air could escape, no sound. I was trapped in someone else's dream. Someone else's nightmare. I forced my eyes shut, burning tears oozed as I waited for an inevitable doom that never came.

I pried one eye open, unsure of what to expect. Madness. Death. To my great surprise, I found myself inside a countryside cottage similar to those in Luffield. The idyllic surroundings should have put me at ease, but the sense of dread refused to dissipate. Stone from the nearby quarry mirrored the exterior walls, the thatched roof doing the same above. Drying herbs hung above the sink. I still could not breathe, but there was no need. My vision refused to clear, reminiscent of when I would don Sister Agnes' spectacles as a child. The stone hearth, normally a place of warmth and comfort reeked of cold hatred. A kettle screamed over the fire. I turned my head to glance out of the window, but my gaze was restricted to the movements of another. I was nothing more than an observer, seeing through someone else's eyes.

"Shut that damn thing up," a woman yelled. My voice yelled. Sound entered my ears as if through water. The speaker's words were as muddled as the vision, but comprehensible.

A lanky gentleman garbed in brown from head to toe jerked the kettle from the flames with an iron hook and dropped it unceremoniously on the stone. Its scream petered out as the woman turned her gaze to the family I had not realised were there.

"And you," her scratchy voice said. The group of six huddled in the corner of the room, cowering. "What part of the letter was unclear? Your kind isn't welcome here. Not in our town. Not in our country. If I had my way, not on our Earth. You are a pestilence in need of extermination."

"You don't understand," said the bespectacled man through a tremulous voice, the father judging by how he protected the others. "The money offered wasn't enough. It would be impossible to uproot my family and relocate for such a paltry sum. And to surrender our home…"

"It wasn't a suggestion, was it, Love?"

"No. That it wasn't," said the lanky one, facing her.

The young man appeared significantly younger than the woman sounded. Tufts of tawny hair stuck out from beneath his cap. His cornflower eyes stared at her—me—with eyes desperate for approval.

"Please tell us what harm we caused you. We'll try and mend it," pleaded the mother, holding a baby tightly to her chest as it started to whimper.

"Existing." The woman dragged out the word, savouring its flavour.

She snatched an all-too-familiar candelabra from the centre of a laden dining table, covered with the meal the duo had interrupted. She twirled the antique as she gazed at the glimmering bronze intently. "Seems like you had the means should you have wanted to leave. I wonder what else we'd find should we dig deeper."

"Y-You don't understand. It-It's a family heirloom! The only thing of value we own. Take it. Take anything you want. Just leave me and my family be. We'll go wherever you want. I'll-I'll find a way."

"Oh, it's too late for that." The lanky man of nineteen or twenty bit into an apple he had nicked from a wooden bowl on the table.

"Your lives," said the woman.

"Wh-What?"

"I want your lives."

With icy cool calm and no hesitation, she swung the bronze implement with as much force as her small frame could muster, smashing it into the side of the man's head. His cracked spectacles shot across the room as eyes rolled back into his head. His body collapsed lifeless to the floor as a pool of blood began to seep from his temple. The woman screamed as the infant followed suit, crawling towards her deceased husband's body.

Still armed with the iron from the fireplace, the man swung the hook into the top of the woman's skull, instantly silencing her screams as the baby tumbled from her clutches. The young girls whimpered as an early adolescent boy jumped to his feet. Slinging the angry tears from his eyes, he charged the woman. She easily dodged his attack and brought the heavy candelabra's base down where his skull met his spine with a sickening crack. He fell, his body spasming. His discontented attacker brought down the weapon repeatedly until bits of blood and bone masked the patinated bronze underneath. The vision became even less clear as my eyes flooded with tears, my body racked with heaving sobs.

The two little girls and baby remained, shrieking from the floorboards. The woman nodded to the man, whose hesitation betrayed his reluctance.

"What are you waiting for? Do it! Do it now!" she shouted, her unquenchable thirst for violence making my stomach heave.

The young man advanced towards the three remaining children with the iron hook.

I screamed and thrashed, desperate to escape the vile memory that ensnared my mind like steaming, pestilent tar. I clawed at my head, sobbing as I willed it to end. Hands reached into the nightmare, grabbing my shoulders. I fought back with what little strength remained.

"Sophia! It's me!" Peter released my forearms as I scrambled backwards towards the wall, disoriented, drawing myself into a ball.

I recognised Peter's voice and parted the curtain of sweat-soaked hair. My fingernails held traces of blood and hair from where I had driven them into my scalp in such panic. I was trembling, and even the hands which I had found so comforting earlier singed my skin like a red-hot brand. The eternity that I had spent in the memory had elapsed in a moment for Peter.

His face revealed the battle between deep concern and utter confusion, but he gave me the space I desperately needed. "What the hell just happened?"

I shook my head, unable to form words, my mouth so dry that they would not have come out anyway. How had Mother had the presence of mind to drag me home after such a horrific vision? I desperately wanted to crawl into a hole and disappear but lacked the fortitude to do even that.

Peter massaged his nape, unsure of how to proceed. "Let's get you home." He held out his hand. At first, I shied away, but my grasp of reality gradually returned. Once I realised that his concern was genuine, I forced myself to allow him to help me to my feet. "I'll get your candelabra."

I jerked my hand from his and slammed the trunk closed, kicking it so forcefully that I broke through its side panel and sent it skittering across the room.

"Umm… We'll leave it then." Peter looked more confused than ever, coughing on the dust my action had stirred. Not offering his hand a second time, he motioned for me to walk ahead of him, holding both his lighter and his candle aloft. I needed little prompting as the lingering wisps of evil compelled me forward. Once we reached the hidden door, he closed it behind us as though it mattered. As if one could trap such evil. With the moonlight sufficient to light our way, he extinguished his flame. Struggling to keep up with my hurried pace, Peter silently yet swiftly guided us back to the unchained door through which we had entered.

We stepped out under a cloudless sky. The stars that had been so beautiful and mesmerising before now felt distant and cold, the sounds of nature ominous and threatening. The bitter wind that had driven us into the shelter of the house had turned and drove us away. As if to punctuate our expulsion from the manor, a murder of crows swirled overhead, crying obnoxiously before descending down the hill and out of sight.

"That's bizarre." Peter returned his gaze to me after having craned his neck to look skyward. "They usually roost at this hour." He looked at me hoping for a response. When he did not receive one, he returned his focus to the path ahead, disappointed.

A fitting omen. Crow. A slur that I had heard used against my mother more times than I cared to count. What better creature to usher us from the property?

My throat tightened as we descended through the now eerily quiet countryside, and I began to hyperventilate. Peter lightly rested a hand on my shoulder as he whispered calming words. Gradually the episode subsided, and we were left with only the gravel's crunch keeping the traumatising silence at bay. His attention never left me, unsure of what to do or say. Once we reached the innocuous statue that had spooked me before, he paused.

"Look, Sophia, I have no idea what happened in there." He gnawed on his cheek, wrestling with how to continue. "When you're ready, I need you to understand that you can tell me."

I stared at him for a long moment before giving him an almost imperceptible nod. He rubbed his hands together, and we continued our journey towards the gate without further delay. I took one last look at what had once been such a magnificent manor. In the revealing light of the full moon, I could just make out a hulking figure standing in the double-arch bedroom window, watching our progress as we left the premises. He *had* been following us. At that moment, I did not care, using every bit of my remaining willpower to place one foot in front of the other. Assimilating the evening's occurrences would come later. Much later.

The uncomfortable silence continued all the way back to the station. The last bus of the evening had already run, so Peter telephoned a cab to carry us back to London at what must have been great personal expense. We rode along the winding country roads, every headlamp suspicious. I managed to mumble Milly's address to Peter who passed the instructions on to the driver. For the entire journey, he kept a cautious eye on his late-night passengers through the rearview mirror, but his hefty commission kept him from asking any questions.

The moment we pulled in front of my host's still illuminated building, a worried Milly bustled down the steps and wrapped me in a large blanket. Her eyes shown like embers, smouldering with barely contained rage. "The hell did you do to her?"

"Not his fault," I mumbled as she whisked me into the foyer.

Peter looked on helplessly from the street as Mei shut the door and locked it behind us. She disappeared to draw a hot bath while Milly brewed me a fresh cup of chamomile. I did not remember them tending to my scalp or dressing me in an evening gown, but the next thing I knew, I was in bed downing a glass of medicine-laced sherry at my friend's behest. I slept so deeply that not even nightmares could penetrate the veil. I remained in such a state for days before I uttered another word.

Chapter XVII

Milly barged into my room on the fourth morning of my bed-stricken state, rousing me from the cocoon that I had created against the outside world. "That'll be enough of that, Dear. It's time for you to rejoin the land of the living."

I forced myself up to seated, raising my arm to block the sunlight blasting in through the windows as she flung open the heavy damask curtains.

"It's a beautiful, crisp morning in London, and I don't intend on you wasting it. Now, you promised to tell me all about your trip, and I know you to be a woman of your word. That fellow of yours has been worried sick as well, coming around every day to check on your wellbeing."

I groaned, reluctant to speak. I collapsed back down and made to roll over.

"There'll be none of that." Milly jerked off the duvet and pulled me to standing. With Mei's help, they disrobed me and thrust me into a shower far cooler than my liking. After a vigorous towelling off and less-than-gentle combing, they had me dressed in a cosy cotton outfit and downstairs in front of a demitasse of crema-topped dark espresso.

"I figured this morning you could use the good stuff. A sip of that will get your blood flowing faster than a cuppa tea ever could. Those Italianos know their coffee."

I had tasted the overly rich beverage a couple of times, but had never taken a shine to it. I took a tentative sip of the rich brown broth and almost spit it back into the cup. It was unbelievably bitter and stout enough to hold a spoon erect. "I'll need some sugar cubes."

"She speaks! Mei, the sugar."

Once I'd downed the petite cup, I suddenly needed to speak at a rate to make up for the past three days. I drank a second when it was offered and for the first time, I think I out-talked Milly. To my host's chagrin, every time the conversation turned to that evening, I'd change the subject.

"Whoo, you're wearing my old ears out." Milly grinned from cheek to cheek as she jokingly wiggled her little finger in her ear. "I've never been around someone who spoke so much and revealed so little. You still owe me, you know."

I took a deep breath, allowing the pace of my heart to settle, and smoothed out the non-existent wrinkles of the fabric on my lap. "I am a woman of my word. You'll get your story, but I'm not ready. Milly, I… I experienced something. Something that I can't relive just yet."

"And you promise it has nothing to do with this Peter who's been sniffing around?"

"I promise. He's a good soul. I owe him as much of an explanation as you."

"Figures he gets one before I do, ha! He'll be here at a quarter till to take you to Kew Gardens. My suggestion, by the way. You'll never find a more soothing place for the soul than nature, which can oft be hard to come by in Londontown."

"Thank you, Milly." I placed my hand on hers.

"Thank me with your story. The curiosity is driving me absolutely batty."

"Let's see how the day goes first."

"I'll be waiting with anticipation. In the meantime, I think I'll practice my archery. Mei, my things!"

Before I could utter a response, my face spoke for me.

"What? A well-to-do woman can't enjoy the shooting sports? I'll have you know I would put myself up against most men in the art."

Mei proffered Milly a gorgeous recurve bow and full quiver before struggling to maneuver a cumbersome circular target out the front door to the park across the street.

"Is there anything you can't do?" I asked, laughing.

Milly grinned as she shrugged, happy to see me smiling again. "There's not much I can't do, but there are a few things that I won't." The rosy-cheeked woman winked. "Mei's quite talented as well, she can—"

There was a knock at the door.

"That'll be your suitor. Try to stay in one piece this time."

I could not help but roll my eyes. Milly may have been a perpetual joker, but I knew she had my best interests at heart. She guided me to the door where Peter stared up at me from under the brim of his watch cap. His eyebrows knitted together as Milly grasped the fact that she was holding a weapon.

"I must look the fool." She cackled. "I'll leave you both to it. She closed the door as she set off across the street to where Mei was setting up her target. With the neighbourhood children at school, the only impediment to

Milly's training was the older couple feeding the birds at the far end of the park.

"Quite the friend you have there." Peter leaned against the iron railing with his hands buried in his trouser pockets. He watched as the woman barked commands at Mei to perfectly position her target.

"She's something else, isn't she?"

I watched as she loosed the first arrow which impacted the white edge of the target, almost off of it completely. Even from the distance, I could hear some foul utterances coming from her direction. The elderly pair, driven away by her unladylike conduct, left her and Mei to themselves. It would not have surprised me if that had been her intent all along.

I turned to face Peter. His eyes shown with relief as a pang of guilt hid behind mine. I had put this new friend through a lot of turmoil over the last several days. Frankly, I was surprised that he had not turned tail and run. I would not have blamed him had he done so.

"How have you been?" Peter asked as he walked me down to a sporty car parked at the curb.

I heard Milly whoop and glanced up to see she had buried an arrow in the yellow centre of the target. A brief smile passed between us.

"I've been better."

I eyed the petite cabriolet Peter had arrived in with uncertainty. The peculiarly small open-air Singer seemed marginally safer than the Triumph motorcycles that were growing in popularity among English gentlemen. Admittedly, I frequently felt the urge to mount one myself, but after so many stressful days, I craved more protection than what was parked in front of me.

"I hope you don't mind if I drive us to the Gardens. It's too beautiful a day to be shut inside a dark metal box." Sensing my hesitation, he added, "This Nine is quite safe. I've had an engineer rework the steering. I promise that I'll drive safely."

I nodded and climbed down into the navy sports car as Peter held its comically small door open. In the brief time that I had known him, he had never struck me as a daredevil, so I trusted his judgement. He jumped into the driver's seat, donned a pair of leather driving gloves, and wrapped his hands around the wooden steering wheel. We took off with a start down the road at speeds the small car magnified in a way that made me positively giddy. Instead of fear, it was quite the opposite. With the roar of the tiny engine and the wind dragging my curls aloft, I began to feel like a normal human being once more. For that moment, I had not a care in the world. I whooped loudly as we caught up with the older couple from the park. The lady stared as the gentleman shook his head.

"I thought you might like it," he yelled over the noise. "Simon said this car is one of the only good decisions I've made."

I smiled inside and out. When I was with Peter, something simply felt right. It was hard to believe that it was only our second day together. Somehow it was as though our spirits had known each other for ages. The fascinating gentleman was beginning to emerge from his shell, and I was finally allowing someone into mine. We bounded along, laughing gaily as we sailed over every bump, our stomachs lurching into our throats. Even at low speeds, the tight turns felt like they would spill us out onto the asphalt, which only served to increase the thrill. When we pulled onto the

Gardens' grounds, a smile was permanently adhered to my face.

Peter helped me out from the low-slung car and after purchasing a pair of tickets, led me into the most beautiful gardens I had ever visited. After my giggles subsided, we meandered through the numerous exhibits for hours, each sight—glass architecture, marble reliefs, carnivorous flowers, poisonous trees—each prompting yet another discussion of antiquity. Peter could speak at length on the minutiae of the antique world. He could recall the most mundane details to an impressive extent and, from what I gathered, could repair or restore just about anything.

My knowledge of the ancient world, while extensive, paled in comparison to his. My love for such dated objects centred around sentimental and cultural importance, whereas Peter's interest of the ancient was deeply rooted in a love of the past. Under Simon's thumb, Peter's knowledge had primarily been used for financial gain. However, as I got to know him, I understood his motives to be quite different. When Peter came across something new, he would meticulously study it until he felt as though he had learned everything from its provenance to its historical significance. If something was mysterious or intriguing, he found it all the more captivating. Between my gift and interests and Peter's knowledge of languages and texts, I couldn't help but think that we would make a formidable presence in the world of antiques.

I watched Peter scrutinise a plaque below a cactus which was eerily reminiscent of the candelabra. My stomach churned. *You consider yourself a businesswoman? You can't even keep your wits about you, Sophia.* I shoved the dream aside. My thoughts would be shackled to that of the vision until I had brought the parties behind the grisly murders to justice. Peter saw me staring and grinned. I smiled politely back. He was no less bound than I. Under the oppressive grip of his belittling brother, he was not going anywhere. Not as long as Simon could profit from his presence.

After hours of enjoyable but light-hearted conversation we had a seat outside of the facility's large greenhouse at a small whitewashed iron table, letting the gentle breeze reinvigorate our exhausted bodies. Peter looked at me questioningly, and I knew that the moment had come.

"Before I tell you what happened the other night, I need you to promise me something."

"Anything."

"Promise that you won't think I'm completely mental."

"Are you?"

I gave him a dirty glance.

"I won't. You have me at my word. I would just like the truth."

After seeing my intense reaction to contact with the candelabra, there was little I could do to hide the truth. I chose in that moment to trust Peter. I told him everything beginning with Mother's experience with the candelabra in his father's shop. The awakening of my gift with the communion chalice. Perpetually feeling like an outsider in my own country. The years that I had spent locating his father's business. Most importantly, what I had seen when I touched that cursed item in the trunk. When I had finished, the sun was kissing the horizon and the Kew Gardens employees were hinting that it was time for us to depart.

"Wow. That's a lot to take in." Peter stared at the ground.

"You don't think I'm mad, do you?"

He shook his head as he stood and stretched, before offering me a hand up. "No. In all of my research, I've collected some pretty outlandish accounts. While I've always been inclined to the rational, it hasn't stopped me from pursuing such stories and artefacts. The prevalence of such events leads me to believe there's more out there than just what we modern humans understand."

"Thank you."

He nodded as we headed toward the car park. "Most importantly, I believe *you*. Not to mention, I think it's highly unlikely that you could fake such an intense reaction like the one you had at the Wilbanks Estate." Peter helped me into the car and we began the drive back to Milly's, albeit less enthused than on our initial journey.

"You're awfully quiet," I said as he pulled to a stop and set the parking brake, but left the car running.

He helped me up and walked me to the door. I saw Milly's head vanish from the parted curtains. *Busybody.* The rustic odour of roasted pheasant filled the air. I guessed that the archery had given my host a taste for game. "Sure you won't come in for dinner?"

"You've left me with a lot to process. Give me a day or two, and I'll be right as rain."

I had little right to protest after spending three days in bed without so much as a telephone call. Peter gave me a peck on the cheek, climbed back into his car, and disappeared down the street before Milly opened the door to usher me inside.

Chapter XVIII

Days ticked by with nary a word from Peter. *Did I scare him off with the truth?* It's no more than he wanted. Perhaps I was the fool for giving it to him. True to my word, the day after my visit to Kew Gardens, I provided Milly a detailed account of what had transpired. Considering Peter's reaction, I refused to divulge anything pertaining to the supernatural. I seemed to have lost one friend, and I did not care to lose a second. In the explanation to my gracious host, I chalked the emotional overwhelm up to confronting the relic that had impacted my mother so. Mildred, being who she was, had desperately wanted to pry but showed impressive restraint. She was, above all, proving to be a most loyal friend. She deserved the truth, and I promised myself to one day give it to her.

A week after the trip to Kew Gardens, I was still passing my days in the guest room doing little more than sleeping and overthinking every detail from that fateful night. Milly would come and chat, but with no conversation able to drift past small talk, she would perpetually leave disappointed. Day after day, Mei faithfully brought me each meal and drew a bath when requested. If not for the anxiety inspired by the vision, it would have been a restful escape. I knew I would eventually have to confront my fears and dig deeper into the strange occurrence if I wanted to bring any resolution to the departed family.

"I'm tired of you moping around the place, Sophia. Let's get you outside." Milly busted into my room and parted the curtains like she was wont to do, bathing the room in brightness. Sporadic rays of sun broke through London's omnipresent grey clouds, fingers of light caressing the city. "Maybe we can catch enough sunlight to get you feeling like yourself again. Now, up and at-em."

Milly all but dragged me from bed, instructing Mei not to take her eyes off me until I was ready to walk out the front door, lest I return to my depressive state. We passed the morning eating a leisurely breakfast, at which I chose coffee over the more traditional tea. With a little extra momentum from the strong coffee and hearty meal, our outing continued at Milly's favourite shoppes. Each boutique was further out of my meagre budget than the next. Mei followed along silently carrying our purchases as they piled up in her short arms. Milly would insist I try on outfits that I couldn't afford, then purchased them for me, refusing to take no for an answer.

The woman had been right to force me out of that stuffy room. The sun did help, and perhaps the buzz of new garments did as well. However, none of it changed the loneliness that sat like a lump in my breast. In a mere few days, I had fallen for Peter, making the connection with a kindred spirit for which I had been wholly unprepared. I had given others parts of myself, but Peter Northrop was the first of which I had given my heart. He was the polar opposite of the type of gentleman I would've taken home in the past—tall and lanky, clumsy and soft-spoken—but he had captured my affection with something so pure, so unadulterated, that radiated from his being. And I had run him off.

"Heavens, would you look at that!" Milly admired a shimmering black dress on the mannequin at a little shop named Thea's. The cleavage dipped remarkably low and it had a far higher hem than most proper British women would consider modest. "If only I had your hips and your youth, Sophia."

I laughed politely as she rubbed the fine material between her fingers. All I could think about was the notion of wearing such an exposing dress in front of Peter. The thought made me weak at the knees.

"Peter would go into arrest if he saw you in this." I teared up and Milly's wide grin faded into motherly concern. "I'm sorry, Sophia. You've known me long enough to know that my mouth runs faster than my mind." She paused for a moment. "You know what? We've done enough shopping, and he's done enough stewing." She let the dress fall back into place and nearly jerked me out the door of the shop to the awaiting car Milly had hired for the day.

"Where's this shop of his, Dearie?" She said once the three of us were seated in the back of the luxurious sedan and our bounty nestled safely in the boot.

"Oh, we can't, Mildred. When he's ready, I'm sure he'll give me a ring." I doubted my own words as they cascaded from my mouth.

"He's had enough time for that. I'm not going to allow him to let a catch like you slip through his scrawny fingers. Hell, I'm half tempted to put you in that dress before I carry you to him."

I couldn't help but laugh. "We can't show up uninvited."

"It's a place of business, is it not?"

"Is it, but…"

"Then tell the man where it's located."

There was no talking Milly out of an idea once it was set in her mind. "The British Museum, please. We will walk from there."

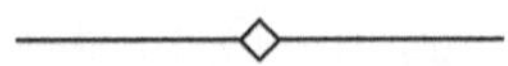

I'd spent the entire car ride in dread. Not the pleasant thrill like darting through the tight London streets in Peter's little cabrio, but a gnawing in my stomach that threatened to bring up the heavy traditional breakfast I had chosen this morning. The driver pulled to a stop in front of the museum on the far side of the road. Milly climbed out, staring at me until I followed.

"Mei, take our things home, and give the driver a tip, would you?"

"Thank you, Mum," said the driver as he shut the door.

"It was well deserved. Now, let's go."

I stood paralysed on the sidewalk as I watched a family of museum patrons climb the steps, running off a flock of pigeons. The children were too similar to what I had witnessed in the candelabra, bringing back a wild twist of emotions. I took a deep breath and forced myself to turn away. Milly flashed a look of concern before letting the issue go. I led her down the side streets that led to Simon and

Peter's shop, dragging my feet so as to delay our arrival as much as possible.

"If you don't speed up, It'll be Saint George's Day by the time we arrive."

"I don't think he'll appreciate us dropping in on him like this. His brother's shop, it's…"

"Not exactly above board. I get it. From what you've told me, Peter's not a part of that, so we've got little to fear. He on the other hand… That boy's going to get a piece of my mind."

I led her to the entrance of the alley where I was immediately spotted by the two men who'd given me the cool greeting on my first trip to the shop as an adult.

"Welcome back, Miss. I see you've brought a friend along."

"Let us through, boys. We have some business to attend to." Milly was already making her way towards the door.

The one named Jas, if I remembered correctly, moved aside to let her pass. The other never bothered to lift himself off the wall. I heard Jas mutter to him, "Mmm. I like a woman with a little fire," before Milly barged through the wooden door, straining the little brass bell above. Its little tinkle seemed insufficient to announce the presence of Mildred G. Foster.

"Who are you?" Simon asked, dropping his newspaper to the counter and rising as Tim peered out from his place in the shadows. Simon's face flashed with something. Not fear. I saw his hand drop to his side and for the first time it occurred to me how much my compatriot looked like trouble. Considering the possibility of violence, I rushed behind Milly to slow her down. When the pair saw me, they both relaxed slightly, but not completely. "You again?"

"We need to speak with Peter, immediately, if you please." Milly demanded.

"He's busy," said the voice from the shadows, his accent deep, akin to gravel pouring from a lorry. Judging by the silhouette framed by a frosted window, he was staring me up and down in a way that made my skin crawl.

"Sorry, Mum," said Simon, "but unless you or your friend are here to do business, I'm going to ask you to leave."

"Peter, get your arse in here and speak to this woman face-to-face." Milly started to storm into the back room, but Tim moved far faster than his bulky figure would lend one to believe and blocked her path. "Sonny, I will eat you for breakfast if you don't get out of my way."

Tim grinned, revealing teeth yellowing from years of smoking in a smile that couldn't have been more menacing. "I'd like to see that."

I swear Milly was about to roll up her sleeves when Peter appeared from the rear of the store and rested a hand on Tim's shoulder. Tim turned and eyed Peter's touch with such disdain that he quickly withdrew it. With a nod from Simon, the wide-shouldered menace stood to the side.

"Sophia. Could we talk in private?"

Milly looked at me questioningly. I nodded and followed him to the back room. With little more than saloon doors to block the sound, the room only provided the impression of privacy. After the drama that had unfolded in the showroom, I had no doubt that the shop's occupants would be listening intently. I fervently hoped Peter would choose his words wisely.

He pulled a wooden stool from under the workbench and motioned for me to sit. The stool's top was marred with indentations and scrapes, an alternate work surface for the tinkerer. He sat on another tattered stool himself. "I've been meaning to stop by; I really have." His nervousness was apparent. I glanced at the disarray of the normally obsessively organised space and realised that he had been burying himself in work to avoid confronting his feelings. The room was littered with open references, scattered papers, and loose bits and bobs. The floor needed a good sweeping and the air held the heavy haze of pipe smoke.

"Peter, I—"

"I'm sorry to interrupt, but please allow me to speak first."

I nodded, happy he was talking to me at all.

"The last few weeks my mind has been spinning like a coaster. Meeting you is the most interesting thing that's ever happened to me. My world was dusty and monochromatic before you arrived trailing vibrant colours and wafts of spring flowers. When I'm with you, I forget about my work. When I'm at work, I can't stop thinking about you. My predictable existence has become anything but—in the best way possible. What I was ill-prepared for during our visit to the Gardens wasn't only what you shared with me, but also the intensity of the feelings I held for you. Still hold for you. I didn't know how to process what I was feeling, so I returned to the mundanity that I understood until I could gather my bearings." He gestured to a pile of coins of various origins he appeared to be painstakingly cross-referencing and cataloguing.

"And what about now?"

"I've always been reluctant to let people into my life," Peter said, taking both of my hands in his, "but I want you in it. Every part of it."

I wrapped my arms around his shoulders, nuzzling into his sweater and taking in the faint smell of grease and old paper that clung to him like a close friend. I did not know where the journey that we had been presented with would take us, but I knew that I could not complete it without Peter at my side.

Chapter XIX

As we emerged from the back room, it was apparent that the shop's occupants had heard our every word. Milly grinned from ear to ear. Tim scoffed as his eyes rolled. Simon loosed a bored sigh and returned to his newspaper. The shop's single patron cleared his throat and feigned a sudden interest in a wooden Bangwa Queen from the French Cameroons.

"I believe I have it from here, Milly."

"I figured as much. Gentlemen, I take my leave." Tim preceded to walk her to the door, but with a stiff glare over her shoulder, he returned back to his corner. The patron did everything he could to blend into the wall.

"Let's take a walk, shall we?" Peter walked to the rack by the door and grabbed his coat, scarf, and cap.

No sooner than we were out of view of Simon's minions, Peter slipped his hand into mine. I returned the gesture with a coquettish look, making him nearly fall off the curb. I could not help but laugh. I pulled him back up to the sidewalk by his scarf, gradually bringing him closer and closer. Then I planted a lingering kiss on his lips that left his head reeling. Peter's hand caressed the nape of my neck as he took over, sending a surge of electricity throughout my body. Something about his demeanour had changed. He still clearly lacked grace, but his confidence was emerging like the daffodils that had begun to dot the roadsides. He turned to me with flushed cheeks and flashed a broad grin. I could not have been more grateful to Milly for forcing me into action.

Once we were out of the alley, we quietly made our way to Bloomsbury Square Garden, hand-in-hand. Each time I stole a glance at Peter, I found him to be doing the same. A warmth would rush to my cheeks, and action oft repeated. In the Garden we were hoping to find some privacy amongst disinterested strangers concerned with nothing more than their own affairs. Upon our arrival, the place was scattered with ladies and gentlemen seeking the escape into nature that was becoming harder and harder to do in the ever-growing city. Peter and I made several rounds before either of us broke the silence.

"As much as I would like to spend all day strolling with you at my side, I imagine you're anxious to continue your search."

I let a mirthless laugh escape, and Peter did not press the issue. "I am." The leaves crunched underfoot as we meandered along the moss-covered cobblestones. I sighed, hesitant to part with the warm tingles of the morning in favour of the harsh reality of the vision. "What I experienced will haunt my mind until I bring those bastards to justice." The sudden vulgarity shattered the park's serenity, drawing a few looks. A mother tugged her child away swiftly by the arm. I felt a pang of guilt, but was no less upset. "With any luck, its resolution will bring peace to Mother's spirit as well." I turned to face my companion. "Peter, we have to figure out where that candelabra came from. If we can determine that, it could lead us back to where that horrific crime took place." I shuddered thinking back to the memory and shoved it from my mind. Every time I allowed the scene to replay, I would succumb to panic. There were important details held within that memory, but I was not ready to relive it. Not yet.

"There's only one place the records would be, and we've already been there."

"The warehouse? If it's that simple, then what are we waiting for, Peter? We could be there before the hour."

I began walking swiftly towards the street, but I noticed Peter was not following.

"Sofia, there was another reason I didn't come visit you."

"Why? What happened?" I had turned around and was biting my lip, nervous about what he was about to say.

"It started when I returned to work the morning after Kew Gardens. Simon confronted me the moment he noticed the downtrodden look across my face."

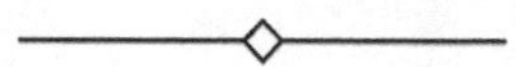

"The prodigal son returns." Simon tossed his ever-present newspaper onto the marred counter and leaned back in his seat. The man and the chair each groaned. He pulled another cigarette from the crumpled pack in his vest pocket, lit it, took a long drag, and expelled the plume into Peter's face. "Dame move on?"

"Sod off." Peter waved away the smoke and disappeared through the saloon doors, setting his satchel down on the floor next to his workbench with more force than necessary.

"Sounds like a yes," said Tim, bathed in his own haze of cigar smoke.

Simon rose and stretched before following Peter into the workroom. He gave him an overpowered pat on the back, making his younger brother cringe. "Couldn't figured out what she saw in you, Little Brother. Did you at least have it off with her?"

Peter sprung from his chair into Simon's face.

"Whoa, there, filly." Simon raised his hands in mock surrender.

"Must've hit a nerve." Tim absentmindedly flicked his lighter open and closed as he watched the drama unfold.

"You've no right to speak of her like that." Peter maintained eye contact with Simon unlike the few times in the past he challenged his brother.

"You two have had quite the time playing ne'er-do-well, running around town and countryside, dressed as fools, trespassing wherever you deem fit. My warehouse. The Wilbanks place. Ring any bells?"

"How could— Oh." Peter glanced toward Tim, the sunlight reflecting off of the metal-clad lighter the burly man toyed with.

"You think I'd let you run around on your own with some trollop? It's my job to protect our family's interests. I knew the moment I saw her hand on your leg that she was nothing but trouble." Simon drove a stout finger into Peter's chest. "And you followed the whore like a love-sick puppy."

Peter sent a fist sailing towards his brother's face, but his wild swing more than announced his intention. Simon easily intercepted the blow with his much stronger hands and the only sound in the shop was Peter's knuckles cracking under the pressure. Simon easily forced Peter back into his workbench without releasing his hand.

"Now, I promised Father I would take care of you. Far be it from me to go back on my word, as damned foolish as it was. Best thing you can do is forget about that dame."

Peter stared down his brother, confidence wavering. Finally, he dropped his head in submission, exactly what Simon expected. "I can't. She needs my help, Simon, and I intend to give it to her. And *not* because I'm being manipulated, but because I am choosing to."

"Suit yourself." Simon sighed and let go. "Waste all the time you like, but I expect your work to get done. I'm not paying you to spend time with that floozy. And I don't want her in the warehouse again. I just found a buyer for the altarpiece, and the last thing I need is the Yard sniffing about."

Peter slammed his hand down on the workbench, surprising Simon. "We need access to the records there! What am I supposed to do, bring every single one of Father's ledgers back to the shop? There's barely enough room for me to work back here as it is."

"For Christ's sake." Simon rolled his eyes as he took another deep drag and stared at the clouded window for a moment. "How much faith do you have in this woman?"

"Complete faith."

"Let's hope it's not misplaced." Simon moved until he was almost nose-to-nose with Peter. "If she breathes a word of anything she sees, or if I get the slightest inkling that she's not who she says she is, I'll have Tim slit her bloody throat while you watch."

Peter nodded, doing his best to restrain a gulp. He wouldn't get any more leeway from his brother than that.

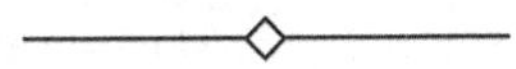

"So if I act in the least way suspicious, Simon will have me killed?"

"He's done…" Peter paused. "He's not one to make idle threats."

"Why do you continue to work with such a fiend? All this work, all this running around we're doing is to put killers like him behind bars. You two couldn't be more different. You have a moral compass. You're kindhearted and intelligent. I know you said you feel the need to carry on your father's legacy, but could you not do that without him?" The intensity of my words surprised even me. I could not bear seeing Peter lose what made him so unique, so special.

"You don't understand."

"You want me to be part of your world, right? Then help me understand," I pleaded.

"He controls everything, alright?" Peter's face flushed and fought back tears, exasperated. "I have nothing of my own! Nothing. Father left me with half of his estate but under Simon's care. My brother can't use it himself, but he dangles it like a carrot on a stick. If I walked out, it would be without so much as a farthing."

My financial predicament was equally as perilous. My savings was running out quickly, despite the generosity of my benefactor. Unless something happened soon, I would not have anywhere near enough funds to accomplish my dream. My heart broke as Peter divulged the full extent of Simon's control. His volume increased in tandem with his emotions, turning heads as he shattered the park's tranquillity.

"I'm sorry, Peter. I'm so sorry." I took his hand and we sat on a bench, its hunter green slats damp from the misting rain that had begun. I pulled him close as he struggled to pull himself together, listening to the pitter-patter of the condensing rainwater as it fell from the trees onto the carpet of decaying leaves. Any onlookers eventually turned away, and Peter slowly calmed. He sat up, massaging the bridge of his nose as he surreptitiously wiped away tears.

"Peter, we're knowledgeable in our respective fields. What if we opened our own antique shop, together? I'm sure Milly would loan us the necessary funds. And we'd pay back every shilling if I had to sneak them under her pillow while she slept."

"You'd be willing to go into business with someone you barely know?" Peter leaned back and chuckled, a sincere sound. "And you truly believe we could pull off something like that?"

"I *know* we could. I have no doubt that your brother would make life difficult for us in London, but we could start fresh anywhere in Europe. Sister Agnes taught me quite a bit of Latin, and you've studied enough that you can read foreign documents in most European languages."

"Your idea holds merit." Peter nodded. "And you'd do that with me?"

I nodded excitedly.

"I don't know what to say."

Smiling, we rose and made our way to the street where we could hail a cab to carry us to the warehouse. With how dramatic our visit had been, I could not help but think the park's other occupants were happy to be rid of us.

"Before we move forward, Sophia, are you sure you wish to carry on chasing this memory? You've proposed a novel idea that could give each of us the independence we crave. We could start anew. Leave our past behind. I wouldn't blame you for backing down from your pursuit given the circumstances."

"If this is about Simon, I don't give two bits about his threats. My mother and I were endowed with this ability for a reason, and I can't help but think we were meant to find that candelabra. I would never forgive myself if I stopped now, and not just for my benefit. Those murderers could still be out there, Peter. Imagine if I stopped and more innocent people died on my account. I can't let that happen."

"Between your optimism and your resolve, you are a force to be reckoned with. It's no wonder Mildred likes you so much." Peter whistled for a cab, holding his hand high in the air. "I wish I had half of your strength."

"You do."

Chapter XX

E ven with the emotion-wrought morning, I could only ignore my hunger so long after such an extensive walk in the park. We stopped at a small outdoor cafe where Peter and I each ordered an egg and cress. By the end of the meal, we were laughing over tea at our surprising appetites. Part of me was anxious to go to the warehouse, but the other part—the part filled with trepidation—was stalling. I went to refill my teacup for the third time and Peter gently blocked the motion with his hand.

"It's time."

I nodded, taking a deep breath. The smile on my lips faded as I faced our imminent departure from the superficial world to its crime-ridden underbelly whose existence everyone wilfully ignored. We took a taxi to the family's warehouse, having the driver drop us off a few streets shy of our destination. Whether we were being watched as we entered for the second time was no longer of any import.

For the time being, Simon no longer concerned himself with our whereabouts.

Peter unlocked the door and flicked on the lights. The illumination drove the darkness away as I hoped to do with the grisly murder of the family that haunted my thoughts. Peter led me back to the familiar record room, the odour of moulding paper filling my nostrils and harking back the bookshop from what now seemed like a past life. As he led me through the array of desks near the entry, I could not help but notice the blinds Peter had lowered on our first visit had been raised. Everything beyond them in the warehouse was now covered in dark grey shipping blankets, concealing all traces within from my view.

"Simon isn't one to take chances." Peter touched the centre of my back, guiding me gently towards the back room where the records were kept. "Wait here for a moment." Peter disappeared for no more than a minute before returning. "We're alone. I had to make certain so that we could speak candidly."

"I can't say I blame you." I smiled at Peter, but he was all business.

"Forgive me for not understanding how your ability works, but could you perhaps do it again?" Peter gestured to a set of three wooden filing cabinets to which the moisture had not been kind. Each had a brass handle and label frame gradually succumbing to verdigris. Most of the old card stock documenting the drawers' contents was discoloured or smudged, the light pencil strokes of the brothers' father no longer legible.

"I'll do my best." I reached out and touched the first handle, half expecting nothing to happen. A feeling, free of all imagery, surprised me. A sad yearning tugged at my emotions as an unfamiliar melody echoed in my mind. I touched each consecutive handle, each with no more information than the last. At some point I had absentmindedly started humming.

I opened my eyes to see a shocked Peter. "What made you do that?"

"Do what?"

"What made you hum that song? That particular song?" Peter was growing agitated, his eyes growing moist with an emotion I could not easily decipher.

"I… I don't know." I shook my head apologetically. "It just came to me."

Peter grew distant as his agitation dissipated. "My mother sang that to me every evening before I went to bed." I reached for Peter's shoulder, but he shied away. "Please don't hum it again. It's difficult for me to bear."

"I'm so sorry, Peter. I won't do it again." I touched the last of the drawers, feeling the same longing sensation. I could almost hear a woman's voice singing, but the words were as foreign as the tune. The voice behind the melody was soft, but carried behind it a subtle strength.

"Forgive me. I overreacted. You couldn't have known." Peter's eyes rose to mine. "It's an old folk song Mother was quite fond of called *In the Quiet Night.*' She died when I was just a lad. I don't have near enough memories of her, but that song has stuck with me all of these years."

I desperately wanted to ask more questions, but Peter changed the subject so abruptly that he clearly had no interest in continuing the conversation.

"Have you found anything?"

I shook my head. "I'm sorry, no. At least, nothing that would help us."

"Then we use the old-fashioned way. It's worked for centuries."

Peter pulled the first drawer out with a squeal, the warped wood rubbing its swollen counterpart and requiring more coercion than expected. The smell of forest decay hit my nostrils as a plume of spore-filled dust clogged the air. Peter sputtered a few times before spitting into a nearby trash can. "Sorry about that. I'll be surprised if my lungs don't grow fungus after whatever we just inhaled."

I chuckled, glad that the Peter I knew was returning. Below that calm demeanour was a profound sadness I had barely touched upon. I had shared so much of my story with him over the last few weeks. I hoped before long that he would trust me with his.

"Father organised the entire cabinet by year, so we needn't look at anything past 1920, the year you first visited the shop. That only leaves us with everything between 1883 and then." Peter sighed and rubbed the back of his head. "That's nearly four decades of records."

"Thirty seven. Considered by some to be an auspicious number."

Peter chuckled. "Thirty seven. Considered by me to mean we'll be here for a while."

We had started our search standing, but within the hour, our backs were aching, stooped over the low cabinets. We had dragged over two desk chairs and alternated taking drawers. At a quarter past five, we finally found the record we had spent the afternoon searching for, written in the same hand we'd been staring at for hours. My exhaustion faded as I read aloud.

"November 1917: Victorian bronze candelabra. Believed 19th century. Lions around base. Five candle arms. Superb craftsmanship. Purchased for 6£. Anonymous seller. See Plymouth Gin Crate."

Peter and I looked at each other before diving back into the cabinet. The crate's card was the next entry in the drawer.

"November 1917: Cedar Plymouth Gin crate. Gorgeous natural patina. Stamped 1866. Original shipping label: 'Destination: Chatham Manor, Luffield.' Ilse smitten with it. Acquired for 0£. Anonymous seller. Used to package Victorian bronze candelabra. See previous entry."

My heart froze mid-beat. Luffield. How? Perhaps it was nothing more than a coincidence. Someone looking to package a candelabra would have used anything nearby. This crate had clearly been in existence for a long while. I could almost feel my mother's hand on my shoulder. Mother never believed in coincidences.

I had grown up playing in the shadow of Chatham Manor, a grand home which sat high on the hill above the town, looming over us like a lord over his vassals. Despite England's transition to a constitutional monarchy, Lord Chatham was still of the mind that Luffield was under his jurisdiction, a belief not too far from the truth. Little occurred in Luffield in which he did not have some degree of involvement. As the town's largest patron, Luffield's inhabitants had little objection. If he was involved in the murders, which I believed was in the realm of possibilities, we would have a difficult path ahead.

"Ilse was my mother's name." Peter whispered as he ran his fingers pensively across the entry. "Luffield. Would you believe that? Life has a funny way of coming full circle."

I nodded, still in a state of shock. "I didn't know if I'd ever return, much less this soon."

"It's not much of a lead, but we have little else to go on."

"No, you're right. I have a few fond memories of Luffield but more that I'd hoped to escape."

"No one can outrun their demons. Not all of them, at least." I nodded as Peter helped me up from the creaky wooden chair. "Do you know anything about this Chatham?"

I brushed the dust from my skirt and attempted to massage my sleeping backside without Peter catching on.

"Very little. Lord Chatham is somewhat reclusive, but he's thought of well by the townspeople. Though his title is honorary, he behaves as though it is not. With as much of his personal wealth he contributes back to the town, we would need a mountain of evidence to turn public opinion against him."

"So… not a place we can saunter into and start asking accusatory questions."

"Exactly. The people of Luffield are friendly enough, but they aren't fond of outsiders, especially overly curious ones. When Mother and I settled there, we weren't only outsiders, but we were different. Dorothy Tate was a single mother, haunted by madness, and more spiritual than religious. Naturally, the locals held us at arm's length. A number of mothers wouldn't allow their children to play with me. Only the sisters at Grafton treated the two of us like the humans we were. In all my years of living and working in Luffield, I never felt accepted into the community."

"That's a shame, but it's their loss." Peter came forward to embrace me, resting his chin gently on top of my head. "You're right about evidence. Not only will we need a mountain, as you say, but it will need to be ironclad. Someone has to know what happened. You can't tell me that an entire family was murdered in cold blood and no one took notice. Even the smallest English towns have busybodies."

"Ugh," I moaned, thinking of the nosy, rumour-spreading ilk that was Camille Hart-Watts.

"Whoever you just thought of, that's clearly the person we need." Peter grinned menacingly.

"I'd give anything to avoid her."

"Including leaving this entire ordeal unsolved?"

He was right, as much as I hated to admit it. I could not let justice slide because I was too haughty to put aside petty differences, even if it meant talking to Camille.

I stood erect, looking him in the eyes. "I'll do whatever it takes."

"That's what I was hoping to hear." Peter took my hand and kissed it, blushing.

I leaned in to kiss him, savouring the lingering taste of spearmint on his tongue. "At that pipe again?"

Peter pulled back, punch-drunk. "I had to do something in your absence."

I laughed, drinking of his lips deeply as I wrapped my arms around him.

With strength unexpected from his thin frame, he hoisted me awkwardly up onto the desk as I giggled. Gradually moving his kisses down my neck and across my clavicle, he drew my shoulder strap down as the light pecks continued. "Come back to my apartment with me." His voice quavered as he spoke.

I stared him in the eyes. "Are you sure?"

"I've never been more sure of anything."

Chapter XXI

When I awoke, it took me a moment to get my bearings as I recalled the events of the prior evening. Peter had invited me back to his flat where we had barely made it through the door with all of our clothes. Any inexperience he may have had in the bedroom, he made up for with his caring patience and meticulous devotion to detail, driving me to inhuman madness.

A warmth flooded my cheeks as I reminisced and beheld the room for the first time in daylight. The apartment bedroom could not have been that much larger than Peter's workshop. The narrow room was lined with windows covered by shutters of some foreign hardwood. Through them I could just make out a stunning view of the London skyline making up for the cramped confines. Sunlight peaked through the gaps where it shone onto my chest, only partially obscured by the bed linens. I stretched, my left arm and leg limited by the incongruous cheap panelled wall against which the bed rested.

Squeaking shower knobs and a gurgling drain choking down the last bit of water announced an end to Peter's shower. Moments later, he stepped into the room garbed only in a towel. The sun's rays caught the droplets on his smooth chest and twinkled like diamonds. One would never guess from his loose-fitting clothes that underneath was a trim gentleman with a subtly athletic build. Alone in his place of comfort with someone who had seen him at his most vulnerable, all traces of the stumbling, nervous person I had initially met had vanished.

"Sleep well?" Peter's face held a giddy grin.

"When you finally let me, yes." I returned his smile.

Peter was not the only one who was more comfortable than they had been in months, if not years. I collapsed back onto the bed in a sigh of pleasure, anxious for breakfast after the night's expenditure. Our adventure was far from over, but I allowed myself to enjoy the moment, however fleeting it might be.

"Milly's probably worried sick."

"Phone your friend. Tell her you're safe and sound."

Knowing her, she was probably already tearing London apart looking for me for failing to keep her in the loop. I rang her immediately and told her not to expect me home for the evening. Peter tickled my neck with light kisses as Milly fussed over the telephone, and it was all I could do to stifle the giggles. The sounds of merriment dispelled any doubt in my friend's mind as to what had kept me engaged. Once her mood had shifted, she put forth a number of risque suggestions before finally let me off the line.

"I have to admit, I kept expecting one of your neighbours to complain about the noise."

"Unlikely. Simon and I own the building."

Peter let the towel fall to the floor. He smirked as I overtly observed his body. He climbed back into bed and rested his head on my breast. His smooth skin was warm, still damp from the shower. The smell of fresh-cut sandalwood mixed with the lingering hint of sweat in the air made me melt back beneath the sheets.

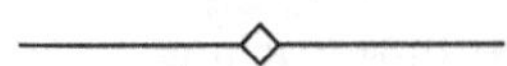

It was lunchtime before we escaped the warm embrace of Peter's bed and emerged onto the busy streets of London. Matching my mood, the heavy cloud cover had dissipated, leaving a sprawling expanse of blue. One could almost forget the chill of the season basking under the warmth of the bright midday sun.

Despite the flat's small size, Peter lived in Soho, one of the more fashionable neighbourhoods in the city. Spending most of his waking hours with his nose in a book or fingers in some ancient mechanism, the bachelor space was more than adequate for his needs. In fact, he seemed to prefer the tight confines. As we strolled through the borough, one by one, the shopkeepers greeted him by name as we made our way to his favourite restaurant.

"Are you sure you're okay with this?" Peter asked, tucking into his *jambon-beurre* with gusto. I guess he had worked up an appetite.

We sat in the tiny French bistro with an air heavily perfumed with the pleasant aromas of the kitchen. The choices and the portions were more akin to lunch at gran's than some fancy gourmet establishment. A tuxedo-clad waiter dropped by our table, asking if the meal was up to snuff in heavily-accented French. I did not need my limited familiarity with romance languages to get the gist of his question. Without missing a beat, Peter responded in what sounded like native-level fluency.

"Peter, you've been holding out on me." I smirked.

My companion blushed. "I'm not one to gasconade," he said with affectation.

I laughed and threw a piece of the baguette I had just torn from the loaf at him, earning a glare from the adjacent table. My childish behaviour was the epitome of deplorable manners in such a fine eatery, but I could not have cared less. Peter laughed deeply, a rich sound when it was not stifled as he so often tried to do.

"To answer your question," I began, still giggling. "I have no choice but to be okay with it. There's no love between Camille and me, but she has no reason to turn down my call." *I don't believe,* I failed to add. I swallowed a spoonful of my stew, savouring the rich flavour of the *cassoulet's* broth. "The woman has a nearly preternatural sense. She seems to know what will happen before it does."

People arched an eyebrow. "Such abilities seem to be commonplace in Luffield."

I playfully stepped on Peter's foot under the table.

"I don't actually believe her awareness extends to clairvoyance, but she is deeply invested in the business of others. Despite how I feel about her, she's quite adept at using her streams of information to predict what will happen next, much to her husband's chagrin."

"She sounds like she would make a hell of a politician. Might I ask why you don't care for her?"

"Our arrival into Luffield was hard enough as it was, being outsiders. From the moment we set foot into the town, she did nothing but propagate rumours about our questionable lineage and values, likely generating said rumours herself."

"Then she's done you a great disservice, but fate has a way of keeping everything in balance. The Dharmic religions refer to it as karma, but the concept is evidenced in other world traditions as well."

"What goes around, comes around."

"Exactly."

"What are you suggesting, Peter? We tell her she can balance the cosmic scales in her favour by helping us?"

"I'm suggesting that we appeal to her better nature and imply that she might benefit in the long run."

"So we threaten her."

"Only if that's how she interprets it."

Peter shrugged, his friendly smile quickly erasing the mischievous look in his eyes, leaving me to question if I was the source of his newfound confidence. His idea had merit, but if it backfired, it would leave us worse off than before.

Peter lifted a finger and the *maitre d'hotel* appeared at his side, leaning down to hear his whisper. The stocky gentleman quickly scampered off. "I hope you don't mind, but I already made the assumption that you would agree. Philippe has ensured that we have tickets on the next train to Luffield and is fetching them now. While you were in the shower, I took the liberty of phoning Ms. Foster. Mei will have your bags packed, and we will pick them up on the way to the station. Are you ready?"

My head reeled from the speed of Peter's decision making, but I had spent too long lollygagging and needed the spur into motion. I took a deep breath as I pulled the napkin out from my lap and placed it delicately on the table. "Yes, but let's go before I get cold feet."

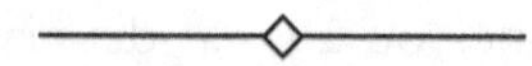

From our view on the train, the countryside flew by like the past few weeks. Peter held my cool hand as I overly anticipated every scenario we would face in the small town. I made sure to fill Peter in on my interaction with Augustus Klemp on the chance that we would run into his goons again. Peter assured me that if worse came to worst, one mention of the Northrop name would be sufficient to see us to safety. While meaning to put me at ease, it made me wonder how far and dangerous Simon's reach truly was. Mostly, I could not help but think that the grave danger we would be placing ourselves in would be more dangerous than anything Klemp could devise. Anyone who would murder an entire family would have no qualms over further killings to keep their actions secret. It would be the noose at best for the guilty parties if discovered.

Even without the loquacious Milly seated next to me, the journey was still a quick one. Peter was always pleasant company but nowhere near as chatty and did his best to keep me from becoming overly anxious. When the train pulled into Citadel Station, my stomach fluttered. Sensing my nervousness, Peter squeezed my hand reassuringly.

I glanced back at Simon's muscle, Tim, who had graced us with his presence. With him following our movements, I doubted that we would need to drop the Northrop name during our visit. Unlike our previous errand, Simon's thug made no effort to conceal himself. "Just ignore him," Peter said.

Once the porter returned our baggage, we made our way off of the train and onto the sparsely populated platform. No matter how hard I tried, I could not ignore the twin cold points on my back where I felt Tim's eyes. Peter was speaking, clearly not for the first time.

"Where to first, my dear?"

Warmth flushed my face as Peter used the pet name for the first time. I leaned over and kissed him on the cheek, not giving a damn what Tim or anyone else saw. "Straight to Camille's."

"I can't imagine this Camille would appreciate us showing up unannounced."

"She can't possibly think me more uncouth than she already does. She'll either help us, or she won't, but I don't think showing up without notice will change anything. We might even limit her scheming, catching her off guard."

"Seems logical enough." Peter looked up at the ominous clouds rolling over the town, hopefully not taking it as an omen.

The brisk morning would not have prevented me from walking to the Hart-Watts residence, which was no great distance from the station, but the drizzle changed my mind. In such a quaint town, the notion of cabs was an unnecessary novelty, something you would only need in a city of size. Fortunately for us, one of the few cabs in the city was parked outside of the station. Without waiting for Peter, I opened the rear door of the vehicle.

"I'm off duty! Can't you see the sign?" The man started mouthing off before seeing me. The familiar look was not one of recognition, but rather attraction. "Oh. Pardon me, mum." He dusted the crumbs from his lapel. "I'm just having a spot of lunch. If you'll allow me to finish my sandwich, I'll happily take you wherever you wish."

"How much to forget about your sandwich? Peter said, flipping the cabbie a crown.

The flash of disappointment that I was not travelling alone disappeared as fast as it had appeared. Peter was obviously a man of means, but it was interesting how he chose to utilise his wealth. Simon kept him on a short leash, but I had the impression if he had every farthing, little about Peter's spending habits would change. He ate well and lived well, but each was done simply, never more than necessary. His most surprising attribute was his unfailing generosity. Everywhere we went, he happily overcompensated people for their services.

"That'll do." His eyes grew wide as the coin disappeared as fast as his disappointment had. He nearly jumped from the car to collect our bags and we were off.

Chapter XXII

The tires squealed as the cabbie made the tight turn into the drive and pulled under an arched entrance sizeable enough to comfortably fit a carriage led by a team of horses. Barring our access to the grounds were enormous iron gates, preventing the Hart-Watts residence from being overrun by anyone considered common rabble. The vehicle's exhaust puttered, echoing against the blocks of the century-old walls as we waited for the home's slow-moving butler to arrive at the gate. After fiddling with the lock in no great hurry, the ageing gentleman approached the cab on Peter's side.

"May I ask who is calling?" The butler could not have sounded more pretentious had he tried.

"Sophia Tate and Peter Northrop," I answered.

The gentleman ignored the breach of etiquette. "The lady of the house prefers her guests to request an audience at least three days prior to arrival. If you would be so kind as to request such an audience…"

"Who does she think she is, the bloody Queen?" I whispered to Peter, who snorted loudly.

The butler ignored the interruption, merely annoyed at being drawn out into the miserably cold weather.

"Pardon our intrusion, but it is a matter of dire importance," said Peter.

"Matters of dire importance already have the mistress' attention."

The butler turned to leave, but Peter coughed suggestively. When he turned, Peter placed a gleaming crown into his gloved hand. The butler stared at it blankly, then back at Peter, who added two more coins.

"A matter of dire importance, you say?" The coins disappeared as the gentleman turned to open the gate, no more excited than before. "I suppose that it is possible that this matter may have escaped her attention."

"A Miss Sophia Tate and a Mr. Peter Northrop, madam."

"Do I not pay you enough, Gerald, that a simple bribe will bring anyone into my presence?"

"No, madam, you do not."

Camille Hart-Watts huffed from her partially reclined position on a well-loved chaise lounge, dismissing him with a flick of her fingertips. A handsome woman of her late forties, she hid her age well. Her low cleavage drew the eyes away from the wrinkles accumulating in the corners of her face. The grey strands that had begun to adorn her head blended in seamlessly with her golden waves so as to almost escape attention. Gerald pulled the double doors to the drawing room closed with a soft click. "Well, have a seat. The least I can do is treat my guests with more dignity than they show me."

With great effort, I avoided rolling my eyes. Peter and I sat on a Victorian settee that had all the earmarks of authenticity, until I saw that what should have been gold-leafed was, in fact, painted. Given Peter's attention to detail, he was seeing through the mask as clearly as I. Wrinkles were far from the only thing Camille was attempting to conceal.

"Thank you for having us." Peter fidgeted, struggling to sit erect on the oddly rounded cushion.

"Mmmhmm. And what, may I ask, brings you here in such a rush that you can't be bothered to call first? I realise that Sophia was raised without proper etiquette, but you strike me as a classical gentleman."

I dug my fingernails into my palms, hoping my face was not betraying my irritation. If not for the necessity of her observations, I would have contently lived the rest of my life free of her conniving machinations. The passe socialite clearly had nothing better to do with her time than relish in the misfortunes of others, likely adding to their troubles as often as not. As I beheld her, seeing through her veil-thin disguise, I almost pitied the woman. Almost.

"Mrs. Hart-Watts, I—"

"Do call me Camille, Peter," she said, batting her eyes at my companion. "We'll be here all day if you insist on using my family names, not to mention that they are a constant reminder of my burdensome husband."

"I'm sorry. Your husband…?" Peter asked, unfazed by her flirtations.

"Darnell, if you insist on reminding me. Dull wit of a man. Once a tycoon of real estate, now nothing more than a boy with his bloody trains. Not even the notion of a good romp will pull him away from his damned toys." Camille rolled her eyes. "Don't look at me like that. Not a soul in Luffield doesn't know of his… decline. Now, are you or are you not going to explain your unexpected presence here?"

"Camille, I know we haven't always seen eye to eye—"

"Haven't seen eye to eye?" Camille's face flushed as she loosed a mad cackle. "My dear, you could never hope to see the world at the same level as I. You and your mother are just one more example of how my cherished Luffield is going to the dogs."

I was enraged, ready to storm out of the door save for Peter's tightening grip of my hand. "*Your* Luffield? Peter, we don't have to stand for this! Am I to understand that my mother and I somehow spoiled *your* precious city? How, pray tell?"

"Because your whore of a mother managed to lure away *my* Darnell from *my* bed."

I was flabbergasted. My hand fell from Peter's as he was as stunned as I.

"You didn't know?" Her eyes narrowed as she scrutinised every twitch of my face.

Mother's madness had on occasion allowed her more lucid days when the sisters and I could almost forget the battle that raged in her mind. At times, she would leave Grafton Nunnery to visit the shoppes in town, often insisting on making the trip alone. It had never once occurred to me that she may have taken on a lover.

Camille rose and made her way to the window. Her tense shoulders relaxed as her demeanour shifted. She sighed, staring out over her gardens a long moment before speaking.

"I don't suppose that I can throw all of the blame towards your mother." She shook her head. "Darnell was a womaniser and a bastard at the best of times, but that doesn't mean that it didn't hurt every time."

"Camille, I—"

"So what business brought you here?"

"Of course." My head spun from Camille's rapid shifts in mood, causing me to stammer. "We've discovered, well, what we believe to be a matter of grave importance regarding Luffield."

"Go on." Camille was enticed as a cat who had cornered a mouse, all traces of the previous conversation had vanished.

I smoothed my skirt as I bolstered my confidence. Peter took my hand once more, a motion that was not lost on our host. "We believe we came across evidence of a gruesome murder that took place. Here, in Luffield."

Camille's melodious laugh filled the air. "Luffield doesn't have murders, Sophia. Not only is it the most beautiful town in the English countryside, but also the safest. One could search high and low and struggle to find any instance of violence more heinous than a husband over-disciplining his wife."

Maybe we had come to the wrong place. Camille's interest seemed to stop at the river where crime was commonplace. The detachment of wealthy individuals from the average townspeople was as reliable as the sunrise. I doubted that she had ever deigned to cross the Nene. Why would she need to when everything was brought to her?

We still had the evidence pointing towards Chatham, but without concrete proof of his involvement, we may as well have been empty-handed. If Camille's knowledge was a dead end, Peter and I had no other promising leads.

"There must be something. Some unusual event that left people scratching their heads." Peter leaned forward on the cushion, struggling to find the balance point between sitting up and falling on his face.

"Hmm." Camille stared off into space for a moment before returning her focus to us. "Now that you mention it, there was a strange occurrence, but that was nigh on twenty years ago. Surely that's of no interest to you."

My senses perked as my hair rose on end. "That's precisely the type of information we are interested in."

"It was so long ago that I'm struggling to recall the details. A number of Darnell's colleagues were involved in real estate, making a handsome income from the influx of residents. Luffield was even more ideal than it is now. Everyone knew everyone. The town was composed of good English people with traditional English values. The most undesirable behaviour was overindulgence at the pub." Camille's eyes glazed as she seemed to forget our presence.

I cleared my throat.

"I should have known that the investments made by my husband and his colleagues would draw more outsiders to our humble town. It hasn't been the same since." She sighed again. "To the matter at hand, I… *overheard* Darnell and his friends discussing some strange occurrences in the housing market. Several families moved out of Luffield in a matter of months. All within the same neighbourhood. All without notice or explanation. All without witnesses. Making the case more peculiar, several of the families had already paid their rent for the next few months. I remember my husband congratulating them on their free earnings. Surely you're not implying they were murdered."

"The truth is we don't know exactly what happened, but the least we can do is investigate further. Do you have any information regarding these families? Please, Camille."

She huffed again. "Alas, you appeal to my good nature. The one to ask would be my husband. Be forewarned, even if you can pry him away from his precious trains, I doubt you'll gather anything of use. Most of what he says are the nonsensical mutterings of a lunatic."

"Thank you, Camille." I proffered my hand. After staring at it for a moment, she reluctantly shook it as though I had the Plague.

"Do whatever is necessary to lighten your consciences, and then leave Luffield in the hands of the capable. Gerald, I know you're eavesdropping. At least have the decency to show our guests to my husband's study."

A muffled cough and a scuffle echoed in from the hallway, and a flushed Gerald entered the room. "If you'll follow me to the Master."

Peter nodded his thanks to Camille who flashed him a subtle smile before extending to him an invitation which clearly didn't apply to me. "You are welcome to call on me again." Her eyes followed him down the hall like a predator sizing up prey.

"I think this will be my one and only visit to the Hart-Watts residence." Peter said once we were out of earshot.

"What's the matter, did you not find her attractive?" I arched an eyebrow.

"No, umm, yes?" I enjoyed watching him squirm as I teased him.. "She was fair for an older woman."

"More fair than I?" I mockingly placed my hand on my chest.

Peter stopped and faced me, all traces of squirming gone. "No. No one's more fair than you, Sophia. You've captured my heart and imagination." He kissed me on the nose.

"Good."

An annoyed Gerald cleared his throat, and we continued down the hall, grinning at each other like the young lovers we were. As he led us through the maze of corridors, I could not help but notice that the artwork lining the halls were reproductions, their frames painted like the furniture in the drawing room. Everything in the house gave the appearance of wealth without actually possessing it. The house itself was far from cheap, but Camille was clearly putting on airs. It made me curious as to what else she was hiding.

Chapter XXIII

The shrill blast of a steam whistle echoed down the lengthy corridor as we approached Darnell's study. The sound was immediately followed by a childlike impersonation, "Woo! Woo!" coming from a room at the far end of the frigid Victorian-inspired hall. The longer we remained in the home, the more we noticed subtle attempts to reduce operating costs, like the pervading chill around every corner. Frankly, I was surprised Camille still had a butler. I could not decide if I had earned some modicum of trust that allowed me this glimpse behind her facade or if she did not consider me a threat to her social wellbeing. The commotion grew steadily louder as we reached the room to which Gerald had escorted us. Through the cracked door, we could hear one squeal of delight after another. The butler gently pushed it open and announced our presence.

The room's once ornate wooden floor immediately drew my eyes, marred and worn clear through its veneer from the constant traffic of its sole inhabitant. Lining the walls were the room's formerly elegant tables downgraded into workbenches. Each was cluttered with a bizarre assortment of materials and glass bottles filled with all manner of liquids, every crate or vessel meticulously labelled. The master of the Hart-Watts residence was crouched in the middle of a sprawling miniature countryside, elaborately constructed in painstaking detail. Within a few moments, it occurred to me that I was observing Luffield, albeit with a few modifications to allow the train to run its course throughout the town.

Gerald cleared his throat and announced us a second time, his voice sounding more nasally in his effort to ignore the stale odour of urine that clung to the room. Darnell Watts lifted his balding head and observed us through thick spectacles which lent him the bulbous eyes of a toad. What was left of his hair was grey and thin and hung down to his shoulders in an oily mass. Unlike the hallway outside, the room was stifling. The intense heat that radiated from the fireplace did not prevent Master Darnell from wearing a heavy tweed coat the colour of worn leather. With nary a word, he turned back to his trains and continued making noises to supplement theirs.

"I'll leave you to it." Gerald departed with haste, leaving us alone in the room with the dementia-addled gentleman.

"Thanks." Peter said in a voice laced with sarcasm once the door had shut behind the butler.

Peter ventured ahead. I found a comfortable vantage point along the crowded wall and pulled out a dusty rocker, removing the stacked yellowing periodicals before taking a seat. I stifled a yelp when a mouse ran across my boots. Peter turned with a raised eyebrow, but I acted as though nothing had happened. I pulled out my notebook and fountain pen, making a few scratches to get the cool ink moving.

"Excuse me, Mr. Darnell." Peter approached him cautiously, but could only get so close. The master was inside the model, standing in a cutout between bridges where the Nene would normally be packed with boats shuttling wares from one side to the other. "We have a few questions we'd like to ask you."

Nothing.

I looked at Peter pleadingly.

He took a different approach. "Darnell. May I call you Darnell?"

The ageing gentleman nodded, briefly meeting Peter's eyes.

"May I join you?" Peter gestured at the hollow in which Darnell was standing.

The older gentleman nodded again.

Peter climbed onto all fours and crawled under the model, making his way carefully through the sturdy, black supports until he reached the opening and stood. Between the two of them, the slim Peter and the more rounded Darnell, there was barely enough room to maneuver.

"Are the trains running on schedule?" Peter spoke in a gentle voice mimicking the snappy syllables of a conductor. His voice mirroring what one would use with a child but absent of any condescension.

"That they are," the gentleman said, leaning over to watch the train closely in wonderment. "Number 401's engineer has been at the bottle again, but it hasn't stopped him from doing his job." Darnell reached up and tugged on a tiny steam whistle mounted to the ceiling which released an ear-piercing squeal. "All aboard the six o'clock to Northampton!"

A model passenger train pulled to a gentle stop at Citadel Station and waited for the static tin figurines crowding the platform to board.

"Darnell, can I ask you a question about some people in Luffield? This would've been from long ago."

Darnell seemingly ignored Peter and handed him a wired control for one of the freight trains circling the town. I could not take my eyes from the elaborate toy, bright and smoking as it toured the down-scaled English countryside. "Don't go too fast. You might think 'Oh, I could shave off a few minutes,' but too much speed and—" Darnell flicked an idle train car off the tracks where it fell to the floor.

"I understand." Peter didn't so much as touch the dial controlling the train's speed, only toying with the various switches controlling the lighting around town.

In addition to being an accurate replica, so many aspects of the model were interactive, be it lights, movement, or sound. I could see the allure. "I understand you dealt with local properties before your… retirement."

Darnell stared at me, as though seeing me for the first time. He nodded, his gaze returning to the black and gold engine storming up into the hills towards the nunnery. Peter had identified the controls for the crossing gates and alarm bells and was hastily trying to operate them in timing with Darnell's speeding train and chuckling at his own ineptitude. There was something endearing, watching Peter interact with the child trapped in this gentleman's body. I rested an elbow on a table of African blackwood, looking on with admiration. Peter finally gave up the frivolous pursuit and his face grew more serious.

"Master Darnell, as much as I love your trains, we came here to ask you an important question. Sophia and I understand there were several families that went missing under unusual circumstances. Does that ring a bell?"

"Ring a bell." Darnell laughed, reaching up to ring the brass bell hung next to the whistle, which did my ears another disservice. "End of the line!" he yelled as the black train marked 401 pulled into Citadel Station station for the second time of the day. "Stewards to cabins H7, C8, V13, Q2, and G36."

"Do you recall any strange stories of people missing? Do you remember where they lived?"

There was a loud crash as Peter's train barrelled into the rear of 401, scattering train cars everywhere, engine wheels still spinning like mad. Pooling beneath Peter's engine was an oily puddle. Darnell turned to Peter with anger in his eyes.

"I'm sorry, Darnell. I wasn't paying attention. Here let me help—"

Darnell jerked the controller from Peter's hand and powered down both locomotives. The room grew quiet as the last traces of smoke disappeared. "End of the line!" His eyes darted back and forth between Peter and me, clearly wanting us to leave immediately.

Peter nodded sullenly, and ducked under the table. When we looked back, Darnell was meticulously placing each train back into place, carefully examining each for damage as he wiped up the spill.

"I'm sorry, Sophia. I thought we'd learn more than that."

I looked down at the utterances I had scrawled in my notebook, tempted to wad up the page and throw it in the raging nearby fire where it would disappear like all other evidence of the heinous crime. Instead, I flipped it closed and shoved it into my pocket with a huff.

When we emerged in the hallway, Gerald was waiting for us.

"You were able to get more out of him than most. Most visitors he ignores completely."

"How long has he been like this?" I asked.

"About eight years." Camille answered, coming up from behind. She looked through the doors at her husband with a tenderness she could not hide as easily as her own grey hair. When she spoke of him, it had been as a burden, but there was clearly still love there. "It started with a forgotten meeting or a misremembered price. Within eighteen months, his partners had to take over the business, but not before they had bled him dry, the turncoat bastards."

"Language, Madam."

"Do shut up, Gerald. I have little else to hide."

Gerald shrugged.

"They took advantage of his feeble mind, and we were left with little more than what was in our bloody accounts. Had him sign over most of his stakes and assets before I caught on. I shuttled him to our solicitor in time to have what little remained changed to my name, but much of the damage was done. I've had to sell most everything of value to maintain this skeleton of a lifestyle." With shaking hands, she pulled out a cigarette and lit it.

"I'm sorry to hear that. Truly I am." I reached for Camille's hand, but she retracted it.

"I'll stand on my own two feet without any help or compassion. Now, I think it's high time that you leave us be. I bid you good day." Camille vanished into Darnell's study, shutting the door behind herself.

"I'll walk you to the door. I believe your cab is still waiting outside."

"Why did you stay, Gerald?" I asked. "I don't imagine it's for the money."

"Master Darnell has been gracious to me since he took me on as a boy. I am merely returning the favour. Madam Camille provides me with room and board plus a small monthly stipend. It is all I need."

Gerald opened the large oak door to the courtyard to let us pass. As Peter left, I saw him place something in his hand. I did not know how much it was, but the butler's attempt to conceal his sniffles told me all I needed to know. With a pat on his shoulder, Peter and I descended the semi-circular marble steps and climbed into the awaiting cab.

Chapter XXIV

I sighed as the cabbie pulled away from the mansion, the imposing edifice of marble now nothing more than a crumbling facade in my mind. For years I had harboured resentment towards Camille and her vicious rumours, but now… Now I only felt sorry for her, whether she desired my pity or not. For a moment I considered it karmic reprisal, but quickly relinquished the thought. I could not help but draw parallels between my mother's demise and her husband's. Warmth returned to my hand as Peter took mine in his.

"Sorry, my love. It would seem that Master Darnell's condition has done a number to his mind." He flashed a smile meant to cheer me up. "The trip wasn't in vain. Camille confirmed that several families went missing. Surely there is more information about such a strange occurrence. Perhaps we could start with the landlords, they…"

My mind trailed off as I chewed on my lip. Something was nagging at the back of my mind. Something we had missed. The moment I realised what it was, I interrupted

Peter. "Do you remember what he said when you asked him about the missing residents?"

Peter laughed, shaking his head in response to my outburst. "Umm, sure. He rang the bell and yelled 'End of the line,' in my ear. It was a moment before I could hear anything else." Peter wiggled his little finger around in his ear, feigning temporary deafness. "Why?"

"Think about it Peter, what if he was telling us something?"

"Doubtful. I think they were nothing more than the musings of a weakened mind."

"End of the line could mean death. What if there was some part of his mind still operational, and he was communicating through the only means he could?"

Peter sat up, turning to face me. "Let's suppose you're right. That would imply that he knew more about their disappearances than he let on."

I stared at him, waiting for him to make the connection.

"Oh." Peter looked at the floor shaking his head. "Oh my. What did he say after that? Something about stewards and cabins. God, I wish I could remember which ones!"

I flipped open my notepad. "H7, C8, V13, Q2, and G36. Thank the universe I wrote it down. At the time I was so frustrated, I nearly threw the page in the fire."

"I'm thrilled you didn't." Peter pulled my face to his and kissed me on the forehead.

"I thought it was quite strange. Any normal person would have said something more consecutive or logical."

"Sophia, you're brilliant." Peter wrapped his arm around me and placed his lips firmly on mine.

"Snogging will cost you extra," the driver joked. "We're nearing the hotel, so feel free to restrain yourselves for a moment longer."

We pulled ourselves apart, blushing like schoolchildren caught beneath the stands.

"Those numbers are no less peculiar now as they were then." I smoothed out the wrinkles on my dress, avoiding both Peter and the driver's eye contact.

"What did you say those numbers were?" asked the driver.

"Not really your business." I said, staring at him through the rear view mirror, all traces of embarrassment gone.

"Look, mum, us drivers hear everything. It ain't nothing personal. I'm only saying I'm a veritable font of information at your disposal."

Peter rolled his eyes. "What's the harm?"

"Alright. H7, C8, V13, Q2, and G36."

"That's what I thought. Sounds like cabbie shorthand." The gentleman held up a clipboard with pick-ups and drop-offs, all hastily scribbled in an abbreviated fashion. "Give me a moment."

The cabbie stroked his chin, his fingers sounding like sandpaper on wood against the stubble. "I think I have it! High Street has a number seven. Crescent has a number eight. Victoria Road has a thirteen. Queens Road has a two. And Green Lane is the only road with a thirty-six. All in the same borough to boot."

"Well I'll be damned. He was telling us the houses exactly as I'd asked." Peter had a huge grin across his face. "That man's mind still has some sharp edges."

"Now, will I be getting a tip for that extra bit of knowledge?"

It was my turn to roll my eyes as Peter handed him another coin on top of the pile he'd already given him. It was fairly earned and had probably shaved off days of research. He pulled to a stop in front of Luffield's few small hotels and collected our bags. The sun was dropping low in the sky, bathing the town in gorgeous hues of purple and orange.

"Don't forget, If you two need to go anywhere, I mean anywhere, give me a ring. Name's Phillip." The cabbie handed us a slip of paper with his number before disappearing among the carts and vehicles roaming the streets.

I could not blame him. With Peter's unbridled generosity, the gentleman had probably made more in a day than he normally did in a month. Peter held the door as we entered the drab hotel. Judging by the sizeable collection of keys on the wall, we were two of very few guests. After filling out the obligatory paperwork, the clerk escorted us to the balcony ringing the lobby and showed us to our suite. I was knackered and my feet ached for some attention.

"I hope I wasn't being too forward, booking us the one room." He flashed his trademark smile, and my body filled with a warmth that made me forget about my exhaustion.

With a hand on his chest, I pushed his back against the door frame with a loud thunk and planted a lingering kiss on his soft lips. I could feel his shoulder's slacken as the day's tension drifted from his body. "Is that being too forward?"

An elderly lady emerged from the adjacent room and upon seeing my body pressed tightly against Peter's, returned to her room muttering angrily and shaking her head. Keeping up appearances for the sake of others was no longer my concern. I had spent too much of my life in a vain attempt to fit into Luffield. That confirmed my conclusion. Peter had changed me as much as I had him. *Let her believe what she will.*

Peter fumbled with the knob as I continued pressing my face against his. "That lady is going to say something to the front desk if we keep this up," he managed to say.

I leaned so close to his ear that he could feel the heat of my breath. "Let her."

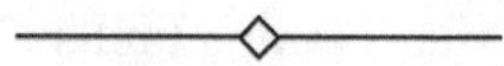

No one evicted us during the night, so any ruckus we had made during the night and again in the morning must have been muted by the walls. When we left our room in the morning, our neighbour happened to be standing on the balcony, looking down on the lobby and puffing away on what remained of a cigarette. I waved, smiling at her. In response, she crossed herself and disappeared, slamming the door behind her.

"So much for country hospitality," said Peter with a mock posh accent. If his grin had been any wider, it would've split his face. I playfully shoved him over.

We left the hotel in search of any restaurant serving breakfast. Unlike London, Luffield's upper-class population did not wake up quite as early as the working class, making it difficult to find a dining establishment.

After the stuffy hotel room, the short walk through the brisk air proved quite pleasant. Laughing and talking, I led Peter to a small storefront that served a simple breakfast. Thatch-roofed like so many of the surrounding houses, the whitewashed building held a warmth that the chilly morning could not steal from it.

"Sophia." The deli's owner nodded, greeting me by name, but little more.

Peter and I ploughed through several egg and tomato sandwiches between the two of us, washing it down with stout tea and a splash of cream. I found myself missing my dear friend Milly, wondering what she was up to on this very same morning, likely unaffected by my absence. Of Tim, the friend we had unwillingly brought along, I had seen no trace. That did not mean he was not nearby, watching our every move. My appetite waned at the thought. Fortunately, I had nearly finished the remaining portion.

"I say we go in order," said Peter, wiping his mouth with a cloth napkin. "I don't imagine that there was any logic to the sequence in which he spouted off numbers, but I can't imagine it would hurt."

"High Street is only a few blocks over. We can walk to all the addresses, much to the chagrin of Phillip." I said, rising.

After bidding goodbye to the owner, Peter left the payment on the table and held the door as I stepped back out onto the frigid cobblestone thoroughfare. The door's forest green paint drew my mind to the woods, one of the places I had reliably found solace as a child. The strong urge to grab Peter's hand and flee there was palpable. Running away would not resolve anything, and I was so tired of running from my problems.

We had to bundle tightly against the wind, but the weather was almost pleasant. I could sense the coming of spring in the not too distant future as the days drew gradually warmer.

We made the right onto High Street, watching the numbers fall as we wound further down the hill. Number 7 was no different from the houses around it, a simple abode with a thatched roof that hung down so low that it would nearly scrape the heads of would-be visitors. A woman in a blue and white striped apron peered through the front window. She saw us staring and came to the door.

"May I help you?" She dried her hands on the flour-dusted apron as a toddler clung to the hem of her skirt.

I spoke before Peter, sensing the woman's trepidation at our presence. He may have had a calm demeanour, but he was still a man and a stranger at that. "We apologise for intruding like this. This may come across as a strange request, but we wanted to know more about the history of your home."

She sized us up for a moment. "Inside with you then. I'll be Susan."

I knew instantly that it was not the home from the memory, albeit not dissimilar. Herbs hung drying by the window, likely from the garden out back. The majority of the house was the joined kitchen and sitting room. The woman gestured to a rocker for Peter, then sat with me on a cushioned bench. We listened to the fire crackle as we watched her son play with a hand-carved wooden car for a moment before the woman spoke.

"I hate to be a disappointment, but I actually don't know much about the house. My husband neither. It's our landlord you'll be needing to see. A Mr. Reed Bailey. Though the only time I seen him is when he comes to collect the check." She rubbed her hands nervously. "Not a friendly man, that one. If the house didn't belong to him, he wouldn't be welcome here."

The child climbed up onto her lap and with an unceremonious drop of her blouse, began suckling from her breast. Peter paled, but dutifully kept his eyes where they belonged.

"Not friendly?" Peter choked out.

"You see my little one. His brother is out with his Da. It's all we can do to make rent, and I haven't believed for one moment, he wouldn't think twice about throwing us out on the streets the instant we failed to pay."

"Has he ever been hostile? Threatened violence or anything of the sort?" I asked.

The woman stared at me through squinted eyes. "Nothing like that. Now, I be needing to put this one down for a nap. You'll understand."

"Right. Thank you for your time."

We made our way to the door under the woman's cool stare. Behind me I could hear the clink of the coins Peter was leaving on the table. *That's one less month's rent they have to worry about.*

Chapter XXV

"We must have come on too strong," I said. The door shut behind us with slightly more force than necessary. We paced down the walking path away from Susan's home, the grass between each stone searching for sunlight as desperately as we were information. "The moment she perceived us as a potential threat to her living situation, she shut down tighter than Wandsworth."

Peter took a deep inhalation of the cool air, blowing the steam out like smoke from his pipe. "We'll have to be more subtle if we want answers. We'll have the opportunity for one, maybe two questions unless the inhabitants of these homes are feeling particularly talkative. I'm afraid that asking directly about Bailey won't be an option. You're more acquainted with Luffield than I am. Do you know anything about this chap?"

"No, but we still have a number of leads." I began moving in the direction of Crescent Number 8. "The remaining houses, this landlord, and Chatham."

"I still don't know how we're going to get to Lord Chatham. He's not one that we can saunter into the home of and begin interrogating." Peter absentmindedly snugged his watch cap, nervousness creeping into his voice. "If he's as influential as you say, one misstep and he could turn the entire town against us. Men like him could even have the law in their pocket. Not to mention that we don't even know if he's involved. The candelabra was in a crate with his name on it, but that could've come from anywhere."

"Something horrible happened here, and if that means confronting Lord Chatham, I will. It's not right for someone to escape justice because they have money or power."

"If only it were that simple." Peter chuckled. "It may come to that. I'm just saying we need to proceed delicately. Wait until we have something more tangible than a vision."

What I had observed was tangible enough. If I forced myself to dwell on the memory, I could still smell the smoke from the fireplace, still hear the mother's pleas. Plenty sufficient evidence in my mind for an arrest had only the villains' faces been clear. Fate had chosen Dorothy and Sophia Tate out of forty some-odd million English citizens to endow with this gift, and I refused to believe it would bestow such a gift without the ability to bring peace to the fallen and justice to the perpetrators.

I arrived at Crescent Number 8 with no memory of my transit thanks to being lost in thought. Number 8 was a larger home than the last and far larger, in fact, than the one in my memory. The home was of similar construction common to all the homes from that period of Luffield's history. A greying thatched roof topped its brick and flint walls. Under the windows hung baskets overgrown with flowers in desperate need of tending. Overgrown tubers from the nearby garden lifted the cobblestones of the path to treacherous angles.

Even knowing it could not have been the site of the murders, anxiety tickled the walls of my stomach at the prospect of coming across the actual location. No one greeted us as we made our way up the narrow path, so Peter gave the stout oak door a knock, dislodging a few flecks of peeling paint which drifted to the ground. The faint odour of menthol tobacco escaped as an elderly woman greeted us with a simple "Yes?"

Judging by her bleary eyes, we had awoken her from her afternoon nap. Her large-lensed eyeglasses were perched so far forward on her nose that at any moment they might fall off if not for a chain dangling back around her neck. Loose grey curls hung unkempt from her frilly mobcap. Behind her, a copy of *Murder on the Orient Express* was upside-down on the side table next to a rocking chair.

"Pardon us for the intrusion, ma'am. I'm Peter Northrop and this is Ms. Sophia Tate. We are historians looking into Luffield's past. We were hoping to ask you a few questions about your home's history."

Historians was a new angle, but not a lie.

The woman hesitated. I thought about suggesting that we could come back, but I was afraid to lose the opportunity. Before I could respond, the woman turned into the home, beckoning us to follow. "How do you take your tea?"

I smiled at Peter and followed her into the warm home. Moments later, we were cosy in front of a warm radiator in the woman's sitting room. It was easy to see why the woman, who had introduced herself as Marta, had fallen asleep. I sipped the strong English tea, waiting for its ingredients to keep me from doing the same.

"About the house, you say? Hmm."

"Yes. Anything you remember," I said.

"My husband, Lloyd, God rest his soul, and I moved into this house in January of 1918. I remember because it was a bloody awful day, if you'll pardon my language. Lloyd had been laid-off from the mines, and we used what little savings we had to purchase this place. He died a few years later from black lung."

"I'm so sorry, Marta."

She waved my apology off. "You've got nothing to apologise for Dearie. It's not as if you killed him." She chuckled with the laugh of a lifelong smoker, pulling a cork-tipped cigarette from a box emblazoned with the Ardath logotype. "Do you mind?"

Peter and I shook our heads, also declining her offer to share.

"You're probably thinking of the irony: Her husband chokes to death on that foul dust, and here she is doing no better. Well, you'd be correct." She let another raspy laugh escape as she lit the end with an engraved 19th-century lighter and took the first pull. "The way I figure, we're all going to die of something out of our control. Might as well have a say in the matter."

"I can't say I blame you," said Peter, who smoked for nostalgia more than anything else. I could not help but wonder if he had given much thought to the correlation between the habit and its negative effects on health. He sipped his tea as he took in the plethora of photographs dotting the room. "Who did you buy the house from?"

"Some chap named Bailey, if memory serves. I only remember because his name reminded me of the criminal court building in London."

Peter leaned back and looked at me. "Would this be a Reed Bailey?"

"That sounds right, but as I said, it was long ago."

"Would you mind terribly if I looked around? I promise not to disturb your things."

Marta waved me on and proceeded to tell Peter in great detail about each picture hanging on her wall. I wandered the low-ceilinged room, ducking under the exposed beams and looking for anything that might provide some hint as to what tragedy may have occurred here to its previous occupants.

When I had touched the candelabra, the deaths that I had witnessed were violent, bloody. So much so that it would have been difficult to remove the stains from the natural wood floors common in this area. I examined the cottage's floor but nothing seemed amiss on the aged wood planks. On the wall, I spotted several copper pans that did not appear to have been used in a long time. A rich patina had begun to develop, just showing the first hints of verdigris.

"Marta. Are these pans original to the home or did you bring them?" I asked, raising my voice loud enough to be heard in the adjacent room.

"Those were there when Lloyd and I moved in. Every time I made to take them down something stayed my hand. Now they are as much of a part of the house as the floor you're standing on." Her voice trailed off. "This was my nephew when he…"

I stared at the copper pans knowing full well what I had to do and prayed any reaction I had would not send our host into a frenzy. The day would come when I never wanted to see copper or its alloys ever again. Without further hesitation, I touched the bottom of the pan and was sucked into another reality.

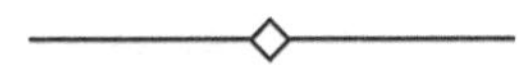

"The devil are you playing at?" The voice came from a middle-aged man I could not see, as if through water.

"I don't understand! We've done nothing wrong." A man stood between the speaker and what I presumed to be his wife and adolescent daughter.

"You and your kind are a conniving lot, puppet masters behind the curtains of our precious town. Pulling our strings so that we dance to your tune. You have no place here."

"Puppet masters?" The man was distraught and confused. "I don't understand. I… I run a fishing company. I have no aspirations past providing for my—"

The speaker backhanded the man, leaving his lip bloodied and bruised.

"Don't you speak to me like I'm a bloody fool. You soil our lovely town, manipulating us into doing whatever your kind wants. That won't happen after today. Cooperate and we might let you and your family leave town alive."

"But this is my home," he pleaded. "I've paid my debts, been an upright citizen, followed the Lord's teachings… What more do you want from me?"

"You shut your bloody yap, and leave your god's name out of this! Leave on the first train out of town and never return." His voice grew more sinister. "All your property is forfeit."

"You can't do that to us!" His wife, a stout woman in her own right, burst out from behind him, grabbed the copper pan from the wall, and marched towards the voice in a fury.

As her husband screamed, she raised the pan into the air and froze. She slowly looked down at her chest, from which a knife had sprung. Blood pooled out from the wound like a poppy in bloom.

"You son of a bitch!" With tears in his eyes, the man sprung at the assailant and there was an ear-shattering pop. He fell to his knees clutching his chest.

"You idiot!" screamed the voice, nearly drowned out by the cries of the daughter.

"I'm… I'm sorry," said a familiar voice, one I knew to belong to the young man from the other vision.

"It's a wonder the whole neighbourhood isn't up after that. If they know what's good for them, they'll stay in their bloody houses."

"What do we do about the girl?"

"Don't have much choice now, do we?" The man pulled the knife from the woman's chest and strode towards the girl who was using her feet to back herself into the corner. "Such a waste."

The vision went dark. I gasped for air as if I had been underwater the entire time. My ears rang from the shot as though the gun had gone off right next to my head. I braced myself against the counter to avoid collapsing to the ground in a heap. *My god, here too?*

When I had composed myself enough to walk, I stumbled my way back to the sitting room. Instantly recognising the pale look on my face, Peter sprung to help me to a seat.

"Why, Dearie, you look as if you've seen a ghost."

In a way, I had.

"I have just the thing." She disappeared and returned with a schooner of sherry.

I knocked it back at once, surprising the woman and letting the fortified wine do its job of calming my nerves.

"Thank you." I clasped the old woman's hands. "Sometimes I have spells and feel faint."

She did not appear completely satisfied with my explanation but let it slide. From the way her eyes flitted back and forth between Peter and me, I think she had assumed that I was pregnant. There could be worse conclusions, not that I had a reputation to protect.

We sat in her living room long enough for me to recover my faculties while Peter and the woman made small talk. The point of digging had passed. With my spell, the woman's suspicions had risen just as in the previous home. I imagined had it not been for sympathy, she would have already made an excuse for us to leave.

Once I had recovered, we thanked her graciously for her hospitality and patience and saw ourselves out. Thankfully, the shock from the vision was not as profound as it had been the first time. I could ill-afford spending another three days in such a stupor. We walked over a kilometre back into town before Peter spoke.

"Are you willing to share what happened?"

I nodded. "I'm going to need a pint."

Chapter XXVI

Following the traumatic experience, Peter diverted from our next stop to The Second Star, a small pub not too far from Crescent 8. I stared at the decades of scrawled wishes pinned to the dusty ceiling by previous patrons and drained a pint of lager as the chef prepared our lunch. I immediately ordered a second, garnering a shout of encouragement from a pair of local drunks.

"Slow down, Soph." Peter placed his hand over the rim of my second glass before I could raise it to my lips.

"Aw, let her drink!" shouted the bearded drunk.

"I like a woman who can hold her drink," muttered the craggy face beneath a watch cap.

Ignoring them, Peter continued. "I can't imagine what you witnessed, but I'm sure that drinking yourself into a stupor is not the best course of action."

I complied and drank the second pint in a more timely manner until our food arrived. We took our lunch to the nearby Hughes Park to escape prying ears and overly vocal patrons. The wind had died down to a whisper. The sun edged out from its cloak of grey, raising the temperature enough that we could enjoy our meal out of doors.

We took our seats on a vacant park bench, and unwrapped our meal. I relished the warm rays on my face as the buzz of the drink slowly calmed my agitated state. I took a few bites of the battered fish before divulging the entire experience, sparing no details. By the time I finished, I half expected Peter to turn back to the pub for another round himself.

Peter rose and paced nervously to and fro in for a moment before slapping his hand on his forehead. "This is almost too much to believe."

Before I could despair, he corrected himself.

"Not that I don't believe you," he said, waving his hands. "This whole scenario grows more interesting, for lack of a better word, by the minute. It makes me question how long this subterfuge has continued under everyone's noses."

"Someone had to know." My face twisted into a snarl. "If not the people involved, there had to be others who wilfully ignored the signs. Perhaps even witnesses whose fear won out over their decency."

"As much as I would like to think better of humanity, fear is a powerful motivator." Peter took his seat and began mindlessly chomping away on his sandwich. "So you believe the primary speaker in this vision to be this Bailey chap?" he asked through a mouthful.

"I can't be certain until we meet him, hear his voice. Not that I'm looking forward to it given the insight into his character."

"I doubt you would be. If we could connect these houses to Bailey, we'd be that much closer to the motivation behind the savagery. Given Bailey's social status, I find it unlikely that he is masterminding this alone."

I nodded in agreement. "A woman, a younger man, and Bailey. But what's their connection to Chatham?"

"I'm not even sure there is one, but we should be all the more careful the deeper we dig. We're bound to be noticed if we haven't been already. The people behind this have proven the lengths to which they are willing to go. Dispatching two nosy pests would be nothing more than an afterthought to them."

"Sometimes I wonder if death would be a relief from this burden, so much so that I'm not scared of it anymore."

"Please, Sophia, don't say that." Peter clasped my hands in his cooler ones. "You have the power to make the world a better place, but even without that, you've made my world better."

I stared into those amber eyes of his, letting everything else drift away with the soft wind that rustled the leaves lingering on the surrounding trees. The brief moment of dissociation from my haunting thoughts sparked a new wave of clarity. "What do you think they meant by 'your kind?' I heard that in both visions."

Peter shook his head at the rapid change of subjects. "I can't imagine. You mentioned that the locals used to call you and your mother names because you were different, but your life was never under threat, correct? Well, not until you threatened someone yourself." Peter smirked.

"True." For some odd reason, this made me break down into a fit of laughter. I still felt proud of myself for turning the tables on Klemp. "We know that at least one family was murdered prior to 1917 when your father acquired the piece. This one felt like the same time period, but I would have no way of knowing precisely when. We should visit the rest of the homes."

"I fear that they will be much the same. I also don't believe continuing as we are to be a wise choice. Any more visits could put your mental health in jeopardy and only serve to draw more attention to our investigation. The natural next step is to confront Bailey, which should lead us to the answers we seek, but that's a matter better suited for the constabulary."

"The constabulary?" I laughed, a loud sound free of mirth. "And what would we tell them, Peter? That I'm some sort of clairvoyant? Because Northamptonshire doesn't have the greatest history when it comes to those accused of possessing supernatural talents outside of Christendom."

"Sophia, it's not the 1600s," Peter said, exasperated. "We can't confront Bailey ourselves, he may be a cold-blooded killer. How would you and I ever hope to defend ourselves against that? Maybe we could use your visions to collect some solid evidence. It'll take time, but…"

I assessed Peter's figure as he carried on. Peter was thin, though far from frail. He had grown in confidence so much since the day I'd first met him, but he was correct. We weren't the type to stand up against criminals, especially unarmed. The only time that I had, I attributed my lucky escape to a combination of quick thinking and happenstance. I briefly considered contacting Jack Davies, the young officer I had met, when I saw Tim, leaning against a barren maple on the far side of the park. He took a deep drag from his cigarette, making no effort to feign disinterest in our affairs.

"What if we had help?" I nodded in Tim's direction.

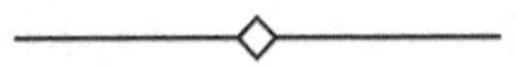

"You want me to do what?" Tim answered in a Cockney accent so thick that it was difficult to follow. The burly gent loomed over the picnic table, refusing to sit on a bench that now looked childlike when compared to his abnormally large frame. The weathered wood flexed as he rested his hands on its surface.

"It's just as we said," Peter began. "We need to speak to this gentleman—"

"This Bailey?"

"Yes. We need to ask him a few questions that have the potential to upset him. If things go sideways, we'd like you there to prevent us from getting hurt."

"Killed's more like it." He lit his third cigarette since the beginning of our conversation, an unfiltered abomination as harsh as the man who burned it. The giant seemed to care for the acrid smoke more than fresh air. "Simon told me to protect your arse, but he didn't say nothing about confronting the leader of some local gang. I've got half a mind to put you both on the next—"

"We think he's responsible for the death of children," I interrupted. "Children, Tim. I refuse to believe you have no sympathy for those who can't defend themselves."

Tim muttered a chain of expletives punctuated by grey plumes. "No child killer deserves the safety of the Code." Tim shook his head. "I must be out of my blooming mind."

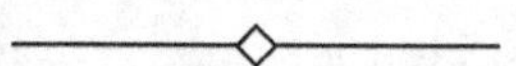

It was not difficult to ascertain the location of Reed Bailey's office. As the owner of a considerable number of Luffield's properties, his homes-for-let signs dotted every notice board across the county. His building was located on the far side of the river, just shy of the town's industrial sector. Peter led the way until the three of us found ourselves parked in front of a window reading, "Reed Bailey, Estate Agent" painted in flaking black and gold letters. His office, if one was being generous, was embedded between a seedy pub and boxing gym, neither of which appeared reputable. Rubbish littered the pavement.

"I guess this is it," said Peter, through a closed nose. The inescapable heavy odour of oil and grease normally associated with the area was overpowered by the smell of cheap booze, sweat, and vomit drifting into the street from the neighbouring businesses. Cracked green vinyl blinds shrouded Bailey's windows and the mildewed awning was at least a decade overdue for replacement.

Before Peter second-guessed the decision, I charged forward into the dimly lit office. The place reeked of stale tobacco and unwashed bodies, offering no reprieve from the stench outside. In the lobby, a secretary with frazzled dyed-orange hair and smudged lipstick exited a back office and pulled the door closed. Adjusting her plaid beige skirt back to where it belonged, she took a seat behind a large wooden desk, one of few furnishings in the largely barren room.

"What can I do for you, love?" she asked Peter in a whiny voice, as if he was the only person in the room. She pulled a piece of gum from a crumpled pack and threw it in her mouth, all the while batting mascara-caked eyelashes at Peter.

I watched, mouth agape as she smacked her gum loud enough to be heard on the opposite bank of the Nene. I had never been a stickler for propriety, but the woman's mannerisms were atrocious. Hesitant to cross the ocean of stained carpet, I spoke from where I stood. "We need to see Mr. Bailey."

As if seeing me for the first time, the secretary eyed me up and down as though she was assessing competition. Then she glanced toward Tim and, despite the copious amounts of makeup, her face lost some of its colour. "I'm afraid Mr. Bailey is out on business. He won't be back until…" she feigned a glance at her crumpled desk calendar as she dragged out the word, "tomorrow."

No sooner than she had finished speaking, a rotund man in an ill-fitting white suit emerged from the same back room, pulling up his zipper and dabbing his sweaty forehead with an already-saturated handkerchief. He couldn't hide his surprise.

"Oh, Mr. Bailey! I didn't expect you back so soon."

A questioning look flashed across his face before he played along with the obvious charade. "You know how urgent matters can be in this business, though I always make time for in-person visits. Who are our guests, Ivy?"

His recognisable voice sent shivers down my spine, making my blood run cold. The man standing in front of Peter offering his damp hand was none other than Reed Bailey, who I knew to be a cold-blooded killer. Peter read every emotion inscribed on my face. Reluctant to shake the man's hand, Peter feigned sudden interest in the local maps adorning Reed's dark-panelled wall.

Ignoring the slight, Reed began to brag about his control over a significant portion of the housing Luffield had to offer, waving an engorged finger toward each pin marking a possessed property. At Tim's suggestion, we had agreed for Peter to play the part of potential investor, someone any greedy magnate would likely be more than happy to entertain.

Despite his nervousness, Peter had little trouble playing the part. Thanks to the expectations of his brother, his tailored clothing was of noticeable quality, even if Peter's stylistic choices were odd for that of a wealthy Londoner. Due to Milly's recent spending spree, I was well suited to be at his side. Tim's presence as our protective detail only added to a false impression that Peter was a man of significant means.

"What brings you here today, Mr....?"

"Ellsworth." Peter answered with a posh tone ringing with refinement, convincing even me. "I own a significant stake in a number of regional housing markets, and I'm interested in adding Luffield to my portfolio. With your substantial assets and local knowledge accompanied by my financial backing and business acumen, we can have this town by the bollocks. What do you say, old chap?"

Reed grinned, a devilish sight which bore his yellowing teeth. "I say I think we can do business."

Chapter XXVII

"So why Luffield, Mr. Ellsworth?" Bailey said as he led us back into his office.

Behind me, Tim whispered, "Why don't you knock off early," to the secretary, followed by the clink of coins being passed discretely from one palm to the next. The next sound that I heard was the chime above the door announcing her departure. She had not taken much convincing.

We made our way into the agent's office, a room of nearly equal size to the lobby with the same dingy burgundy carpet and dilapidated wood panelling. A pervasive odour of sweat and sex clung to the air of the room, turning my stomach. I could not have been more grateful when Bailey cracked open the window of his own volition, though the air from the adjacent alleyway was only a minimal improvement. The portly man shuffled his way behind his desk, having a seat under an unrealistically flattering oil painting of himself with his right hand on a bulldog. Peter's nose twitched at the ambient smells, but if it bothered him, he showed no sign of it.

"Luffield is a quaint little village in the heart of the English countryside. Not too far from London. A ripe market for short-term rentals to those on holiday, I do believe."

"Short-term rentals, eh? An interesting notion that I haven't given much thought. Sounds like it has the potential to be quite lucrative." Bailey splayed his hands as he leaned across his desk. "I'll be forthright with you, Mr. Ellsworth. At the end of the day, I'm a businessman. You'll forgive me if I ask what's in it for me."

"I collect properties, Mr. Bailey, for which I would require someone local to procure and manage them. I live and work in London and own land from the Channel to the Midlands. I can't be bothered to deal with such trivialities in person."

"You'll have to understand, Luffield is a very... traditional community." Bailey began to absentmindedly rearrange the items that had been scattered across his desk during the recent interlude. "People like it here because it's quiet and beautiful. Serene, I dare say. But Luffield has always been reluctant to change. The town is rife with Luddites so opposed to it that they still prefer a horse to an automobile, if you believe it. So you'll understand me when I tell you that people won't be in a hurry to relinquish their homes, regardless of price. Believe me, I've tried."

Peter leaned forward, his voice taking on a more aggressive tone. His voice sent chills down my spine as he played into Bailey's desires. "If financial incentive doesn't sway the owners, there are *other* ways of encouraging them."

Bailey leaned back, drawing a cigar from a wooden box on his desk. The chair groaned as he reclined. He twisted it between his fingers for a moment before snipping the end, and igniting it with a fat, leather-bound lighter. I thought it curious that he did not offer one to Peter. "It's one thing to offer to buy someone's home, Mr. Ellsworth." He took a deep drag, blowing a cloud of smoke towards the window before spitting an errant piece of tobacco leaf onto the floor. "It's an altogether different matter to *encourage* them."

"I'm sure we could make such a matter worth your while."

"Then I'm your man," Bailey said menacingly. The estate agent grinned, a sickening sight under his beady, greedy eyes. "Anything else you'd require? You'll find I'm a man of many talents." His revolting gaze fell upon my figure, making me acutely aware of how shapely the dress I had chosen for the day made me appear. I suppressed the wave of nausea that followed, thankful when his focus returned to the potential client in the room. I failed to see what attraction his sagging, greasy features held for his buxom secretary who was not unattractive in her own right.

"The residents of London will be flocking here in hopes of an escape. They seek comfort without effort. When we acquire these properties, I'd like them to remain fully furnished, lacking only comestibles."

"That can be arranged," Bailey said with a chuckle, palpably excited by the notion of evicting innocent residents for easy coin.

"Of the utmost import: Would-be holidayers prize a certain… atmosphere. We want them to feel secure. Comfortable. Undesirable elements could make them ill at ease. We want them returning, do we not?"

"And what traits, exactly, do you consider to be undesirable?" Bailey spilled onto his desk, almost licking his lips maliciously, raising my gorge.

"I'll be honest. I'm not here by happenstance, Mr. Bailey. You've come highly recommended in your line of work. That being said, I think you know exactly what traits I consider undesirable."

"The goddamned Jews."

Caught completely off guard, a squeak escaped my lips, instantly giving away our ruse. My eyes darted towards Peter in panic, who had paled himself from the revelation.

Bailey rocketed back in his chair, eyes narrowed. "What are you playing at?"

Peter, Tim, and I exchanged panicked glances. Bailey dove towards his desk drawer where he undoubtedly kept a weapon. Before Peter or I could react, Tim was across the desk and had the Bailey pinned to the wall beneath the painting as the estate agent's likeness stared down upon the scene unfazed. Bailey's feet kicked at the empty air as Tim compressed the man's thick neck with a bulging forearm.

"What's this all about?" the crimson-faced man gurgled, spittle frothing at the corners of his mouth.

Tim glared at Peter, awaiting instruction. Simon's muscle was accustomed to acting under orders. Instinctively, he had neutralised the threat, but without further guidance, he was unsure how to proceed. With Peter frozen in shock, I had no choice but to take the initiative. I signalled to Tim to keep the vile man aloft.

"Why Jews? They are a kind people. What did they ever do to you?" I moved forward until the acrid stench of his struggling breath overwhelmed my nostrils.

"Exist." Bailey's face was turning the hue of the pickled beets that had been a staple of my low-income childhood. "A blight… to Britain." His vitriol would have continued to spew forth had it not been in competition with his oxygen.

My mind swam with far more questions than I had time to ask. "You wanted to run them out of town with nothing but the clothes on their backs. You get your perfect little village and free properties with which to start a business."

Bailey nodded. I searched his bloodshot eyes for any trace of guilt but found none.

My ire skyrocketed. "When they didn't waltz away from the lives they had spent years building for themselves, lives that they had every right to, you took matters into your own hands." My voice began to crack. "You slaughtered entire families, didn't you?"

Bailey ignored me, his eyes beginning to roll back into his head. If Tim's hold continued any longer, he would pass out.

"Didn't you?!" I screamed.

"Not alone!"

I took a deep breath and realised tears of fury poured forth and were streaming down my cheeks. Sorrow would come later. I nodded to Tim, who let the pathetic man crumple to the filthy carpet where he gasped for air through a rattling throat. The giant must have done some permanent damage, but I felt no pity. Peter had stood as Tim dove over the desk, but he had since fallen back into the faux-leather chair, looking more pale than ever.

Recalling the other strangers from my visions, I lowered myself to a squat so that I could face the monster eye to eye. "Who else?"

The agent shook his head vigorously, sitting up. "They'll kill me if they find out I squawked. I'm no bloody grasser!"

Tim picked up a heavy stained glass-shaded floor lamp, jerking the cord from the wall, the action alone sufficient to back the withering Bailey into the corner. Turning his shorn head towards me, he held the lamp high, giving me a brief opening to stop his impending action. The moment came and went. Tim slammed the lamp's iron base into the estate agent's knee, obliterating any bones between it and the floor.

Bailey loosed a blood-curdling scream. "Hackett! Agatha Hackett, you bloody bastards!"

My mind spun as I stared at Bailey, sweat and tears cascading down his face in rivulets. What had been his knee was nothing more than a muddled mass of sinew and bone, rapidly dying his right pant leg crimson as the pulverised joint bled out onto the carpet. Despite what he had done, I felt a pang of sympathy, but brushed aside the feeling as fast as it had come. "Who's Agatha Hackett?"

"Please!" he begged. "Take me to a doctor, and I'll tell you everything you want to know." He reached for my hand, which I jerked away.

"Who. Is. Agatha. Hackett?"

Bailey shook his head, not even parting his lips. The greedy, cocksure bastard who had pounced at our promise of easy coin had all but vanished, quickly replaced by this whimpering character cowering in a corner. The similarity Reed Bailey held to his innocent victims during their last moments was not lost on me. Tim lifted the bloody lamp again, aiming for the other knee.

"Chatham's head housekeeper!"

Peter sat up, finally roused from his stupor. "As in Lord Chatham?"

Bailey nodded.

Peter looked at me as our suspicions indicating Chatham were confirmed. After divulging the connection to the manor, threats were no longer necessary. Bailey began haemorrhaging information as rapidly as blood. "She recruited me after a guildhall meeting. I'd opposed the influx of outsiders seeking labour. Save for the few times I helped her, she'd eliminate the squatters. Her lover, some footman, would aid with the cleanup. I'd only handle the property and fence the belongings. Everything she didn't claim for Chatham was my profit. I've only killed two people in my life, I swear it!"

Tim surprised me when he spoke. "Squatters? By that you mean families? With children. Them?"

Bailey nodded sluggishly, his face paling.

All emotion left Tim's face, making the man more ominous than I had ever seen him.

"You disgust me," I said to Bailey. Part of me wanted to take the lamp for myself and deal a few blows. The other part could not believe that I had stood idly by and allowed such a violent action, an action that was slowly leading to the agent's death. "I hope when Agatha finds you she shows you no more mercy than you showed those families."

The broken man formerly known as Reed Bailey merely whimpered.

"Let's go," suggested Peter through a strained voice. "We'll call for an ambulance when we're safely away."

I rose. Colour had begun to return to Peter's cheeks. The three of us made our way towards the door. Just as I reached out for the knob, I heard the unmistakable cocking of a revolver. Before I could react, Tim spun. In a practised fluid motion, he drew his own automatic from a shoulder holster concealed beneath his jacket and fired two shots side-by-side into the man's chest. Bailey's revolver fell to the floor with a heavy thunk. Foamy blood sputtered from his mouth as fell face-first into the carpet. I muffled a scream, my feet frozen to the carpet. Tears clouded my vision.

"Somebody will have heard that," uttered Tim. "Best we get a move on."

Shocked into action, Peter took me by my upper arm. "Sophia, we need to leave. Now." He urged me towards the door as Tim drew the building's blinds to a close.

I stared at him, dumbfounded. He took me carefully and guided me out of the office lobby and onto the street where I promptly retched on the sidewalk. I struggled with the emotional maelstrom that raged in my gut. In the visions, death felt like a first-hand observation, yet somehow removed. Reality had never been more than a breath away, and what had occurred had done so long ago. But I had watched Reed Bailey's death firsthand, a death that would not have happened had we not gone there in the first place. *How can I bring light to such atrocities if I must commit atrocities to do so?* My head swam, threatening another bout of vomiting. Peter's grip never lessened as he guided me across the Nene as fast as possible without raising suspicion. Everything after that was a blur.

Chapter XXVIII

I came to my senses sitting on the foot of the squeaky hotel room bed. I had been immobile for so long that the quilted pattern from the comforter had imprinted into my palms. I craved nothing more than crawling into Peter's comforting embrace, but across from me sat the broad-shouldered Tim. After what I had seen the man do, I could not bring myself to so much as make eye contact with him. Crouched in front of me, Peter was speaking as if through water. As the seconds passed, his voice became clearer.

"…back in the hotel. Everything's going to be okay."

Peter's trembling hands betrayed his calm demeanour as he placed them atop of mine.

"We killed a man." I looked Peter in the eyes. Unlike me, he bore no tears, but his sympathy was evident.

"You didn't do nothing," said Tim. "And I was defending meself."

"We have to report his death to the constabulary. If it was in self-defence, we were within our rights to protect ourselves, weren't we?"

"They won't see it like that. Remember, I smashed his leg to smithereens."

He did not add that I had had the chance to stop it and did not. My head fell into my hands, and I spoke through sobs. "How are we any better than the people we're chasing?"

Peter lifted my chin so that I faced him, wiping a stray tear on my chin with his thumb. "Sometimes we have to do uncomfortable things to reach our desired end. I don't like that we had to kill him any more than you, but he was going to kill you, Sophia. That barrel was levelled at your head. I'm not about to lose you."

At me? The realisation took me aback. "What about the body? It will lead back to us. His secretary knows what we look like. Knows we paid her to leave."

"You've been out of it for a while, love. I stayed behind while Peter brought you back here. You needn't worry your pretty little head about such a thing."

His response made me deeply uncomfortable, but I did not have the emotional stamina to inquire further. Down in my chest, I knew the truth. Simon and Tim were old hands when it came to nefarious deeds. If not for Tim, I doubted that I would be alive, but at what cost? What Mother Superior and I both believed to be a gift felt more like a curse given our predicament. "Maybe we should stop, before someone else gets killed."

"Sophia, I know you. You'll never forgive yourself if you stop now. Someone must answer for these heinous crimes. Darnell told us about several homes, but those are only the ones he knew about. The truth is we have no idea how many murders have occurred in Luffield. I hate to say it, but the death of that sleazy low-life is a small price to pay for bringing these murderers to justice."

The entire reason that I was conducting this investigation was to shed light on the happening directly under the noses of Luffield's oblivious residents. Peter was right. If I gave up now, the memories would haunt me to the end of my days, just as they had my mother. I had nowhere to go except deeper into the mire. I hoped that the life of Reed Bailey was the highest cost we would incur.

"Okay," I nodded, taking the proffered handkerchief and wiping my eyes as I took a deep, shaky breath. "Bailey said that Agatha Hackett worked for Lord Chatham. That's another finger pointing in his direction as the mastermind behind this all. It stands to reason that he would want to model Luffield after his own expectations and is one of the few with the power to do so. We have to find a way to question his housekeeper."

"That's where I'm going to stand in your way." Tim interlaced his fingers behind his head and reclined against the back of the cheap chair to a chorus of its pops.

"Excuse me?" My head snapped up almost as fast as Peter's.

"I can't let you go meddling about Chatham's affairs."

"And why not?" asked Peter, unsteady as he confronted his brother's minion. It was all too easy to forget where Tim's loyalties were when he had been defending us, looking to us for guidance. However, the moment our plans conflicted with Simon's, they became quite clear.

"That lord's one of your brother's most profitable clients. It wouldn't do to upset 'im would it?"

Of course! Why wouldn't he? After running Luffield's silent pogrom, what's dealing in black-market sundries? I stared at Tim for a moment, mouth agape. "I need some air." I stood and swooned a bit before collecting myself.

"Here, let me—"

"I'm fine." I shrugged off his hands and stormed out of the room, not even bothering to shut the door behind me. I knew Peter had turned a blind eye towards Simon's dealings, but that had not stopped him from accepting his brother's money. Money that may well have come as a result of the very matter we were seeking to expose. He was guilty by association. An apathetic accessory. I left the hotel, my eyes stinging, and walked halfway down the street before the breeze reminded me that I had forgotten my coat. "Damn it all," I muttered, pulling my collar tight. Dusk was close.

"Sophia. Sophia." Peter's raised voice came from behind, rising above the din.

Peter ran up to my side, winded. "You forgot... your coat."

I paused as he took the opportunity to drape it over my shoulders. I resisted the urge to jerk it from his hands and don it myself. "Did you know about him? About Lord Chatham?"

Peter paused, but would not meet my eyes. "Not to this extent."

I spun on my heels, striding away in a huff.

Peter rushed to keep pace with me. "You know that my brother's dealings haven't always been above board. I've never deceived you about that. We've purchased things from Chatham before, but we purchase a great many things from a great number of people. He never gave us any indication that he was involved in more dastardly dealings, much less a private genocide."

"But you didn't ask questions, Peter. You never asked questions! You sit in that back room with your head down, doing anything and everything your brother asks with no thought of your own. At some point you have to take ownership of your involvement."

Peter's head dropped, chagrined. "You are absolutely right." He took my hand, which I allowed. "If you're still willing to do business together, I'd walk away from Northrop's Antiques. For good. We would start with nothing, but it would be an honest living."

"It's the right thing to do, Peter. Whether with me or not. Simon may not be murdering people for who they are, but you can't deny that at some level, he's complicit in all of this."

Peter nodded as an older couple walked by, heads huddled together for warmth.

I pulled him into a niche where we could speak with a little more privacy. "If we stop now, Agatha, the footman, Chatham, anyone else involved will all be getting away with countless crimes. We have to circumvent your brother and his muscle and follow this lead to Chatham ourselves."

"We can't, Sophia. It's one thing to walk away from the family business, but interfering with Chatham will directly oppose my brother. Simon may not murder innocent people, but he's not kind to those who stand in his way."

The inner strength that Peter had exercised began to fade away in the shadow of his brother.

My tears returned as my volume rose, drawing more attention from passersby. "What happened to 'You'll never forgive yourself if you stop now,' Peter? Are you that fearful of Simon? He can find new clients. Hell, if we told him what was happening, he might even take our side. Peter, you have to stand up to your brother."

"I can't, alright?" A slow drizzle began to drift down from the smoky sky above, dampening Peter's face and masking his tears. His eyes fell to my feet. "I don't know what types of dealings he has. What crimes he's committed. I've lasted this long under his protection by not asking questions. He vowed to Father to protect me, but if I were to start causing problems for his business…"

"I don't understand." My eyes grew blurrier by the moment. "You'd rather not ask tough questions than bring someone to justice for the murder of innocent children?"

Peter didn't respond.

"You're a bloody coward." I spun and charged across the street.

The rain grew heavier by the minute. I had no intention of heading back to the hotel, and the Women's Lodge was on the far side of town from where I was. I trudged along, alone under the deluge when everyone with sense had taken cover. Within a few moments, I realised that my feet were pointed towards the convent. My one reliable refuge. My mind was so agitated that I hadn't noticed the automobile pulling alongside me.

"I thought that was you, Miss Tate." Officer Davies yelled over the pouring rain. Before I could respond, he was out of the car. "You shouldn't be about in weather like this. Let me give you a lift." He threw a dry trench coat over my shoulders and opened the passenger door.

I nodded my thanks and climbed in.

"I didn't expect to see you back in Luffield so soon. Is there anywhere I can take you?"

"Grafton Nunnery, please." I forced a smile.

"And you were planning to walk there? In this? You're braver than I thought." He peeled away from the curb and headed out of the city, climbing the winding road that led up the hill to the convent.

Davies spoke constantly throughout the trip, but I had little to say. His worried eyes kept darting to the rear-view mirror to check on his passenger. The thought crossed my mind to divulge everything, but that would only serve to incriminate myself. Owning up to my participation in a crime was a reality I could face. What I could not face was that without evidence, Chatham and the others might escape scot-free. The other side of the river had no shortage of men like Reed Bailey. Like sharks, they'd be fighting over the tasty morsels he'd left and be more than happy to accept Chatham's employ.

The young officer pulled to a stop in front of the tall chapel doors as Mother Superior opened them, curious as to what visitors would be calling at this hour. "You sure you don't need anything else, Miss?" Davies asked as he opened the door, rain sheeting off of his cap.

"No thank you, Officer Davies. I appreciate the lift."

"Have a good evening." He climbed back into the driver's side but waited to drive back down the hill until I was safely inside the convent.

"Get in here, child, before you catch your death." Mother Superior took Davies' drenched coat as well as my own, handing them to one of the nuns who scampered off with them. "Go have a seat by the fire. I'll have Sister Therese bring you something from the kitchens. Praise God we finally have an abundance of food in our larder," she added, crossing herself.

I couldn't help but smirk at that. If nothing else, Klemp had held up his end of the bargain.

I made my way to the roaring hearth, where Sister Maria

was more that happy to relinquish her seat. Pushing the worn high-backed chair closer to the fire, they whispered to each other as I warmed myself back up. I gratefully accepted a cosy blanket from the caring women, allowing the deluge of the day's chaotic emotions to dissipate. Before Sister Therese returned with food and drink, I was fast asleep.

Chapter XXIX

By the time Mother Superior roused me from my slumber, the torrent outside had calmed. The fire had died down considerably, making the vaulted room positively chilly. My teeth began to chatter as the damp from the clothes soaked into my bones, sending the abbess into a tizzy.

"You poor dearie. Lord forgive me for not immediately fetching you fresh garments."

Sister Therese strode into the room with a cup of warm milk and a hunk of bread, placing it into my trembling hands. The handsome Burrows clock that had been donated when I was a child read just after midnight. With no regard to the late hour, Reverend Mother dispatched Sister Maria, who was roughly my size, to procure some dry apparel. Nuns kept few articles of clothing aside from their habits, but the funereal dress I ultimately found myself in was at least comfortable.

"Thank you for this," I said as I emerged from the larder where I had changed.

The Reverend Mother waived it off. 'Inasmuch as ye have done it unto one of the least of these…'"

"To what do we owe your presence?" Sister Therese asked impatiently, ever the curious one. "I didn't figure we'd be seeing you anytime soon."

"Leave the poor girl be, Sister. Can't you see that she's exhausted?" Mother Superior faced me, cheeks radiating her warmth. "You have a place here as long as you need. You know that. Right now, you need some rest."

A flash of lightning illuminated the space, followed closely by a clap of thunder that made the nuns loose a startled yelp.

"And the Lord agrees," laughed Reverend Mother. "I'll show you to a room, and we can speak in the morning."

To Therese's chagrin, Sister Maria was assigned to show me to my room. The stairway lights that had been retrofitted after the electric bulb had become commonplace were no longer working. Like so many aspects of the convent, they too had fallen into disrepair. Between the significant decrease in funding and its ailing caretaker, I feared for the nunnery's future.

Sister Maria guided me up the winding stone staircase, a narrow, twisting, low-ceilinged chamber of stone carved centuries before that would induce claustrophobia in even those not prone to the condition. The original building had been constructed long before proper nutrition was commonplace. As such, the passages had been designed with a smaller-statured populace in mind. The light from the nun's candle did little to dispel the pressing darkness. Our shadows danced across the moss-covered wall as we wound our way up to the dorter and into the empty common room surrounded by the nun's cells. A fire blazed in the room's hearth, expected to warm each individual room, but I knew from experience that it failed at the task.

"Here's your room, Miss Sophia." She opened the iron-bound wooden door with a creak and made her way in to ignite the candle on the dresser. "Mother Superior said this was the room you and your mother used to share when you would stay with us."

I nodded, the memory-filled cell threatening to bring back the torrent of emotions from earlier. At least the nostalgic images swirling my mind were my own.

The sister placed a comforting hand on my shoulder before leaving me alone with my thoughts. Thunder receded into the distance as the cloud cover parted to reveal a bright, moonlit night that filtered through the minuscule elevated window. The single candle bathed the room in a warm glow short of the warmth itself. The room was spartan, as was to be expected in a facility such as this. The simple furniture consisted of the double bed that Mother and I had shared, a heavily used desk with a small built-in shelf, a three-drawer dresser with wood so warped that nothing would close correctly, and a *prie-dieu* that had not been used in ages.

Once alone, I disrobed to the chemise, let my hair fall, and climbed between the cool sheets before the chill could set in any further. The bed was little more than a thin mattress laid across noisy springs and topped with a rough-spun blanket, but I was too tired to care. An emptiness ached where Peter had carved out a space in my heart. Unlike past suitors, I had given my entire self over to him. As much as I had fallen for his humorous quirks and unrelenting kindness, I could not tolerate his cowardice, especially not when it mattered most.

"Bastard," I muttered aloud as the door cracked open.

"I'm sorry, Miss. My apologies." Therese began to back out of the door rapidly.

"No, no, no. Not you, Therese." I wiped my eyes on the bed sheet. "Please, come in."

Sister Therese sheepishly opened the door and shut it behind her without a sound. "I hope I'm not intruding. You gave me a fright there for a moment."

"I'm sorry, Therese. I was angry and talking to myself."

For the first time I noticed the pair of pewter cups in her hands, and under her arm was an extra pillow. "I know it's late, but I thought I'd bring you something to help you sleep."

"Your presence is a welcome one, Therese." I arranged the two pillows so that we could sit up and patted the bed for her to sit.

She climbed in next to me, offering me one of the cups. The dated springs groaned with the added weight.

Once she had settled in comfortably I took a sip of the wine. My eyes went wide. "Is this…"

"Sacramental wine?" She winked and whispered, "I won't tell if you won't."

I stifled a laugh. It would not do to wake up half the convent and be caught drinking, much less with communal wine that was supposed to be the blood of Christ.

"Anyone can see you have a lot on your mind. What I find most helpful is sharing the burden with others, so I wanted to offer a compassionate ear. That is, if you want it."

I took another sip. After having spent time with the more affluent Milly and Peter, my taste had become more refined, making the merlot little more than tolerable. Nevertheless, it would temporarily take the edges off the heartbreak I was enduring.

"You can tell me anything, Sophia." She put her arm around me and pulled me close, miming zipping her lips. "Confidential as the confessional with none of the forgiveness."

I laughed at her silliness with regard to the sacrament, but the wall of fake composure that I had constructed crumbled, and I began bawling. The fat tears fell onto Therese's habit, darkening the material. Therese sat there patiently, smoothing my curly hair as she repeatedly hummed "The Oak and the Ash," a song she knew from before taking her vows. I could not help but wonder if the choice was intentional. Though I was not exactly a maiden, perhaps straying into the city had been a mistake. Perhaps Luffield was where I belonged, and I was denying it. Even if I chose to settle in the country town, I would be no better than Peter if I turned a blind eye towards the suffering to which I had been privy.

I was unsure how long I cried before my sobs ceased. I felt as though I had run out of tears, emotionally spent. I sat up, and took another swallow of the middling wine. "Something's happened, and I don't know what to do."

"Our Lord in Heaven! You're not supposed to be having anything stronger than small ale if your pregnant." Therese moved to take the cup from my hands, but I held it beyond her reach, my laughter at her excited response after such sobbing sounding strange in the cramped space.

"I'm not pregnant," I said, laughing under my breath. I sat up and wiped my eyes, thankful for the sister's unintended humour that had snapped me out of my self-pity.

"Thank the good Lord. So what is it then?"

I started regaling my friend with everything that had occurred over the last few weeks, originally only hinting at the things I'd discovered. Whether it was the wine or the camaraderie, I began to spill my entire story to the sister, supernatural abilities and all. I told her everything, the candelabra, the murders, even the estate agent. When I was finished, her arms were wrapped around me, and she was crying as hard as I had been. My spirit felt far less burdened, and I could not have been more grateful for a neutral confidant.

"Oh, Sophia. And here I thought nothing exciting happened in our humble little town."

"Exciting isn't exactly the word I would choose for it."

"Well, no. But there's certainly far more going on than meets the eye."

"That's true." I titled back my cup, finishing the remaining drops. I longed for a second cup, but was not about to ask Therese to risk another trip into the sacred tabernacle.

"You said you didn't, but I think you know exactly what to do. Sophia, you are the strongest woman I have ever met. If you can't do what needs doing, then I don't know who could. Our Lord entrusted this gift to you for a reason. This is your chance."

"I don't know if I can do this by myself. I told you about Tim. I have no doubt that he will be keeping an eye on me. I don't even like to think about what he might do if I run afoul of him. And what would I do even with him? Barge into Chatham Manor and tell them I need to accuse their housekeeper of murder with no evidence in hand?"

"You told me that brute's orders were to keep an eye on Peter. If he's run away, wouldn't Tim follow him?"

I shook my head, fighting the tears that threatened to return at the notion of Peter turning tail and running. Therese reached out and took my hand.

"Tim knows how headstrong I am. If he had to choose between keeping an eye on Peter and protecting Simon's interests, I know what he'd choose. Neither Simon nor Tim have ever seemed particularly fond of Peter."

"Their family dynamic is as unscrupulous as their business practices, if you ask me. Wait… You said Chatham was one of Simon's biggest clients, correct?"

"Yes. Why?"

"The estate agent, Bailey, would fence anything this Agatha didn't claim. That means she was taking any significant items to Lord Chatham. To their owners, the family heirlooms' sentimental value eclipsed any financial one; but to Chatham, those people's most prised possessions would have been worth a great deal. And Peter's brother was selling them. What vile creatures!"

"As if genocide wasn't bad enough, the mongrels were profiting from it."

Therese stared. The realisation of what she was implying hit me like a tonne of bricks.

"Wait, you think Simon is aware of the murders?

Therese shrugged.

"He has no shortage of business. Why would he…" My mind reeled. "Wait. Surely Simon doesn't believe the propaganda coming from that nationalist bastard in Germany. Peter's brother struck me as a common criminal, but not a proponent of this social improvement bollocks. Pardon my language."

Therese shook off the course words. "He doesn't have to share Lord Chatham's beliefs to profit from them. If Simon is as savvy as you make him out to be, he would be wise to know as much about the pieces that came into his possession as possible. The better question is, 'Could Peter have known?'"

Therese yawned. It was getting late, and the nun would have morning duties, tired or not.

I shook my head. "He was as shocked by every revelation as I. He knew his brother didn't conduct business above board, but he never would have supported Simon if he knew his brother was profiteering from crimes of hate."

"You know him better than I, so I trust that you are right. If you consider the dates you told me, though, it sounds like this nasty business began with their father, Wilbur, William, whatever his name was." Therese leaned her head on my shoulder, beginning to drift into slumber. "Simon simply took over where his father left off," she whispered.

"If Peter doesn't have the courage to expose this atrocity, I hope he has the bollocks to walk away from the family business. I don't see how in good conscience he could carry on knowing what he knows now." I stifled a yawn myself. It was getting late, and the wine was having its effect. "You're right. I have to follow this to the top, no matter what happens to me. These families deserve justice."

I glanced down at Therese, but she was sound asleep. The rise and fall of her chest indicated that her rest was peaceful, despite the dark nature of our conversation. As I drifted into the world of dreams, I made up my mind to visit Chatham Manor in the morning, not allowing anyone to stand in my way.

Chapter XXX

The next morning, Sister Therese was already gone, her spot on the creaky bed still warm. I rose and would have slipped back into the borrowed dress, but it had vanished overnight. In its place were the clothes I had arrived in, freshly laundered and, most importantly, dry. I slipped back into them and exited into the hallway, which already bustled with the convent's inhabitants going about their morning routines. I was not disappointed that I had missed the early morning mass, but I felt a twinge of guilt for not helping with the chores.

"Sophia! A pleasure to see you up and about." Mother Superior beamed as she trundled through the others, gaily singing the to-do list in a mock Gregorian chant that had the sisters in hysterics. I refused to believe that all nuns were as lucky as the ones at Grafton to have an abbess like her. "Our good Lord has seen it fit to fill me with joy today. You'll find some eggs and potatoes in the kitchen waiting for you, though they may be a touch cool for your liking. Now, I've got a number of duties that need tending to, but I'd like to see you in my office at the ten o'clock bell."

Before I could thank her or ask how I could help, she had disappeared amongst the wicker baskets of laundry and bodies. I made my way to the kitchen and found the aforementioned breakfast plate sitting on the mantle above the dying fire. In short order, the room would again roar to life with the preparation of the noon meal for the convent. The eggs I found had skimmed over with film, the potatoes stale, and the apple juice diluted, but I was no less grateful for the hospitality. I leaned against the wooden counter top scored with decades of use and downed the food like I had not eaten in days. I cleaned my plate in the large farm sink as I stared out the window through the drying herbs hung from the ceiling, watching the nuns dart to and fro outside. I could not sit comfortably as my hosts toiled so.

Once finished, I made my way to the barn where I found Brother George struggling to haul a heavy galvanised jug of milk he had harvested from Annette. The pleasant aroma of fresh hay filled my nostrils, overpowering any less desirable smells one might find amongst beast of burden.

"Sophia." He inclined his threadbare cap in respect, a grin across his face.

I threw my arms around the old gentleman with no concern about his dusty dungarees and mud-caked wellingtons, knocking the wind out of his ailing frame and nearly making him topple the jug.

"*Oof!* A pleasure to see you as well," he cried happily as he regained his breath. "Seems like just yesteryear you were a wee lass, and I was reading you *Adventures in Wonderland.*"

I laughed. Throughout my childhood, the caretaker, who had seemed positively ancient then, had assumed the role of the grandfather I never had. I helped him load the jug onto the cart to which Mathilde was already harnessed. "Heading into town?"

The groundskeeper nodded. "Our donations have increased as of late," he said, arching an eyebrow in my direction without further comment, "but we still need money for a fair number of items. Annette here is one of the few ways we have left to do so."

I grabbed a rough-handled pitchfork older than I was and began adding fresh hay to the animal's pens while George topped off their water troughs.

"Would you mind terribly giving me a ride to the far side of town after lunch?"

"I don't imagine why not. Not to mention, I'd appreciate the company. Don't have many people to talk to these days except the Reverend Mother, and you know good and well who does most of the talking."

I chuckled politely with a tinge of melancholy. George had lost his wife over a decade ago and had never been quite the same since. He and his wife had had the type of love that only seems to exist in Jane Austen novels. Since his wife's untimely death, the caretaker had seemed half the man he was before, a part of his soul simply gone. Even at his most cheerful, there was an indescribable loneliness that lingered behind those dark brown eyes of his nearly obscured by his caterpillar-like grey brows.

We finished the barnyard chores, and I left him on his own to brush the beasts of burden, a meditative activity in which he took the utmost care, trusting no one to do but himself. I took a meandering route through the grounds, admiring the antiquated natural stonework, local slate roof, and blown-glass windows that were becoming less commonplace in favour of more modern materials. It saddened me to see so many aspects of the convent falling into disrepair. Given George's age and the lack of funds, I did not know how much longer the convent could sustain itself. The gravel ground together beneath my boots as I wound my way to the superior's office, but not before finding myself at Mother's headstone. After verifying that no one was within earshot, I knelt at her foot.

"Wow." I stared down into my lap, fiddling with a long strand of dry grass. I did not know how to begin. I had so much to say, but no idea how to say it. "It's been a while since we've spoken, but I want to tell you that the ability that you've imparted to me… It's changed me in ways you can't imagine. On some days I consider it a gift, and on others, a curse. I find myself reluctant to touch any metal with that damned reddish hue. Some things have filled me with the most profound joy, but then your fingers graze that one item and it scars you so deeply that you never want to touch anything else."

I stared up at the overcast sky, an unchanging light grey from horizon to horizon, as tears began to form.

"I found the candelabra." I could almost imagine my mother stirring at that. "I saw what you must have seen, so many years ago. Now I understand why it drove you mad. I couldn't even finish the memory before withdrawing in terror. If I had held on any longer, it would have done the same to me." I touched the ground, hoping to somehow connect with her spirit, drawing my hand closed around a clump of dormant grass. "I'm no hero, Mother." I started crying. "But, I refuse to believe the universe would provide us such an ability to discover such wounds without the strength to heal them. I'll bring those responsible to justice and honour the memories of those who perished. You have my word."

I stayed in that posture for a time, absorbing the calm I felt from being so close to my mother. When I rose, to no surprise, I found Mother Superior standing in the nearby doorway. "Are you sure eavesdropping isn't a sin?" I asked, arching an eyebrow.

She chuckled the comment away. "Only if the intent is. I'm no different from a confessional in this respect. Truth be told, my window opens to the graveyard, and I can hear when visitors speak. Not to mention that you were running late for our meeting."

I smiled, not offended by her grandmotherly presence in the slightest. "Isn't it a little chilly for an open window?"

Mother Superior fluffed the fabric of her habit repeatedly while patting her ample belly with another. "I'm no stranger to heat. These thin sisters running around keep the sanctuary positively blistering. If I die during prayers, it'll be from heatstroke." She laughed heartily. "I thought I was going to meet our Lord and Saviour when I went through menopause."

We joined in a chorus of laughter. The woman was nothing if not endearing.

"Come in. Tell me all about your troubles."

"Troubles?" I asked, ducking through the squat wooden door frame buried in the rough-hewn wall that made up the older portion of the convent.

It was her turn to raise an eyebrow. "Don't take me for oblivious. That's what the novitiates are for."

I took a seat in the proffered chair, a simple four-legged thing with no cushion, and stared up at the crucifix positioned on the wall above where her head would be. Her white-walled office in many ways reminded me of my cell in the dorter with all the same furnishing, save for a bed. The *prie-dieu* was more ornate than the one in my room and the knee pad was almost non-existent from unrelenting use by the Reverend Mother and her predecessors. Instead of sitting behind the desk where she had been cross-referencing a pair of missals, she took the matching chair next to me. The antiquated furniture wobbled and groaned, but held fast. She took my hand in hers.

"I can piece together a lot of what's happened, dearie, but I need you to fill in the gaps."

I nodded, taking a deep breath. "What I tell you has the potential to put the convent in danger. I fear I've already shared too much with Sister Therese."

"Don't worry about us. Grafton Nunnery has weathered a great many centuries through more ordeals than I could count. I can't imagine that this decade has any more to fear than what the we sisters have faced before. And Sister Therese is a good soul, despite her knack for bending the rules. I would ask that next time you two want a drink, use the non-sacramental wine I keep in the cupboard behind you." She winked.

I could not help but laugh.

"You don't get to be my age and my position if you miss much. Little gets by me these days, including that broken heart of yours."

I broke down before she uttered another word. I would have thought by now that I had few tears left. Sadly, heartbreak could not be resolved in a day. She cradled me, singing comforting hymns softly as my emotional dyke burst. When the sobs finally relented, I confessed everything to her.

I did so much more than fill in the gaps. So many things she never could have imagined. Once I finished my tale, she leaned back in her chair, overwhelmed, a feeling to which even the experienced abbess was not accustomed.

"My God in Heaven. And in Luffield. I never thought I'd see the day." The abbess took a deep, quavering breath, her cheery presence from the morning traded for profound empathy.

"I've asked Brother George to carry me to the manor after lunch. I still don't have any idea what I'm going to do once I reach it. I'm hoping the slow trip will give me a chance to come up with some semblance of a plan."

Mother Superior rose and walked around behind her desk, rummaging in a drawer before pulling out an embroidered handkerchief and dabbing her eyes. She sat, staring down at the surface for so long that I considered slipping out. "Go to the manor's servant entrance," she said without looking up. "Ask for a gentleman named Paul. Tell him I sent you, and he'll help you with whatever you need."

I sat up, excited about the potential lead. "Forgive me if I'm being impertinent. I've known you for a long time, but I've never heard you mention Paul or knowing anyone at Chatham Manor."

"His name hasn't rolled off my lips in nigh on two decades, but I know he's still around." She clutched her rosary. "See him in town from time to time, smiling as he did when we were young." Her lip trembled. All my life, the woman had been a kind but firm presence in my life. The unwavering abbess was the epitome of womanly strength, which made it all the more difficult to watch her facade of strength wane, even if only for a moment. "We were young lovers a great many moons ago. When I felt the Lord's call, I left everything behind. Every time I lay eyes on him, I know there's still love there. From both parties."

I stared at her, perplexed and heartbroken.

She choked out a laugh at the dumbfounded look on my face. "Eventually people will remember that no one is born a nun."

Chapter XXXI

Brother George, ever a man of his word, helped me up into the wagon's box before pulling down the winding drive on our journey to Chatham Manor. My stomach churned like a roiling ocean on the cusp of a squall. As much as I would have liked to believe it was due to the wagon's incessant jostling, the rising anxiety eclipsed all other sensations. *Who am I to barge into the home of Lord Derrick Chatham, a gentleman I had never met, and demand a confession from his head of house?* Or worse, if the corruption extended to Chatham as suspected, my very life would be in grave peril. For one responsible for countless deaths, likely considerably more than known about, what was one more meddling woman? Leading up to this moment I had had Peter, and to a lesser extent, Tim, watching my back. Even if he was not the strongest or most intimidating person, Peter's presence alone provided me with some modicum of safety. But now? Peter's newfound spine had vanished, and Tim, if still around, was no longer on my side. I would be blindly diving into a hornet nest alone and unprotected. This would be the bravest thing I had ever done—or the stupidest.

"Storm's coming, Miss." George tilted his hat back and examined the sky with wisdom born of decades spent out of doors.

"That's what I'm afraid of." I pulled my shawl tighter around my shoulders without so much as glancing upward. The wind tugged at my hair, picking up as we grew closer to our destination.

"I'll wait for you as long as need be."

"That won't be necessary, George. I'll find my own way home," I smiled and gave him a peck on the cheek, causing his normally pale skin to turn a healthy shade of pink.

The wagon groaned as George made the turn onto the estate grounds, heading up a long gravel drive lined with manicured evergreens with sprawling gardens beyond. The classically handsome manor took on an ageless quality when approached by our horse-drawn wagon, but any awe I held for the home's sesquicentennial architecture was driven out by the menacing appearance brought on by the impending tempest. As the dark clouds devoured the sunlight, the house grew increasingly foreboding. Its normally warm-hued walls became ashen and lifeless; the slate-capped roof, a weathered headstone; the pinnacles of the towers, medieval spikes awaiting victims. Doubt replaced resolve. I spun in my seat and stared back longingly at the iron gate, surprised that it had not mysteriously slammed shut behind us.

"All you need say is turn back, Miss Sophia, and I'd do it in two shakes of a lamb's tail. The question is, could you live with yourself if I did?"

I stared into the knowing eyes hidden under the wisps of white hair, surprised, and yet not. I had been a fool to think after spending my youth around the wise caretaker that he would be completely unaware of my talents. His gift of observation might not have been supernatural, but he was acutely aware of all that occurred on the grounds that he tended with such care, and to a lesser extent, Luffield. Honestly, I felt relief as some of the tension drained from my chilled limbs. The more who were aware of the bucolic town's darkest secret, the less likely the perpetrators were to outrun their crimes—or anything they might do to me to keep them hidden. If George did not know the exact reason for my visit, he could surmise enough to grasp its import and my danger.

"No," I said, resolve gradually returning. "Take me to the servants' entrance, please."

"There's the Sophia I know." The old caretaker grinned, snapping the reins and matching the clap of thunder that rent the sky. "You never were one to shy away from what needed to be done."

My confidence continued building as we passed the balustraded grand perron leading up to the main entry in favour of the more humble servant's entry around the side. Catching both of us off-guard, a young servant darted out from the antechamber. "Miss Sophia Tate, I presume?"

"Yes," I stammered, surprised by the anticipation of my arrival.

George urged Mathilde to a quick stop. After the lengthy journey, the old mare was more than happy to oblige. As the servant extended a hand to help me down, the caretaker whispered into my ear, "Find out how deep the rabbit hole goes."

I turned in time to see George wink. I took the servant's hand and stepped down to the wooden footboard as the well-mannered gentleman turned his head to protect my modesty. As I stepped onto the path, the first drops of rain pelted my face.

"I'll see to it that she's returned safely," said the servant, nodding to George.

My old friend gave one last wink, yelled at Mathilde, and was off the way he came.

"Let's get you inside, Miss. Forgive my shortsightedness. I would've brought an umbrella had I thought it."

"I won't melt from a few drops of water," I said, waving off his concern and hiding my discomfort behind the humour.

"Miss Tate." A rigid, immaculately dressed gentleman, who could be none other than Chatham's personal butler, approached me as we entered the vestibule. His haughty manner and well-groomed appearance betrayed his position. His greying hair was slicked back, shining as brightly as his polished shoes. His tailed coat and trousers did not reveal so much as a speck of lint with fold lines that could double as a straight edge. "My name is Preston, milord's butler. I trust your trip by *buggy* was not too tiresome."

Despite the unnerving panic pulsating through my extremities, I felt obligated to participate in the charade of formalities regardless of his condescending tone. "Thank you, It—"

"If you'll follow me. Lord Chatham will see you in the dining room." Tradition did not appear to prevent this Preston from being a pompous ass.

I followed the butler though a traditional manor that defined opulence. Unlike the home of Camille and Darnell, each piece of stunning art that lined the walls was authentic, every frame leafed in actual gold and hung on solid mahogany walls. Each furnishing fit the style of the house so precisely that they must have been custom crafted for the home, every object equally as curated. The more picturesque neighbourhoods of Luffield were extravagant in a cosy, countryside manner, but Chatham Manor was altogether different. If this was Chatham's country home, I could not fathom his London residence. The butler cleared his throat, and I realised that I had stopped to gawk at an original Cézanne from early in the artist's career.

"My apologies," I said instinctively.

"Enrapture is understandable from those not exposed to such refinement on a frequent basis."

"And pretentiousness is understandable from those not exposed to manners on a frequent basis." I retorted before I had thought better of it.

Preston snuffed in offence, turning on his heels and continuing down the hall slightly faster than before. I stifled a laugh. I should not have made such a scathing remark, but his toffee-nosed disdain had instantly become intolerable. Part of me sadistically wished he was responsible for some aspect of the crimes so that he would be forced to play the arrogant weasel in the penitentiary. Let him see how well received it would be there.

As the butler led me on, I could not help but notice a copy of the biweekly Luffield Gazette lying folded on a side table. The headline read, "Two Dead in Murder-Suicide." I suppressed a yelp when I saw the accompanying images. The victims in both images were younger than they had been when I'd met them, but the features of Reed Bailey and his secretary were unmistakable. No matter how much I had lied to myself about Tim's actions, I had known the truth all along. Tim Cooksey was a cold-blooded killer, but it did not change the fact that I felt equally responsible for their deaths. To Preston's annoyance, I had halted again, but this time I was only urged forward by his impatiently arched eyebrow.

He led me to a pair of intricately carved double doors that ran nearly to the ceiling and opened them, gesturing for me to continue on my own. I took a deep breath and stepped into what was likely the most opulent room I had ever experienced. I must have looked as uncivilised as Chatham's butler imagined me with my mouth agape, mesmerised by surroundings all the more enthralling to scholars of antiquity. Perhaps Preston's description had not been entirely inaccurate, as rude as it had been. Studying such breathtaking creations in black and white stills next to an emotionally deprived block of text nestled amongst the pages of dusty compendiums did little justice to prepare one for the actual artefact. Above my head hung a stunning Baccarat chandelier, its French crystals sparkling like the sun in stark contrast to the darkened sky beyond the windows. The Alberti-style fresco ceiling glowed, illuminated in a paint-friendly spectrum by lights hidden by the room's equally impressive Renaissance-inspired friezes. To top off my sense of wonderment, my head swam in the sumptuous odours wafting up from the dinner spread.

In a chamber such as this, I could momentarily forget about any troubles that existed outside of these four walls. A clap of thunder shattered the moment of awe, and I saw that I was not alone. At the head of the table was Lord Derrick Chatham, a doppelganger of the image that the bi-weekly Luffield Gazette favoured. As the white-haired lord rose from his seat, I could not help but admire the bespoke jade-green suit and cravat wrapping his average figure, further accented by what must have been solid gold cuff links, collar pin, and watch chain. The biggest surprise of the room was yet to come. On either side of a silver platter of roast game, rose Peter and Tim. I could imagine Preston's wicked smirk as he latched the doors behind me.

As the grim reality set in, the impressiveness of the hall dissipated. I remembered the origin of much of Chatham's funding and the reason for my presence. How many priceless heirlooms and artefacts had been stolen to pay for the paintings, the carvings, and the sculptures I had seen on my way in the mansion? In Derrick Chatham's mind, how many people's lives were less important than his?

"You must be Sophia. What an absolute pleasure," Chatham said, walking to my side and giving me an unwelcome kiss on the cheek. His overly familiar gesture raised bile in my throat. The rare scent of eucalyptus overpowered the spread as the coarse grey strands of his beard irritated my skin. What had been delicious aromas flooding the dining room were now revolting. "My guests have told me so much about you."

Chapter XXXII

My visit to Chatham Manor had covered the gamut of emotions: fear, surprise, awe, disgust… and now rage. I seethed as I glared at Peter Northrop. His wilfully oblivious over-sized companion sat to his side chomping away contentedly on the fowl in front of him, not even bothering to use the proper utensils like the animal he was. All of Peter's posturing had been bollocks. When it came down to it, he was nothing more than a pawn of his brother, no less a minion than Tim. The betrayal left me gutted, empty and on the verge of collapse. Only the idea of justice for the fallen kept me going. Peter moved to speak, but Chatham filled the space.

"I'm sure introductions are unnecessary." Chatham took my hand and led me to the far side of the table from the door where he pulled out a chair next to Peter. For a moment, the only sound in the room was Tim's gnawing every morsel of meat from a bone. "My friends have shared with me most distressing news."

The rain tapped against the window panes like impatient fingers. I relented and sat, largely ignoring the 18th-century American embroidery on the chair cushion and the authentic Moor-inspired rug gracing the floor.

"Please help yourself." Chatham gestured to the extensive spread in front of us. With my stomach so ill-at-ease, I was doing well not to retch. "If there's anything you desire, simply make it known."

"Thank you, Lord Chatham." It fascinated me to no end that even under the most difficult of circumstances, people tended to observe decorum so long as someone else was doing so. In reality, I wanted nothing more than to climb onto the table, kicking dishes right and left, screaming at the top of my lungs.

"Derrick, please." He flashed the pearly smile of a man who was used to getting anything *he* desired.

"Your friend Peter and his… *colleague*," Chatham began as Tim ripped the last meat from the bone with a snap, wiped his mouth on the pristine linen tablecloth brocaded with Sicilian lace, and began draining a glass of what I assumed to be quite expensive Cabernet, "have informed me that they have in their possession evidence that my housekeeper was involved in some most troubling activities. Is this so?"

My head spun. If Peter had decided to confront Chatham, why had he not involved me, the person who held such evidence? Furthermore, why had he allowed me to continue believing that he was nothing more than a coward? I stared at Peter, whose eyes pleaded with me to agree. I nodded reluctantly, struggling to mask my confusion.

"If what you say is true, which I trust that it is, she has brought shame upon my house and my name. Agatha has been my most trusted employee for over two decades.

Recommended to me by your family, Peter, you'll be surprised to know." Chatham shook his head in disbelief. "I can't allow her exemplary work history stand in the way of what needs to be done, however undesirable."

I stared at Peter, astounded. He appeared equally as shocked as I, but his face pleaded not to push further—a plea I had every intention of ignoring. If we allowed our morality to be dictated by personal benefit, humanity's suffering would never cease. "Lord Chatham," I began as Peter winced, "I find it difficult to believe that you knew nothing of the activities of 'your most trusted employee.' Am I supposed to believe that you profited from the goods she procured without ever questioning their origin?"

Peter placed his right hand on my leg firmly, but I was finished with cowardice and propriety was not far behind.

"Surely you met Reed Bailey, the estate agent. Anyone with a modicum of discernment could judge from his sleazy demeanour that he wasn't an upstanding gentleman."

Peter squeezed harder.

"Reed was, for certain, an interesting individual with faults all of his own," said Chatham. "He provided me with a necessary service that I must now find elsewhere. You see, among other interests, I see myself as a broker of sorts. I use my reach and resources to obtain desired relics for others. It's something of a passion of mine and for which I feel no guilt. Like Bailey, I provide a service. It is true, Agatha was responsible for tracking down a number of these relics for me, a task for which she was sufficiently financed to purchase legitimately. Any crimes she committed were done of her own accord, likely to retain as much of the money I provided her with as possible. It's a story of human selfishness, one nearly as old as time."

"Lord Chatham, for all intents and purposes, you run the town of Luffield. Did you not ever think to question the numerous families that had suddenly gone missing?"

"My dear," Chatham began. For many, the term of endearment was an expression of love. From my experience, when gentlemen like Lord Derrick Chatham used it, it was a tool of condescension, used to make me feel ignorant of the matters at hand, matters which I was more than qualified to address. "Farmhands and labourers bouncing between rural towns and villages is commonplace. Do you honestly expect me to keep tabs on all the comings and goings of our fair village? Our migrant population holds little interest to me. What does, however, catch my attention are striking events such as murder-suicides that never happen in our peaceful little hamlet."

The knot that developed in my throat was so pronounced that I feared if I swallowed, the sound would reverberate through the room like an incriminating drumbeat.

"I find it an odd coincidence that you confront me about Agatha and bring up Bailey the day after he and his secretary were found dead."

My eyes darted towards Tim, who had frozen mid-bite of a small pastry. Chatham misjudged my knee-jerk reaction as ignorance. As much as I was loath to admit it, the lord had me dead-to-rights. I had done my best to justify Tim's initial action as self-defence, but under Chatham's narrowed eyes and the awareness of the secretary's death, my hands felt equally as bloody as Tim's.

"Perhaps I am not the only one guilty of ignorance."

My heart was pounding, my face betraying my inner turmoil. Derrick Chatham was as steady as a sea stack in a typhoon.

"I can't say that I'm shocked." Chatham picked up a dinner knife and began twirling it against the pad of his finger. "Bailey was a prolific womaniser. The fact that his secretary shot him and then herself comes as no surprise."

My mind raced. Lord Chatham was no fool.

"You'll find that in life, the line between black and white often blurs into myriad greys. Sometimes we are required to dabble among those greys to meet our ends, an idea to which you are no stranger."

"But to kill innocent families just because of their beliefs?" I was still righteously angry, but the foundation of truth and justice I stood on crumbled beneath me. "That's not a matter of grey, that's black as can be."

Chatham was unfazed as ever. "I don't begrudge anyone of their personal convictions, Miss Tate. You will understand that I am a humble man of imports and exports focused on the wellbeing of this town and my bottom line. My business is a thriving one which demands much of my attention. You cannot possibly believe that I should be held responsible for the ill will held towards others by those beneath me. Agatha and her colleague will be dealt with appropriately. I always had a bad feeling about the footman, Patrick. I've never known anyone who wished to be called Spivey to be of upstanding moral character.

"Sophia, my dear, you strike me as a shrewd woman. You must understand that I'm deeply saddened that my oversight has led to such atrocities. That being said, you'll find that the town of Luffield has greatly benefited from the contributions of the Chatham family going back for nigh on a quarter millennium. I think you would be hard pressed to find a magistrate willing to hear a case against me."

Peter withdrew his hand in defeat, having proved nothing. He may have brought our information to Lord Chatham's attention, but only in the interest of protecting Simon's client from the threat I posed. This way, everyone could feign an interest in justice and resume business as unusual. With Agatha and Patrick off the board, Chatham's hand in the murders would be forgotten. Given his means, he would have no difficulty finding a replacement for the three cogs he had lost in his machine. Despite what people wanted to believe about our humble town, it, like every human establishment throughout history, was not without a criminal element.

Chatham's emerald eyes bored into mine, and I knew he was correct. He was in control and always had been. I found it infuriating that he considered himself untouchable and, for all intents and purposes, was. He did not care if those he profited from were Catholic or Jew, Muslim or Hindu—so long as he profited. Agatha's antisemitic desires may have been a driving force for many of his acquisitions, but profit was Chatham's bottom line. What a loathsome bastard.

"Preston." Lord Chatham placed the knife on the table and folded his hands in his lap.

Within moments, his butler stood inside the door.

"Show Agatha and *Spivey* to the dining room. Inform the constabulary that we will be needing their services, and ask them to be discreet about it."

Preston vanished with a snappy bow as Chatham turned to me. "When the two of them enter, I would like you to present your evidence against them. We will all serve as witnesses to their confessions."

Any lingering traces of confidence I strode in with had disappeared, replaced by soul-consuming doubt and anxiety.

How could I share evidence from a supernatural source and not be laughed out of the room? As much as anger as I felt towards Peter, his reputation was on the line too. I wished to refuse, but I feared that if I opened my mouth to utter so much as a word, the only thing to escape would be vomit.

Chapter XXXIII

"Enter," Lord Chatham said in response to a soft rap at the dining room door. Even given the intensity of the impending moment, his tone bore no difference from any other command he had issued to his servants during our presence.

An older woman of very small-stature entered, her hair pulled back so tightly that it appeared to stretch the skin of her face taught in a poor effort to disguise her age. Where Chatham masked his dominant persona with a grandfatherly presence, his senior-most housekeeper openly wore the expression of overly strict schoolmarm, anxious to swat a squirmy student with the nearest meter stick.

With her was a gangling footman in his late thirties wearing expensive, estate-furnished livery. The imperfections of his suit—a wrinkle across the breast, misaligned trousers, asymmetrical collar wings—were all the more noticeable in a household where nothing was out of place. Despite a forced grin across his face, Patrick handled his cap nervously and rarely lifted his eyes from the ornate Spanish rug lining the floor. The dishevelled state of the lanky man's red hair and overall appearance must have been a source of constant embarrassment to the lord.

"Yes, milord?" Agatha Hackett's salt-and-pepper eyebrows were motionless as she spoke.

At the sound of her voice, my blood ran cold as ice. Beyond a shadow of a doubt, the woman standing in front of me was the same person that I had witnessed in the candelabra vision massacring an entire family of Jews. My face must have been as pale as that of a corpse.

"I'd like to introduce my guests," said Chatham, waving his hand around the table and introducing Peter, Tim, and myself. "They have informed me of some most disturbing news about your conduct outside of these walls."

Agatha Hackett's eyes questioned her master, but she said nothing further knowing the slightest acknowledgement would be incriminating.

"Sophia, please tell Agatha what you and your friend Peter have discovered."

I swallowed the gorge rising in my throat as I broke out into a cold sweat. I did not know what I had expected to do aside from arriving at the manor unannounced and inquiring about Mother Superior's old friend Paul. In all the scenarios that I had imagined, directly confronting the head housekeeper after Lord Chatham himself had completely undermined my notion of right and wrong was not it. Especially not in front of an audience.

I took a deep breath, reminding myself that I was in the right, only interested in exposing the truth and bringing some semblance of justice to the families that had died. I had not killed Bailey or his secretary. I was not profiting from the death of innocent people. Killing people was wrong, and genocide was worse!

A sense of calm came over me. I could almost feel the supportive touch of my mother on my shoulder. I pulled myself together, and the nausea began to dissipate. Agatha's stern expression gave no hint of weakness, not a single chink in her armour. She was a cold-blooded killer, but where Tim was driven by orders, Agatha was driven by hatred; what Chatham approached as business, she saw as her righteous duty. My eyes fell to her accomplice, Patrick Spivey. He, however... "Patrick."

His head rocketed up, yet his eyes were reluctant to meet my own. Both he and Agatha were surprised that I had addressed him first, a minor breach in protocol, but a breach nonetheless. I caught a twitch at the corner or Agatha's tightly pursed lips. I had found the chink. I donned the aggressive voice I used with Ms. Palmer's son, Perry.

"Spivey, if... if you please, miss. Da's the only one who ever called me Patrick, and then it was Patrick the Pill—"

"Guard your tongue!" snapped Agatha.

"It's quite alright." I waved off the course language, wanting Agatha's dull-witted accomplice to let his guard down. His voice confirmed that he was indeed the last remaining suspect from the visions. It took everything in me to play at being friendly. "Please call me Sophia. What beautiful red hair you have, Spivey."

The footman blushed and leaned on a chair with poorly attempted swagger, taking my compliment as flirting. With every word Patrick and I shared, Agatha's face darkened. Peter's sideways glance bore his shock at my approach.

The footman tugged at one of his ragged curls. "Came from me mum. Irish she was, and Da never let her forget it."

"You were close to your mum?"

Patrick nodded. "Died when I was young, she did. Da lost his job. Took it and Mum's death out on me 'til I up and left. If rumours be true, the bastard died in a bar fight last year. Beg your pardon, miss. Shame. I would've liked to deck him meself given the chance."

"And after you ran away, you found steady work here?"

"Yes, miss, after a few odd jobs that didn't work out. Missus Hackett found me and put me to work."

"And your mum, would she be proud of the work you are doing here?"

"I'm sorry, Miss Sophia, I'm afraid I don't follow."

"You see, I'm aware of what you've done. I'd like to know what your mum would think of what you did to those poor families."

"And wh… what families would that be, Miss?" Patrick managed to hide the stammer, but his confidence was failing. He wrung his hat tightly.

Agatha was ready to pounce should he utter so much as a syllable out-of-place.

"Those families you murdered when you were younger."

All colour had left his cheeks. "How did… I didn't murder no—"

"A hard-working father. A wife, holding an innocent babe in her arms." Agatha and Patrick's faces were shocked. I rose and approached them, my eyes stinging with tears. "Two sweet little girls and an infant. An infant, Patrick! How would your mum feel about them?"

"I only did what I was told!" He yelled, hurt apparent in his eyes. I had struck a nerve.

"Shut up!" Agatha hissed.

"It started when we began shagging. At first it was all talk."

"Shut up!"

"The things she said, they made sense, you know? The Hebes were coming into Luffield and taking honest people's jobs, like me da's. Bringing in their different ideas and forcing them on the children."

"Shut up!"

"One night, after we'd, you know, done it, we found some Hebe drunk in an alleyway."

"Shut up!"

"Agatha picked up an old iron pipe laying on the ground and began to hit the man. She… she didn't stop."

"Shut up!"

"She handed it to me, yelling at me to do it too. Said if I didn't, we'd stop shagging. So I hit him. She kept yelling, and I kept hitting him and hitting him." Agatha was screaming at the top of her lungs for Patrick to shut up, but the words flowed forth as fast as his tears. Tim watched as he picked his teeth with a toothpick. Chatham stared on straight-faced. "She told me to hit his head. By the second hit, his body started shaking, and then it was still. I'd killed the poor bastard."

"You miserable piece of shite! Shut the hell up!"

"From then on, I did everything she asked. Got to the point it even stopped bothering me. She threatened to turn me in anytime I questioned it! I never cared for those Hebe bastards, but I never wanted to kill them. You have to believe me!"

"How many did you kill?" I asked through gritted teeth. Patrick shook his head.

"How many did you kill?" Peter yelled, finally spurred into action.

"All of them!" Patrick yelled, then whispered, "All of them. We didn't leave nary a Hebe in Luffield. Agatha wanted the message to be clear. Didn't want no more Hebes moving to Luffield."

I collapsed back into my chair dumbfounded. Agatha jumped on top of Patrick and began clawing and pummelling his face. The action played out in front of me like watching a film at the cinema, and I, nothing more than a powerless spectator. Tim rose so quickly to join the fray that the hand-crafted chair flipped back onto the rug with a muffled thud. Everyone's screaming came through a thick veil shielding me from my present reality.

"Sophia? Sophia?" Peter was yelling at me, leaning down in my face in an attempt to pull me out of the daze.

Tim held a kicking and screaming Agatha aloft from behind. Patrick laid on the floor, moaning, his face and shirt spattered with blood.

"You miserable bastard!" She screamed. "And *you*, Derrick, your hands are just as filthy in this as are mine! Don't act like you weren't a part of this. You knew what we did. You chose some of the homes yourself."

Chatham approached Agatha with the calmest of resolves. "Don't drag me down with you in this. You heard the boy. Every bit of this was your making. Throwing the blame around is the errand of a desperate fool."

Agatha flailed, but unable to reach him, spit an enormous wad of phlegm into his face. I had no doubt that Lord Chatham was as involved as Agatha insinuated, but without the strongest evidence, I was powerless to bring him to justice.

"Most unfortunate that you chose this path." He took the unused napkin from Tim's place and dabbed at his face, wiping her spittle from his nearly white beard. "Preston, has the constable—"

A gunshot silenced the room. All groans, screams, and chatter ceased in an instant. My eyes fell to Chatham's chest, on which a red poppy bloomed. Derrick Chatham's mouth opened in surprise as he exhaled his final breath and fell first to his knees, then face-first onto his priceless rug.

I turned to see Agatha brandishing Tim's automatic, a wisp of smoke curling up from the barrel. Somehow, she had managed to wriggle an arm from the burly man's grip and grab his sidearm. Everyone else in the room was unarmed and powerless against the remaining rounds in the pistol's magazine. The realisation hit me that she could easily kill every one of us. The hall went deathly quiet. The seconds drifted by like treacle on a winter day until the silence was broken by the thunder of boots echoing up the stairway.

Reflecting the last moments of her victims, Agatha's face contorted in sheer terror. Her voice quavered as she spoke. "I only desired for Luffield to remain pure."

She turned the barrel up against her chin and squeezed the trigger, dousing everyone and everything behind in her in swathes of crimson.

Chapter XXXIV

I had not so much as twitched when the constabulary burst through the double doors, my body as immobile as one of the marble statues gracing the manor's corridors. I tried in vain to assimilate all that had transpired as the growing plash of Lord Chatham's blood oozed off the carpet and onto the herringbone parquet. The inspector, an unknown mustachioed officer, and the recognisable Officer Davies charged in one after another with their revolvers drawn. Upon seeing an elapsed scene of carnage included the town's primary benefactor, they stared on in shock.

"Ring an ambulance!" yelled the inspector.

"Are you alright, Miss Tate?" Davies sprinted to me, grabbed my shoulders and quickly scanned me for wounds, giving me enough time for my mind to catch up to the present.

Tim took his unused cloth napkin from the table and wiped Agatha's blood from his face. Inspector Yarbrough cautiously removed the automatic from Agatha's motionless hand with his boot as he mumbled something about 1903.

"I'm fine, Officer Davies. Really." My mind was a quagmire, a blur of all that had transpired, but physically, I was unscathed.

"Oh, thank God," he said, still struggling to comprehend the unexpected scene. "Who's responsible for this?"

I gestured at Agatha's body, then pointed at Patrick. "The footman was her accessory. He'll need some medical care before you place him under arrest. He should provide you with a full confession."

Davies glanced at Inspector Yarbrough for approval who nodded. The mustachioed officer clapped Patrick in irons and led him out into the hallway until a nurse from the local ambulance service arrived on the scene. Afterwards, the constable squinted at Tim, Peter, and me in turn after he had made all of his observations. Once determined that we were not a threat, he holstered his weapon. "Who are you lot and what the bloody hell happened here? Let's start with why Lord Derrick bloody Chatham is lying in a pool of his own effluence, shall we?"

"I'm Sophia Tate. This is Peter Northrop, and—"

"Name's Cooksey," interrupted Tim.

Inspector Yarbrough eyed Tim once more, his keen intuition likely sounding alarms in his head. It would not take significant effort to uncover Tim's chequered past, so I began speaking in effort to avoid additional investigations that could connect us to his past transgressions. Yarbrough seemed surprised that the explanation was coming from me rather than Peter.

"Peter and I are scholars of antiquity. We—"

"I'm sorry, what?" asked the inspector for clarification.

"Peter and I study and acquire antiques, usually for the purpose of selling them." I waited for Yarbrough to interrupt again, but he appeared impatient for me to continue. "This began when Peter and I were searching for a particular piece and inadvertently came across a tragic revelation."

"And what, pray tell, was that?"

"Chatham's assistant, Agatha," I pointed at her motionless body, avoiding looking at the gruesome scene, "with the help of the footman that your man escorted from the premises, one Patrick Spivey, had brutally murdered several local Jewish families."

"Jesus Christ, is that all?" Yarbrough tilted his porkpie cap back on his head and rubbed his face with his hand. "I long for the days when Luffield's only crimes were petty larceny or drunk and disorderly. "So why the hell would they do something like that?"

"Hatred," I answered. "Should he fail to confess to all that transpired, we will gladly provide sworn statements."

"Is that all?"

"No." I brushed his sarcasm aside. Out of the corner of my eye, Peter grimaced. He may have been content to allow the housekeeper and footman to take the fall, but I could not let Chatham off the hook solely because of his position. "Lord Chatham was profiting from the deaths of the families, selling their homes and valuables through a fence named Reed Bailey." The more I talked, the more the invisible weight on my shoulder lifted. Details burst forth as the dam that had strained to hold everything in ruptured. "Once Patrick admitted his guilt and blamed Agatha for organising the crimes, she attacked him in a fit of violence." The constable inspector listened intently, his line of questioning unnecessary as I carried on without help. "When Tim, err… Mr. Cooksey, restrained Agatha, she implicated Lord Chatham, whose denial drove her into madness. She grabbed Mr. Cooksey's personal sidearm and shot Lord Chatham, then herself before anyone had the time to intervene."

Worry had cropped up in Peter's eyes at the mention of Bailey, but I left out any mention of Simon or my abilities, giving him some sense of ease.

Inspector Yarbrough made humming sounds as he processed everything he had heard while Officer Davies photographed the bodies and made detailed notes. In the meantime, Patrick had been brought back into the room bandaged. Agatha had carved several canyons in his already craggy face. If the cocksure man ever saw daylight again, he would have twice as much trouble bedding another woman.

"Is this true, lad?" Yarbrough turned to Patrick who had been listening from just beyond the door. He nodded his head sullenly. "And you'd be willing to put that in a signed confession?" The grown man, who now appeared nothing but a boy, nodded again. Patrick winced as the officer led him outside to a waiting car. At least he had a conscience, albeit too late in development.

"Now, about this personal weapon…" the inspector began.

"I believe Mr. Cooksey has a certificate for his sidearm," said Peter, speaking for the first time since Chatham's death.

Tim fumbled around in his pockets before producing a crumpled piece of paper.

Yarbrough read through the short document, muttering mostly incomprehensibly, "…is hereby authorised to carry and use a gun in Great Britain…" The inspector handed the scrap back to Tim. "Everything's in order then. We'll take your automatic down to the station to check it against your story, but you should be able to pick it up within the fortnight."

Tim nodded his thanks as a pair from the ambulance service loaded up the bodies for transport to the morgue.

Yarbrough rotated his hat in his hands, staring at the dead bodies as they were wheeled from the room. "There's going to be hell to pay once word gets out. The townsfolk will be begging for blood, but looks to me like Spivey is the only guilty party left alive. I won't see him hanged. I intend for him to rot his life away in a dark hole. Regardless of the source of his charity, Chatham was the benefactor of half of Luffield." The inspector rubbed his face again, looking older than when he had arrived. "I bloody well have my work cut out for me. Chatham didn't have any dependents. If what you say is true, I'll do everything in my power to ensure that a portion of his estate goes to the relatives of the families. It'll be a bear of a task to track them down, but I'll make sure it's done."

"Thank you, Inspector."

"Thank me when it's done." Inspector Yarbrough pulled out a cigar and ignited it, ignoring the scoff of the butler as he entered.

Preston did his best to ignore the bloodstains and cleared his throat. The butler had cooperated with the constabulary as though it was merely another of his duties. If he was affected by the death of his master and colleague, he did not show it.

"Did you have something to add?" asked the inspector.

Preston handed Yarbrough a thick envelope. "You'll find that Lord Chatham was forever a man of the people. His will stipulated that upon his death, his home was to be transferred to the county and converted into a centre for the arts. The curation of the manor's extensive collection was to fall to... *me*." Preston added the final word with disdain, his face holding a similar look to Patrick's as he had been escorted from the room. Something told me that being a public servant was tantamount to a life sentence for the pretentious gentleman.

"I'll see that it gets to the right people." The inspector took the will, making to leave but hesitated. "One thing I still don't understand is why you never alerted us to what you discovered."

I hesitated, unsure of how to respond without revealing my gift.

"We got in over our heads quicker than we anticipated," answered Peter.

"You don't say."

Peter ignored the sarcasm. "We stumbled on evidence of Agatha's misdeeds, but needed something more concrete before bringing it to your attention. Before we knew it, we were here, chatting with Lord Chatham."

"I assure you, we wanted nothing more than to bring her to justice," I added. "We never intended for it to escalate as it did."

"*Hmm.* Not many of your type left these days, folks willing to follow the truth at their own expense." Yarbrough shrugged. "You two don't strike me as complicit in all this, and Jack seems to trust you. That's good enough for me."

Jack's cheeks turned a rosy pink.

"You, on the other hand..." Yarbrough pointed at Tim. "What's your part in all this?"

"I'm a friend of the family. When things got tense, they asked me to tag along."

Inspector Yarbrough arched an eyebrow, but did not inquire further.

"I'll gather your information and follow up on everything you've told me. Luffield may not know it yet, but on behalf of the town, thank you for what you've done. You're free to go."

I released the breath I had been holding, believing us to be in the clear. The inspector had reached the door before he turned back.

"You lot never made it as far as Reed Bailey's office did you?" he said, gesturing to the three of us with the smoking nub of his cigar.

"Never got the chance with him dying and all," said Tim.

Yarbrough nodded, not quite convinced, but departed nonetheless.

Jack escorted the three of us to the front door in time to see the inspector's Wolseley disappear through the gate. The steady rain had subsided and the sun was beginning to peak out from its grey shroud. "Will you be heading back to London then, Miss? If you don't mind me asking."

Peter smirked, but said nothing.

"For the time being at least. I'll be staying with my friend, Mildred, until I find a place of my own. With this tragedy all but resolved, I'm anxious to move on to the next chapter of my life."

"And what might that be?"

"I'd like to open a shop of my own."

"A noble pursuit, Miss. I wish you all the best." The young officer nodded and returned inside leaving us alone as the footman who had first greeted me brought around Peter's two-seat roadster.

I stared at Tim, who took the hint. "I could use the fresh air anyway," he said, lighting one of his hand-rolled cigarettes. He walked down the drive whistling, feigning admiration of the landscaping.

"Should we feel bad for making him walk all the way—"

"Sophia, I'm sorry. I *was* a coward." Peter's head dropped, and I allowed him to continue. "Once I thought better of it, I decided to confront Chatham myself."

"To protect Simon's interests from me?"

"What? No." Peter shook his head. " I hoped that he would let something slip when we brought forth the evidence of Agatha's guilt. He's a clever one, but I was hoping to beat him at his own game."

"And when that failed?"

"I intended on demanding that Simon cease all business with him."

I stared into his eyes, which brimmed with sincerity. I forced myself not to be too excited over his rediscovered courage. "I'm proud of you, Peter."

He nodded, obviously expecting a different reaction. He rested his hands on the marble balustrade and stared at the moon, already visible in the late afternoon sky. I suppressed the urge to go to him. I cared about him deeply but could not handle another disappointment.

"Of course, it only took a matter of moments before I realised that he was untouchable and he knew it. I suppose in a way, we got the justice we sought, just not in the way we expected."

No longer ignoring my feelings, I strode to the balustrade and rested my hand on his. As we faced each other, he moved in slowly to kiss me, giving me every opportunity to reject it. When our lips finally met, every pleasurable sensation returned as I melted into his arms. I savoured the mild taste of spearmint on his tongue that I had come to appreciate. When the kiss finally ended, we held each other for a while before speaking.

"I love you, Peter. That's why it pained me so when you cowed to your brother. If our time together has shown me anything, it's that you are stronger than that."

"You… you love me?" Peter asked.

"I do."

"Well…" He rubbed the back of his neck, blushing something fierce. "I love you too." He wrapped an arm around me and pulled me in for a kiss that lasted even longer than the first.

When the kiss ended, I stared into his eyes. "You know what you have to do, right?"

Peter nodded. "I have to confront my brother."

Chapter XXXV

"You want to do what, now?" asked Simon, lowering his newspaper to the wooden counter of the Northrop family antique shop so that he could see Peter's face.

Simon clearly had heard Peter's request, but he was doing everything he could to maintain his intimidating role over his brother. We had spent a couple days recouping from the ordeal but not so many that Peter lost the will to stand up to Simon. Tim had resumed his normal place amongst the shadows and thick plumes of smoke. What minimal camaraderie we had built during our time together had vanished in his boss' presence.

"I'm formally submitting my resignation, so that I can open my own shop with Sophia as an equal partner." Peter spoke without a hint of quaver to his voice. "One that deals exclusively above board. It will be of no threat to your business. We plan to operate in a different market."

I held Peter's cool hand as he confronted Simon. I feared

that it would make him look weak, but he held it proudly, having insisted that I be present for the conversation.

Simon scoffed. "You can't be serious." He stared at his brother with a critical eye for a long moment, the only sound being the London traffic, muffled by the old building's thick walls. "Well I'll be damned. You are."

"Little brother finally grew a pair," said the shadow.

Simon let out a sonorous laugh which echoed through the shop. "And with what capital, may I ask?"

"My inheritance. I'm only asking for that which is owed to me."

"I'm not going to let you squander your half of Father's money on such a preposterous lark with a dame you barely know."

"What about this is either of those things?" I asked. Peter had already done the hardest part in proving that he could confront his brother. At this point, I did not mind helping the effort along. "You know yourself that an antique business can be quite lucrative. I'll grant you that we haven't known each other for very long, but it's clear that we desire the same things and work well together. Peter's only wish is to continue your father's legacy in a more upstanding fashion than you."

"You keep any mention of my father out of your pretty little mouth." Simon pointed a stout finger at my face.

"She's got a mouth on her, alright," said Simon's minion. "Surprised it hasn't got her killed."

"You have no right to speak to her like that!" Peter spoke with authority, not the whiny voice he had used with his brother when we had first met. "She's my partner, and you will show her more respect than you've shown me all these years."

Simon raised his hands in mock defeat. "If this is truly what you want, I'll give you your share. There's little else I can do with it. But know this: You'll be out of business within the year. And should you come crawling back to me for help, you won't find anything but that backroom waiting for you."

"You underestimate my talents. I've been helping keep this shop stable for years. Sophia is quite the student of history, a veritable encyclopaedia of information."

Tim burst out in a fit of laughter. "You've been keeping the legitimate side of this shop in business for years. And don't forget about contacts. Who you know means everything in this line of work."

"Be honest with yourself, Peter. How do you think we afford a shop in central London peddling this old rubbish?" Simon rose and stood face to face with his brother, carelessly twirling a Phrygian aulos from ancient Greece. Nearly a head taller and twice the muscle, Simon couldn't have been more intimidating as he spun the flute in Peter's face. "Whether you'd admitted it to yourself or not, you've known all along that the majority of our income is from, let's say," Simon stared off for a moment before returning his gaze to Peter. "goods with questionable origins. Wealthy connoisseurs like Chatham don't give two bollocks about the origin of their trinkets. They don't want what just anyone can have. When clients like them tell me they want something, I get it. By any means necessary."

"Even if that means innocent people die along the way?" I asked.

"I'm not killing them, am I, sweetheart? Play at sourcing wholesome goods, but know, one: you will never stop common thievery; and two: the goods you buy *legitimately* likely were stolen at one point in their existence or another. Have you *been* to the British Museum?"

"We may not be able to solve the world's problems, Mr. Northrop, but we can do what little we can, and do it honestly."

"What little you can?" Simon paced as he chuckled. "Like what you did for Bailey? For Chatham?"

His words were a sucker-punch to the gut, taking my breath away like the real thing.

"See. No one's hands are as clean as they choose to believe."

"You're not upset about Chatham?" asked Peter.

"You're damn right I'm upset that you went behind my back, but am I torn to pieces over Chatham's death, no. Chatham wasn't the biggest fish in the pond by far. Now if you'd gone after a whale like Johner, we'd be having a different discussion."

"This whole time I thought Chatham was one of the shop's main benefactors."

Simon let another hearty laugh escape. "Hundreds of Chathams and Baileys dot the Isles. And thousands more abroad. Every little corner of the world has their own equivalent, each resorting to whatever means they see fit to acquire anything they can turn a profit on, legitimate or no. So go open your little antique shop. Pretend you are making a difference."

"We will. This is what Sophia and I want to do. If it means tightening our belts to accomplish our dreams, we'll do what we have to do."

"Don't say you weren't warned." Simon picked up the telephone and rang the bank, asking them to allow Peter access to the funds that were rightfully his. "It's done."

"So, that's it then?" asked Peter.

"That's it."

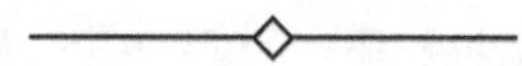

"Where should we go?" I stuck my arm through Peter's as we strolled through Bloomsbury Square Garden, less than a kilometre from what was now exclusively Simon's shop. I appreciated the time to stretch my legs as I assimilated the events of the last three weeks. "I don't think we should stay in London."

"What do you think about Zürich?" he asked. "It's in the middle of Europe, making the entire continent accessible."

"Switzerland? I hear there isn't an unattractive place in the entire country." I grinned. "Only if you're willing to help me learn the languages."

"You understand a fair amount of Latin, and I have talents with others. Between the two of us, I have faith you can figure them out quickly."

"But we know nothing of running a business in Switzerland."

"Running a business is the same in every country, the only thing that changes is the amount you pay the state." Peter laughed.

"We just need to find our own Johner."

"Don't say that."

"Who is he?"

"I don't know. A ghost really. He demanded the utmost secrecy, never meeting Simon face-to-face, and only communicating through cryptic letters. He never contacted anyone other than my brother, and all of their transactions were strictly off the books. That's why I underestimated his importance. The amounts he paid Simon never made him question his identity further. All we really knew about him was that he was shipping everything he purchased back to Germany."

"The fact that you know that much means Johner couldn't have been his real name."

"Probably not." Peter shook his head.

"Do you think Johner was mixed up in all of this?"

"It's possible, but the man had Simon spooked. That's no easy feat. Perhaps it's best in this case if we let sleeping dogs lie."

Peter's response was not what I had hoped. After Chatham's death, I had considered the matter largely resolved. I wanted to follow the trail to its conclusion, wherever it led, but chasing a potential war profiteer into a hostile nation posed an unacceptable risk. I allowed a pent up sigh escape as I stared at the skyline.

"Do you think Simon knew where Bailey's stuff was coming from? He and Agatha must have been at it for years. We know of five families, but there could be considerably more."

"Simon was a criminal and a bastard, but I like to believe that he was more honourable than he lets on. I wish I could say the same for Tim." Peter took my hand. "I'd like to put all of this behind us. What we both need is a fresh start."

"I don't have much, but between your money and mine, we can open a quaint little shop that's in line with our morals. In Zürich, even." I began laughing. I still couldn't get used to the idea that I might be moving to Switzerland.

"As long as I have you, that's everything I need." Peter pulled me in for a kiss and we headed to his car for dinner at Milly's.

Chapter XXXVI

"You sure that's the last truck, Pete?" Milly set down a large hunter green trunk in the middle of the empty storefront with a groan before collapsing on it. "This is why I pay people for help."

"We're trying to save money, Milly." I gave the woman a peck on her sweaty cheek and laughed.

"Leave it to me to break a sweat when everyone around me is wearing a damn *mantel*, that's what they call a coat, right?"

I laughed contentedly. I could not have been in better company as I accomplished my dreams in a land as gorgeous as Switzerland. It had taken us several months to get the documents in order to move ourselves and our inventory across the continent. As I stared at Uetliberg rising in the distance, I could almost feel Mother next to me, smiling. On a clear day, you could just make out the Alps, a few hours by train from the city.

Mei walked in behind Milly, looking like a pack mule with everything she lugged on her back and in her arms, not showing a sign of complaint. Under her petite Asian frame must have been muscles larger than my own.

"Thank God that's finished," said Peter, checking off another crate from his inventory. I did not know how he could make out the writing in the faint orange glow provided by the scant functioning bulbs that dotted the cracked ceiling. "I told you my brother had a good heart when it came down to it."

Our little shop was filling up fast. Once we had leased our business front and had a permanent address, Simon had shipped a fair portion of his store's legitimate inventory to us. Or as he put it, "old rubbish." Well, that "old rubbish" was going to give us the jump start we needed in the foreign city. Unsurprisingly, Milly had affluent friends everywhere and had already put us in touch with an auction house, three potential clients, and an archaeologist with permits to dig in half of the countries bordering the Mediterranean.

"Make sure you tell him thank you for me." I kissed Peter on the lips and watched him go googly eyed.

I took in the panorama from out of the front window, which overlooked the glimmering town lining the hill down to the edges of the Limmat River. Fireworks bloomed, part of the Labour Day celebration, their sparkles reflecting on the calm river's surface. Our shop and the cosy flat above it had an idyllic view, though neither floor of the semi-detached building was much larger than one of the thatched-roof cottages of Luffield.

The business was not the only thing that would need work. Part of the condition of our lease was that we make a number of much-needed repairs throughout the building. The plaster was cracking, revealing the stack-plank construction beneath; several boards in the flooring would need to be replaced and both levels relacquered; several panes of glass were broken and would need replacements. The to-do list went on and on, with each step involving oversight from the local department of historic preservation. One of the first things I had learned in moving to the Altstadt region was that everything in the old district was considered historic.

"You two have all the makings of a wonderful life ahead of you. You both have a good head on your shoulders, but should you ever find yourselves short on funds, you know who to call."

"Milly, I—"

"I know good and well you're going to refuse, but the offer's there nonetheless."

I capitulated. "Thank you, Milly."

"I should be thanking you, Sophia. I was getting bored with the mundanity of life. I don't know how all these rich folks keep their sanity doing the same damn activities over and over again. You came along and brought me some excitement and friendship when I needed it most. I couldn't ask for more."

"You're welcome to stay with us as long as you like, Mildred," said Peter.

"There's no way I'm staying in that closet you call a flat. I've taken the liberty of getting Mei and me a room downtown. We'll be only a phone call away. And you're going to have to start calling me Milly if you have any intention of taking Sophia away from me."

"As you say, Milly," Peter said with some effort.

"This little trip has put some wind in my sails and inspired me to get out and see the world. Once you two get squared away, we're off to lands unknown."

"Let me walk you out." I grinned as I followed Milly and Mei out of the door. Peter chuckled behind me as I waved goodbye to the pair disappearing down the avenue.

I reached into the rear of the lorry and grabbed the last item on board, a covered bronze bust of a Hellenic warrior that Simon had been so kind to send. Part of the protective canvas had come untucked from the rope binding it, and my unsuspecting fingertips made contact with the alloy. My nostrils filled with the odour of freshly burned tobacco.

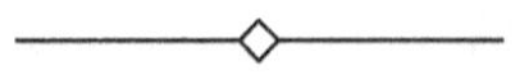

"Guten Abend, Herr Northrop."

The wide-open space was instantly recognisable as the Northrop warehouse, or at least the portion I was never permitted to enter. Everything inside was arranged differently from what I recalled, the space was tidy and well-organised, meaning the meeting I was observing had taken place long before my visit.

"You know I prefer my mother's real name, *Reichsleiter* Rosenberg," said a voice matching the timbre and tone of Simon's.

"Very well, *Herr* Johner. Your mother, *Frau* Johner, was one of our best spies during the *Weltkrieg.* You honour her when you carry her name, unlike those power-hungry *Juden* who stabbed her in the back. The mongrels never left the comfort of their homes during the War." Rosenberg emerged from the shadows, his boot heels clicked on the concrete as he came face-to-face with the speaker I observed from behind. The *Reichsleiter* was not an unattractive man, his blond hair perfectly kempt. Despite the simple beige button-down shirt he wore, his poise screamed military. German military. "I'm excited to see the *entartete Kunst* you have acquired for me."

"Of course, *Reichsleiter* Rosenberg."

Johner walked over to a covered crate and jerked off the canvas tarpaulin covering it. Beneath it I could see a number of simplistic frames stored vertically in a custom wooden rack matching each piece's dimensions.

"Klee, Kokoschka, Kandinsky, Gleizes, Metzinger… a veritable treasure trove of degenerate art." Rosenberg pulled out one piece after another with careless speed for such valuable artwork, not bothering to examine more than the top third of each. "Have them loaded onto the next train to Berlin. The *Führer* will naturally want to examine them before they are publicly incinerated. Would you believe there is talk of that *Arschkriecher* Ziegler holding an exhibition for this *Scheiße?*"

"He has never been anything more than an arse-kissing fool."

Rosenberg shrugged. "The *Führer* likes his art."

"Art has been spiralling the drain the entire twentieth century, including Ziegler's banal work. Without someone as powerful as the *Führer*, we won't be able to put a stop to this nonsense."

"My thoughts exactly. I trust none of their previous owners will come sniffing around like the dogs they are."

"Of that you can be certain, *Reichsleiter* Rosenberg. I have people from Plymouth to Kirkwall funnelling me art, gems and precious metals, antiques—anything of value held in the possession of those swines. They know the mission and execute their tasks well. My own brother is neither aware of the role he plays in my service nor to whom he plays it."

My heart stopped mid-beat.

"Ha! You always were a clever bastard. You do the *Reich* and your *Führer* a great service, Peter." The *Reichsleiter* extended his hand and shook Johner's—Peter's. *"Sieg Heil!"*

"Sieg Heil!" Peter Northrop responded in a booming voice, resounding with confidence, power, and malice.

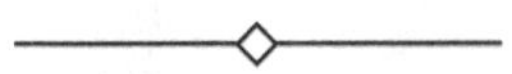

The vision faded and I dropped the priceless Greek bust to the cobblestone, where it began its awkward tumbling descent down the cobblestone-paved hill like a discordant bell.

Peter ran out from the storefront, cradling me in his arms. "Sophia, are you alright?"

"Get away from me!" I screamed, slashing at his face with my fingernails, the only weapon I had at my disposal. "It was you! All along it was you!"

The slump of Peter's shoulders disappeared as he stood confident and erect, a wicked smile crossing his now bloodied face. Every trace of the Peter I knew faded as quickly as the vision had. His awkward, meek persona had all been an act—a boldfaced lie to mask the vile character lurking beneath. And I had fallen for every bit of it. Peter drew a handkerchief from his pocket, calmly dabbing the blood on his cheek. He looked towards the bust that had come to a halt on a storm drain and made the connection. "Such a shame you had to discover that. I knew it was a possibility, but I took the chance."

"Why?" I sobbed, leaning up from where I'd collapsed onto the stone. Cheers echoed from a pub down the way, but the street was abandoned. I was alone with one of the most dangerous men in England. "How could you do that to me? To all of those innocent people?"

"They aren't innocent!" Peter screamed, momentarily losing his calm, before taking on the cool temperament once more. "You, because a woman at my side adds to my legitimacy as a businessman while I work to build a better society—a fascist society. We'll call the lovemaking an unexpected perk. You *Gypsies* are quite… talented in the bedroom."

"You rotten bastard." The sneer nearly rent my cheeks.

"And the *Juden,* because our society requires the extermination of anyone who corrupts it: degenerates, deviants, disabled… anyone who would prevent humanity from reaching its true potential. It's not limited to idealism. I make a great deal of money in the process. The inheritance that Simon gave me was peanuts by comparison. I have more wealth than he could fathom and a high position in the Third Reich to boot."

Images flashed before me of all the memories I had shared with Peter. The most pleasant moments of my life were nothing but a fraud. I hated every second that I had spent with the loathsome villain. "I hate you!"

"Your feelings are understandable." His smile became all the more devious as the blood from his cheek ran between his teeth.

"Damn you." I wanted to excise him from my life like the festering abscess he was, but there was one burning question I could not shake. "Why did you help me?" I snarled.

"Me help you?" Peter chuckled. "You helped me, my dear. More than you could imagine. You single-handedly helped me mop up all the evidence and witnesses to my crimes. With you out of the way, I can operate even more freely than before. I'd offer to let you join me in this new world, but I know you'd refuse."

I spat at his feet.

"That's no way for a lady to conduct herself, Sophia. We'll have to teach you some manners before you face the *Führer.*"

A look of pure shock crossed my face.

"Oh, yes. The *Führer* holds great interest in the supernatural. A woman of your talents would be of great interest to him. Are you familiar with a Doctor Mengele? No? *Reichsleiter* Rosenberg has been anxious to recruit him to the cause. He would be *very* interested to examine you, though I can't promise you will enjoy the experience."

I shook my head, my fury being displaced by fear. "You stay away from me!"

"Resistance will make this much harder than it has to be." Peter offered his hand.

I sprang to my feet and took off down the street towards the loud pub downhill. Peter's steady footsteps echoed down the empty street behind me. I screamed for help, but the majority of the old town's residents were at the riverfront enjoying the festivities, leaving the area virtually abandoned. Peter's footfalls grew continually louder before a blow to the back of my head sent me sprawling across the pavement. My head swam from the impact.

"I'll bring you to the *Führer* if I have to drag your unconscious body to his feet."

I struggled to lift myself from the curb where I'd hit my forehead. Blood trickled down into my eye. My world spun as he reached out to grab me.

"Like hell you will, you evil bastard." Milly barged towards him, skirt hiked in the air for speed.

Peter spun and, without hesitation, drew an automatic pistol and shot her in the chest.

"No!"

Milly was on the ground, gasping. Peter walked over to her and raised the pistol to her face. "Your loud-mouthed friend, I have no need of."

I cringed, waiting for the shot that would end Milly's life, but it never came. I cracked my sticky eyes open and saw Peter clutching his chest. A small throwing knife barely protruding from his splayed hand. He fell back onto the pavement, his weapon skittering across the stone. Mei approached him with a second knife at the ready, poised to attack.

I crawled to Milly as fast as my legs would allow. She was pale and struggling for breath. I fumbled through her thick blouse, desperate to find her injury and slow the bleeding. Unbelievably, the woman began a wheezy laugh.

"I told you these buttons were too damn heavy, Mei. The bloody things can stop a bullet!"

I examined the buttons carefully. Sure enough, one held a flattened chunk of lead as big as the tip of my thumb. "But your breathing…"

"You try getting shot and see if it doesn't knock the wind right out of you."

I could not help but join her laughter as hot tears rolled down my cheeks. I glanced back at Peter, his lifeless body's eyes still staring. Mei walked to his corpse and said something that must have been extremely vulgar in Mandarin with more emotion than I'd ever seen from her.

"Give him what for, Mei," Milly said, chuckling.

"I'm sorry, Soph. I really thought he was a winner." She clasped my hand.

"We all did."

Epilogue

T he colourful explosions above the Limmat River on National Day took me back to that night in May, three months ago to the day. Instead of bringing forward traumatic memories, the crackles and pops of the fireworks and glow of paper lanterns served a similar reminder to that of the Swiss—I was free.

I finished wrapping the garish ceramic toad from Scotland, happy that the hideous piece would no longer be haunting my shelves. Placing it carefully into a cardboard box, I passed it to Emilia, one of my regular clients. For some silly reason I worried that breaking the hideous thing might bring a stroke of back luck.

"*Danke*, Sophia. *Bis bald.*"

"*Tschüss*, Emilia."

The German words still felt heavy on my tongue, but my grasp of German and French was improving. She took the package carefully, and waiving goodbye, went out the door with a tinkle of the little brass bell I had installed. I rested my hands on the counter and sighed. It had been a long day, and I was ready to head upstairs. I made my way to the door to lock up for the night. I had closed the blinds and was twisting the deadbolt as the phone rang. I answered in English, thankful that a large portion of the population were Anglophones.

"Miss Tate, Memories—"

"Just me, Sophia," said Officer Davies on the other end of the line.

"It's so good to hear from you, Jack. How have you been?"

"I'm doing well. How's business?"

"Couldn't be doing better."

"I've got some good news. Yarbrough located Peter's accounts and the stolen inventory that hadn't yet been shipped to Germany."

"That's… fantastic." The news was pleasant, but I was more than ready to put the events of the last few months behind me.

"Look, Sophia, they want to give you a portion of the funds as an award."

My mouth fell agape. When I had opened the business I had been quite concerned about my precarious financial position, but funnily enough, money seemed to be coming from every direction—albeit often tainted.

"Have it sent to the Bevis Marks Synagogue in London."

"All of it? Are you sure? It's a lot of money."

"All of it, Jack. I can think of no better use than to send his-ill gotten gains to the exact people he sought so desperately to repress."

After a long pause, the young officer exhaled.

"If you're sure, I'll make it happen."

"Thanks, Jack."

Jack had become a good friend over the last few months, calling in every week or so to check on me. I think he had reluctantly accepted that I had no interest in a relationship, but that had not stopped him from being concerned about my welfare.

My life was just beginning to feel like my own. For months after Peter's death, the Swiss authorities, Scotland Yard, and the Luffield Constabulary had been in near constant communication, struggling to assemble all the pieces to a puzzle that still had large swathes missing.

Scotland Yard had arrested Simon, but as Peter had said in the vision that exposed him, Simon was completely ignorant of his brother's darker side. The Yard had yet to be able to locate Tim. Jack had said that Simon was still in a state of shock by the revelation as he was being loaded into the criminal transport. Though Simon had refused to confess, the contents of the warehouse was enough to put him in prison for a long time. Anything that had not been confiscated from his antique shop had been transferred to me, surprisingly at Simon's request. I still was not sure about everything he had sent. I glanced over into the corner of the shop where a quiet presence loomed in the shadows, the only sign of his existence the wisps of smoke that curled over his shorn head and out the cracked window. Simon's letter had insinuated that thanks to this particular gift, I would never be in danger again.

Another crackle of fireworks reminded me again of that night, prompting me to further inquire about the investigation. "Any leads?" The question did not need elaboration.

"They don't tell me everything." Jack chuckled. "But last I had heard was that *Reichsleiter* Rosenberg's trail outside of

Germany had gone cold. And you know the investigators won't be going there anytime soon. I'm sorry, Soph."

I nodded, not that Jack could see it.

When I had been questioned by the authorities, it had taken a feat to tell them everything without revealing my abilities. I had done it, but not without a few raised eyebrows. Since Rosenberg had disappeared, I imagined that the network he and Peter had created already had new undercover agents at their helm. Unbeknownst to me, Peter had chosen Zürich for his own agenda, but that had not stopped me from taking what we had begun and turning it into the dream that I had envisioned—but not with Peter's money. That I had donated to Grafton Nunnery.

"At least Peter didn't escape justice." On some level it felt wrong, but I was glad Peter was dead. One less cog in the despicable German war machine.

"Any word from Grafton?" he asked.

"Now that you mention it, yes. I nearly forgot." I grabbed a letter on top of the pile of yesterday's mail and unfolded it. "Mother Superior thanked me yet again for the donation. She said it paid for a complete restoration of the grounds, and there was enough left over to pay for George's funeral and hire a new caretaker."

"I'm sorry you couldn't make it back."

"George knew how I felt about him. The last time I saw him, I could tell he wasn't long for this earth, but that doesn't mean I won't miss him dearly.

"She said in addition to repairing every wire, shingle, and board they even added a few modernities. What she's most excited about is that they have enough means now to resume their food outreach. If she has her way, no child in Luffield will ever go hungry again."

"Good for them!"

Milly had generously filled in the monetary gaps left by my donations. She was not about to let my business fail because I refused to use dirty funds. Contrary to Simon's predictions, the shop was thriving. I would not be wealthy by anyone's standards, but there was plenty of business to pay for the necessities and some extra. Since Milly would not hear of me paying her back, I even had a little extra for the occasional indulgence, like my upcoming holiday to Lauterbrunnen.

There was a soft rap at the door. Tim rose, but with a subtle flick of my finger returned to his stool.

"Hang on, Jack. Someone's at the door. I'll let them know I'm closed."

"Knowing your German, you'll probably tell them that the brothel is four streets over."

I loosed a harmonious laugh. "You're probably right. Oh, it's Fritz!"

"Do tell him I said hello. I leave you to it."

"Thanks, Jack."

I replaced the phone onto the receiver and unlocked the door, letting the fatherly gentleman into the shop.

"Fritz, an unexpected surprise but a welcome one. Tell me you're not working on a national holiday."

He shrugged. "What can I say, I like having an excuse to visit," he said in heavily accented English as he pushed his gold rimmed spectacles further up the bridge of his nose, intentionally ignoring the shop's unofficial employee. "I like your new sign. One day you will have to share its meaning with me."

I had christened the shop Memories of Bronze (*"Erinnerungen an Bronze"* as the sign read). Given the amount of hours Fritz passed in the shop, I could imagine him eventually piecing together the inspiration behind the name.

"You never need an excuse, but what brings you in?"

"I have a most interesting package for you, Sophia." Fritz shuffled over the high counter and strained to place the heavy box on its surface. I rushed to help him, but was merely shooed away. "I may not be as strong as I once was, but I still wish to do things myself, *Ja.*"

I returned his smile. "And what do you have for me, Fritz?" It had been difficult to drop the gentleman's title, but he would jokingly rap me with his cane for even attempting to use formal German around him.

My relationship to Fritz had begun as a necessity as he ran the customs office on the Limmat through which the majority of my inventory entered the country. What had begun as a professional association had become a personal one. He had grown attached to me, reminding him of the daughter he had lost in the Great War, something he still was unable to talk about. It had become commonplace for him to deliver packages well after working hours.

"Something from China. If you'll forgive a gentleman's curiosity, I would very much like to see what's inside. Objects from the Orient ceaselessly fascinate me. Oh, I almost forgot, this letter came with it." Fritz pulled a beige envelope from under the twine and proffered it to me. I instantly recognised Milly's script.

"It's from Milly!"

"I do hope she plans to visit soon." Fritz looked over my shoulder as I broke the seal. He enjoyed Mildred's company as much as I did. A fact that I was sure had nothing to do with her flirtation and Mei's batches of magenbrot. I read the letter aloud.

"My dear Sophia,

We arrived at the Chinese mainland safe and sound. I can't tell you how thrilled I am to be off of that bloody ship, bouncing to and fro over every god-forsaken wave. I've got half a mind to stay here so that I never have to travel again, but then I'd never get to see that handsome devil friend of yours.

Heavens, there are so many people, and I'm the tallest person around. Me! I've never seen such crowds. My trust is completely in the hands of my travelling companion as all the spoken language sounds like singsongy gibberish, and their written words are nothing more than beautifully drawn sticks.

The architecture is the most fascinating I've seen in my life. It makes our English construction positively boring by comparison. Mei tells me the age and history of everything we see. I'm beginning to think the Chinese were writing and painting scrolls when we were still throwing sticks and stones at one another.

Mei took me to the market this morning. The things they do in the street… I saw a chicken beheaded and defeathered right in front of me. And don't get me started on what they eat. I could have tried a seahorse on a stick. I didn't even know such a creature existed, much less that I could eat it. I asked for a simple snack and was given a boiled egg. Sophia, I'll be damned if there wasn't a half developed bird inside. I'll be sticking with the soup, thank you very much.

You'll recall the reason for our visit was Mei's two-timing brother-in-law falling ill. It turns out that it was nothing serious. A stone in his kidneys. Likely from the stress of those two mistresses he has behind his wife's back. Now his poor health will be due to Mei exacting her vengeance."

Tim let a wheezy laugh escape.

Fritz accompanied it with a hearty laugh of his own. "I can imagine her running around, cursing in Mandarin as she chases him with *ein Schuh.*"

I continued through a fit of laughter.

"I found this accompanying bronze serpent at a street stall. I won't pretend I understand your gift, but the incredible piece seemed almost to be calling me, beckoning me to send it to you. If it's nothing special, I won't be offended if you sell it immediately. Hope to see you in a few weeks.

All my love,
Milly."

"Oh, good lord." I rolled my eyes. "That's all I need is Milly sending me every trinket China has to offer. She'll have to shell out for a larger shop if this keeps up."

"It would keep me in work." Fritz chuckled. "Perhaps I will become a collector of all things eastern."

Curiosity got the better of me, and I began tearing the wrapping off of the box. Inside was a wooden crate covered in the beautiful complex calligraphy of Chinese characters. Tim retrieved a crowbar from the shop's back room, and I pried open the lid. Inside, nestled in red velvet, was a mesmerising bronze sculpture of a coiled serpent, appearing more wise than the reptiles were usually portrayed. I had never seen such detail captured by the casting process. I reached both hands down into the box.

"You sure about that?" Tim asked.

"Pretty damn sure."

Author's Note

Being a hardcore fan of science fiction and fantasy, *Memories of Bronze* was a book I never expected to write. My mother was always the diehard mystery fan of the house, reading everything from Ellis Peters to Lilian Jackson Braun and watching everything from *Miss Marple* to *Lovejoy.* Because of her and my father, who enjoyed them too, I was raised watching British television more nights than not. While my classmates were engrossed in shows like *Saturday Night Live* and *Family Matters,* my family was watching *Mystery!* with Diana Rigg or *Masterpiece Theatre.* (I preferred *Cadfael* and *Poirot.*) Apparently, all that mystery content must have lodged deep within my subconscious. Once I finished the *Release Day Saga* and was evaluating what to write next, I couldn't break away from the idea of a period British mystery. I wrote what is now the prologue of *Memories of Bronze* and sent it to my beta readers who loved the idea. I spent the next few years writing the manuscript, constantly joking about whether I would be remembered as the sci-fi author who wrote a mystery novel or the mystery author who wrote a few sci-fi novels—a fact that remains to be seen. I hope you enjoy *Memories of Bronze* and find my British English tolerable. Now if only Mom could be around to see it.

Acknowledgements

There are so many people to whom I owe thanks for the success of this and my previous books. There is no way I can mention everyone who has made this possible. First and foremost, my gratitude goes to my wife and daughters for what they have sacrificed to make my author dream a reality. An extra special thanks goes to my editor and wife, Jessica Matthews, who helps me polish my error-ridden manuscripts into something readable. I also want to thank my beta readers: Deshea Surratt, Mallory Reid, Ariel Wells, and Amy Vaughan who give me invaluable, and often blunt, feedback. I also want to thank Dale Kesterson, who gave me some pointers and encouragement early on in my mystery-writing journey. And thank you to all of the people who have purchased and reviewed my work since the beginning. Words cannot express how important ratings and reviews are in our modern world for indie authors like me. Though I can never understate the importance of good, old-fashioned word-of-mouth.

About the Author

Ryan Matthews is the offspring of a mystery-loving nursing professor and science-advocating environmental chemist who fostered his lifelong love of learning. After working for a decade in the field of graphic design, he felt the call of education. Ryan now teaches English to speakers of other languages, and he is working towards a doctorate in educational leadership. Outside of his work and studies, Ryan enjoys playing games with his family, torturing the French horn, tromping through state parks, and studying foreign languages and cultures. He lives in Tennessee with his wife, daughters, and the family pets—Luna and Coda.

Memories of Bronze is Ryan's first delve into the world of supernatural mystery. His debut series, the adventure-packed *Release Day Saga,* is young-adult speculative fiction.

Ryan Matthews Author
@ryanmatthews501

ryanmatthewsauthor.com

Your Opinion Matters!

To support independent authors like me, please rate, review, and spread the word about all of your favorite reads.

www.ingramcontent.com/pod-product-compliance
Lightning Source LLC
Chambersburg PA
CBHW021033310726
48969CB00006B/1635